BLOOD MEMORIES

By Margaret Durand

ISBN: 978-0-9953197-3-8

For Carolyn, who led the way

This hour I tell things in confidence, I might not tell everybody, but I will tell you.

WALT WHITMAN, 1855

PREFACE

This novel was inspired by letters addressed to my great-great grandparents from their only son, Donald.

In 1860, they lived on a small farm near the village of Chippawa, now part of Niagara Falls, Ontario. Donald was sixteen-years-old, and he wrote letters home while apprenticed as a pharmacist in Ontario and New York. In 1863, he joined the Northern Army during the American Civil War. I read the words of an anxious young boy who matured over the space of four short years and imagined his life in pre-Confederation Canada and during the war. I remembered my Great Aunt Jessie who never married and was a bit of a tyrant, albeit with a soft center. I thought Donald could use a strong partner, and my version of a young Jessie, infatuated with Donald but unwilling to tell him, ended up taking over a large part of the book.

I donated Donald's correspondence to the Canadian Letters and Images Project, and his letters have been digitized and made available to the public.

The lines that accompany each chapter heading were taken from the long poem by Walt Whitman called "*Song of Myself*", first published in 1855 as part of Whitman's collection, *Leaves of Grass*. Whitman attended to the sick and wounded in several Washington hospitals during the American Civil War. I was drawn to the idea of Jessie, having lost much of what she valued in life, finding solace in his poetry.

CONTENTS

Chapter 1: 1860, Chippawa, Canada West 1

Chapter 2: 1861, Chippawa, Canada West 14

Chapter 3: 1861, Fergus, Canada West 39

Chapter 4: 1862, Ingersoll, Canada West 54

Chapter 5: 1862, St. Catharines, Canada West 66

Chapter 6: 1863, Ingersoll, Canada West 73

Chapter 7: 1863, Chippawa, Canada West 86

Chapter 8: 1863, Newark, New York 99

Chapter 9, 1864, Galt, Canada West 112

Chapter 10: 1864, Camp on Dumpling Mountain, Virginia 126

Chapter 11: 1864, Galt, Canada West 139

Chapter 12: 1864, Camp on Dumpling Mountain, Virginia 149

Chapter 13: 1864, Rochester, New York 157

Chapter 14: 1864, The Rapidan River, Virginia 165

Chapter 15: 1864, Bowling Green, Virginia 178

Chapter 16: 1864, Cold Harbor, Virginia 188

Chapter 17: 1864, City Point, Virginia 195

Chapter 18: 1864, James River Crossing, Virginia 206

Chapter 19: 1864, Outside Petersburg, Virginia 221

Chapter 20: 1864, Armory Hospital, Virginia 240

Chapter 21: 1864, Arlington, Virginia 252

Acknowledgements 260

About Margaret Durand 261

CHAPTER 1: 1860, CHIPPAWA, CANADA WEST

Not I nor anyone else can travel that road for you

The raccoon was alive but past caring that Donald and Jessie stood no more than a foot away. The sad creature lay on its side, drops of crimson blood weeping from a wound and melting a hole in the snow. One of the animal's front legs lay under its head with four pink pads facing up, as if pleading for mercy. A black fur mask surrounding the creature's eyes completed the image.

"The little bandit was caught in the act," Donald said, "but it would be cruel to leave him to the birds."

"Joey's father shot him after he clawed his way into their hen house," Jessie said, her voice a whisper. Squatting beside the raccoon, the hem of her long woollen dress formed a tent around worn leather boots. Donald smirked when he imagined the raccoon jumping up to hide beneath her petticoats, but the animal didn't react to their presence.

"Maybe he's paralyzed." Donald leaned forward to see if the animal's chest was moving.

"Or maybe he's smart enough to stay quiet." Jessie gently pushed aside Donald's index finger that hovered perilously close to one of the animal's eyes.

Donald shrugged, acknowledging the possibility.

"Let's take him to my barn and see if we can get him back to rights," Jessie said.

There was a moment of silence while Donald considered whether it might be kinder to kill the raccoon, but then he leapt up when an idea came to him. "I'll get my toboggan and a flour sack to put him in. I have something new to try."

Jessie shouted for an explanation, but he ignored her as he ran for home. For a change, he'd like to be the one to surprise her.

When they pulled the toboggan into the barn and lifted the sack onto the bench, Jessie's father asked the cause for excitement. A blood-stained apron was wrapped around his lean torso, and Donald suspected Mr. Mackay had helped at a difficult early birthing. A sheep bleating in one of the horse stalls confirmed his guess.

"What have ye got there, Donald?"

"A bullet wound, Mr. MacKay." Then Donald realized Jessie's father was inquiring about the creature in the sack, not the injury. "A raccoon, sir, and still breathing."

Jessie's family had emigrated from Scotland a dozen years earlier to settle in Chippawa, but the village had been slow to accept Mr. MacKay as its farrier. Even now, some living along the Niagara River said his ways with horses and other farm animals were unconventional at best. His independent attitude had rubbed off on his only daughter, Jessie. She was unusual too, especially for a girl, but she shared his passion for animals and was willing to pass on what she learned from her father about their behaviour and ailments. Today would be different because it was his turn to reveal something new to the MacKays.

Donald pulled out a stoppered glass vial from his pocket and held it up. "It's called chloroform." He enjoyed seeing Jessie's questioning look.

"Aye, I've heard of that," Mr. MacKay said. "And I suppose Doctor Forbes let you have that wee sample?" Donald shrugged, knowing his father would be dead set against wasting anaesthetic on an animal. "I thought as much," Mr. MacKay said, shaking his head.

"What's chloroform, Donny?" Jessie said.

"It'll make him sleep. It's like ether but not as dangerous near a flame." He could see more questions forming on her lips, but her father asked first.

"Do ye know how to use it, lad?"

"From what I've read, I should place a few drops on a ball of cotton and hold it to its nose, well, snout." It was like pulling teeth to get his father to tell him details about the practice of medicine. He'd only known about chloroform by eavesdropping on his father's conversation with Doctor Aberdeen.

"I've heard chloroform can kill quickly when given in excess," Mr. MacKay said. "One of you must keep a close watch on the creature's breathing." He stared pointedly at Jessie. "When it slows, remove the cotton, and when the beast starts to move again, replace it. I should not have to tell you to avoid breathing the vapours yourselves."

"Let me administer the chloroform, Donny, and you can remove the bullet." That longing in her eyes made him grin.

"Fine, but I need a pair of forceps," Donald said.

"Ours are all too large," Jessie admitted, looking at the wall board displaying her father's well-used tools.

"That's because I use them to pull nails from horse shoes, not bullets from flesh," Mr. MacKay said.

"I should have thought of that," Donald said, annoyed that he'd forgotten what now seemed obvious. His father kept his surgical kit in his desk drawer, and Donald had borrowed his instruments on more than one occasion.

"Do you think Mother's tweezers might do in a pinch?" Jessie said, laughing at her pun. Donald smiled and Mr. MacKay frowned.

"I hope you have a pair of your own because your mother won't be giving you permission to probe around in a dirty raccoon with her personal tweezers," Mr. MacKay said.

"If Donny can borrow the chloroform, I can borrow the tweezers," she laughed and flew out of the barn. Donald heard Jessie's mother calling for her to take down the washing.

By the time Jessie returned to the barn, the raccoon was pressed to the bench on his stomach with Donald holding one set of struggling legs while Mr. MacKay held the other. As fast as she'd returned, Donald knew Jessie hadn't stopped at the clothes line.

"I told you it was a possum," Jessie said, eliciting a smile from Donald.

"He's not paralyzed, that's for sure, and the sooner you wet the lint with the chloroform, the better."

Jessie carefully dripped the chloroform onto the cotton, and they wrinkled their noses as the sharp odour wafted upwards. When she held the cotton close to the raccoon's snout, he struggled harder to escape. "Should this be taking so long?" she asked as the raccoon continued to wriggle.

Donald shrugged and turned to her father. "Don't look at me for help, lad. I've not used the stuff," Mr. MacKay said. Finally, the raccoon stopped moving. Donald could see the creature's breath was too slow, and he motioned Jessie to lift the cotton from his nose. "Remember to clean the fur around the wound with alcohol before you go digging in there," Mr. MacKay said, handing Donald a bottle of medicinal alcohol. "You don't want to carry in any particles of muck."

Donald wet the fur and skin around the shoulder wound and then used Mrs. MacKay's tweezers to gently probe the hole. "I think I touched the bullet, but it's slippery and I can't get purchase on the thing."

"Here, let me try," Mr. MacKay said, taking the tweezers from him and scowling as he tried to grip the bullet with the inadequate tool. Then Donald placed his hand on the other side of the raccoon's shoulder and pushed the flesh gently towards the tweezers.

"Aye, that's helping, lad. Push up a bit more against me, as you're doing." Mr. MacKay pulled out a half-inch bullet with a triumphant, "Yes!" He passed the tweezers with the prize to Donald.

At this moment, the raccoon decided to move again, and Jessie replaced the cotton pad over its nose. It relaxed quickly this time. "The bleeding is under control, so we haven't damaged any large blood vessels, but you must to sew up that hole before you're done here," Mr. MacKay said. "And make sure the cage is strong because this fellow will be angry when he awakens."

Donald held up the lead bullet like a trophy and was rewarded with Jessie's smile. After sewing up the wound, he went to the corner of the barn to reinforce one of their old make-shift cages. When he heard Jessie yell in surprise, he ran to find her pressing a bloody cloth to her palm and the raccoon awkwardly trying to right itself. He pressed the chloroform-soaked pad back back on it's nose while Jessie placed the flour sack over the animal. She pulled down gently on both sides, restraining its body against the table until the chloroform had a chance to work. Donald gently lifted the limp raccoon and set it inside the cage. Within a minute, it started to twitch.

"It's stopped bleeding," he said as he studied the two little punctures in her palm, then washed and bound up her wound. "Lucky for you the raccoon's half asleep." He took a close look at her face. They'd both received a good number of nips and bites over the years, but Jessie never complained. She was what his mother would call plucky. "We'll see who heals faster, you or the raccoon."

Jessie scowled. "It had better be me. He's not even a paying customer."

Three weeks later, when the mid-year exams were over, his teacher told Donald to remain after school. The fire in the schoolroom stove had died down, and the winter's chill penetrated the drafty space. Miss Armstrong, arms crossed over an ample bosom, fixed Donald with a stern gaze. She picked up his report card between thumb and forefinger and waved it above her desk, lifting up the scent of her disapproval along with the faint odour of peppermint lozenge. It bothered Donald to see her more resigned than disappointed.

"Donald, you can do better than this," she said, making annoying clucking sounds with her tongue. "You've made several errors on the arithmetic questions and your spelling is well below average. As captain of the cricket team, the students look up to you. I expect you to set an example." She raised her formidable eyebrow as she waited for his explanation.

Donald shuffled his feet. He'd done well on his home assignments, but his father and even his little sister, Rhoda, had helped him. Reading had always been difficult for him, and arithmetic only made sense when his father took him through the problems slowly. No matter how hard he tried to concentrate, numbers became jumbled up in his head. Donald wanted to tell Miss Armstrong he didn't feel well that day, but he couldn't bring himself to tell a fib, so instead he said, "I know I can do better if I try harder." As he said this, he realized that it, too, was stretching the truth.

"I hope so, Donald, or you will not achieve the grades necessary to attend medical school next fall." She handed him his report card and dismissed him with an impatient flick of her wrist.

Donald doubted his marks would improve even if he studied day and night. He felt his father's disappointment like a heavy weight he could shoulder best when occupied with something he enjoyed. Distracted by the shouts of his school mates headed home to their farm chores, he glanced out the frost-rimmed window panes. Only Jessie remained at the gate, staring at the lamp-lit windows and no doubt wondering what was taking him so long. His mind went back to the problem at hand.

When he was younger, he was sure he would become a surgeon like his father. After Papa had received his training in Scotland, he could only find work as a ship's surgeon, and so began his long career with the Royal Navy. Perhaps if Papa's first year at sea had not been so exciting, or he had he not met his mother after his transfer to Canada, he might have returned to Scotland and led a very different life.

His father's adventures on the high seas intrigued Donald. He would repeat his father's stories to the other boys and watch their eyes enlarge, as his own eyes had done, when he described how to amputate a limb or what happened when an African slaver was caught at sea. Once, he brought one of his father's French leaches to school and terrified the others when he lifted the slimy creature from its jar, placed it on his arm to feed, and watched it swell with his blood. "They use several of these on each patient, not only one," he said. "My father has kept this leach for five years. He named it Phoenix after his first ship."

"What does he feed it?" Joey said, failing to appreciate why the leach was swelling.

"My blood," Donald said in a low gravelly voice, making the younger children shudder. "You're welcome to visit me and feed it whenever you want, Joey. He would like your blood." The class had erupted in laughter.

Donald had conflicting ideas about being a naval surgeon. His father complained of conditions at sea that made proper medical treatment so difficult. Although Papa enjoyed the prestige of being Edinburgh trained, he had decided not to practice medicine when he retired to Chippawa. This disappointed Donald, and having his father described as a farmer, even a gentleman farmer, bothered him since his hoity-toity Aunt Eliza said farmers were as dull as ditch water. Papa said the village had a competent surgeon and didn't need a second one, but he suspected other reasons when he overheard his father confiding to a friend that shipboard medicine had not prepared him to doctor those on land. Besides, he'd said, the townsfolk cannot pay city prices for medical treatments, and even Doctor Aberdeen farmed to supplement his income.

As a small boy, Donald had looked forward to Papa's retirement when they might spend more time together, but Papa attended church and town council meetings, especially during the evenings when Donald was free. His father's cheeks and nose became redder with each passing year, and that told another story. Papa was grumpy most mornings and complained of leg pains, but after a drink or two of his favourite whisky, he became much too jovial. His heavy Scot's accent and recognizable bray made Donald cringe in his company. When they worked side by side for the few hectic weeks of harvest, Papa could never spare breath for conversation. His father often seemed impatient and gruff with him, but Mama gave the excuse that farm life must seem quite dull after being a naval surgeon. Donald wondered if Papa's life was as dull as ditch water. Shaking off these thoughts, he lifted his woollen jacket from the upper row of wooden pegs by the school house door and headed outdoors.

Jessie was still leaning against the gate when Donald left the school house. Her hands were moving in strange but graceful patterns, and when he saw the string, he realized she was occupied with a game of cat's cradle. The witch's broom vanished when the little Mackenzie boy grabbed the string from her hands and ran off. Jessie leaped after him, and within seconds, she had the boy pinned against the fence.

"Give that back, you heathen," she shouted, pulling the string from his fingers. "You shouldn't take what doesn't belong to you. Next time, I'll tie this string around your ear and yank it off." Donald smiled at the image that came to mind, and the boy scurried off without a backward glance.

As he approached Jessie, her frown transformed into a smile. Donald thought her dark dress and shawl did little to soften her boyish figure. Dark blonde hair, held partly in check by a frayed yellow ribbon, fell in tangled waves to her waist. Surprisingly tall for a girl, Donald often felt uneasy looking directly into green eyes that penetrated him as if searching for something he lacked. But when she smiled, her face brightened and came alive with delight. He felt his anger dissipate.

"Did she give you the hickory switch?" Jessie asked, secreting the string along with her smile.

Donald shrugged and kicked at the fence post as they left the yard. They both knew Miss Armstrong needed nothing but her tongue to whip obedience into her pupils. Wagging his head and mimicking Miss Armstrong's high-pitched voice, he said, "You can do better if you try".

He had tried to do better on the exam by stretching his neck to see the answers from the fellow sitting in front of him. Angus usually sat there, and Angus always did well on tests. But he could see only Joey's paper, and Joey struggled more than all the others with school work. Jessie had caught him straining to look and had frowned at him. Later she had asked Donald why he didn't pay more attention in class. He had shrugged, having decided long ago it was better to be thought lazy than dim-witted. "Let's go see if our raccoon wants his freedom," he said.

The next day, Donald stood alone beneath the oak tree outside his house wishing he did not have to face Papa who had asked to see him after school. A skiff of the season's first snow lay on the ground, and heavy gray clouds threatened more. He fingered the initials he had carved into the rough bark five years earlier. Small letters at the time, they seemed to grow at his pace, stretching with the bark of the oak tree.

He rarely spoke to Papa as it seemed they shared few interests anymore. Still, Donald felt the pressure of his father's expectations, and as he picked at his initials on the tree, he wondered what he could say to him to explain his poor grades. He ripped off a desiccated brown leaf clinging to a branch, but when he opened his fist, only a skeleton of veins remained. Like his future, there were many different paths that crumbled when examined too closely. He dropped the remains of the leaf and slouched into the house.

Papa was sitting behind his shabby mahogany desk. A meaty arm supported his bearded chin, and a frown of concentration replaced his usual open countenance. His hair, gray long before retirement, had remained thick, and the fingers of his right hand were buried in it like ploughshares. He was wearing his old tweed coat, patched more than once at the elbows, and Donald wondered, as he always did, why his father did not care more for his appearance. Doctor Aberdeen always sported the latest fashions, and Aunt Eliza said that his deportment and sense of style set Doctor Aberdeen apart. When Papa looked up and saw him waiting at the door, Donald felt himself shrink under critical eyes.

"Sit down, Donald. I need to speak to you concerning your report card."

"Excellent," he said, as he slumped down onto his father's battered sea chest and emitted a sigh.

"Not excellent, in fact, far from it. Can you give me an explanation?"

Donald glanced briefly at his father, trying to judge the depth of his disappointment. He noted the telling flash of silver. The thumb of Papa's left hand unconsciously opened and closed the lid of his small silver lancet case, a habit of many years when he was anxious. His habit had worn away the initials engraved on its surface, and, were he not careful, the small hinges were apt to open and release the sharp lancets within.

"The questions were difficult. I could have done better with more time," Donald said.

"Did you study?"

Donald nodded, still staring at the floor. He had tried to study, but whenever he opened a book, his mind wandered like a hound searching for a scent. Even so, he knew others in the class had done better with less effort. It didn't seem fair, and his anger rose with his colour. Papa knew it took him a while to think through a problem, but eventually he arrived at the right answer.

"With these grades, you will miss getting a scholarship to study medicine."

Donald, eyes still fixed on the carpet, mumbled, "Medicine is not so wonderful." He knew his words would hurt his father, but he was surprised when he felt the pain of his own lie. Truth be told, he had wanted to be a surgeon for as long as he could remember. Now he must accept that he was not as smart as Papa. He kicked the back of the trunk with his heel.

"Perhaps you have a plan for your future you might share with me?" his father said.

Jessie's taunts played in his head as Donald struggled for an answer. "I was thinking I could become a veterinarian, Papa. There's a new school in York, and Jessie and I have talked of opening a business together, to care for sick animals." His father's eyes bulged, and Donald waited for the tirade.

"Why would you consider wasting your time doctoring sick animals when they are so easy to replace," he said. His voice indicated disappointment as much as anger. "You know my opinion on this, and I imagine Jessie's parents are none too pleased either. Really, Donald, I expected more sense from you."

"But we're good at helping animals, Papa, and veterinarians are being trained in Europe and America these days." He recognized Jessie's enthusiasm in his voice.

"Those wild creatures you play with are of no use to anyone. This is Canada, and any veterinary trade will remain insignificant here for many years to come." His father searched through a pile of journal papers and correspondence on his desk, lifting out a single envelope. "You must have a solid profession to support you, a profession like pharmacy. Nowadays, one needn't be a surgeon to run a pharmacy. I have arranged for you to begin an apprenticeship after the spring planting. You will work with Mr. Strathmore at Fergus Dispensing."

"But I would have to leave Chippawa and all my friends," Donald leapt up and moved to stand in front of a window too small to provide adequate light or air. His father's news shocked him. Why hadn't he been consulted before arrangements were made? His back to his father, he clenched the rough window frame and stared out at the open barn door. The cows and chickens were as silent as cats on the prowl.

"You know there is no proper training to be had in this small village," his father said, fingering his lancet case.

The sharp tone and a glance at a florid face told him his father bordered on losing his temper. "I could help out on the farm," Donald said, ignoring the warnings.

"The farm will not support you. It was only meant to supplement my income. You must make your own path, Donald."

"But we could have more cows and sell the butter and cheese."

"We lack sufficient good land to feed more animals."

"I don't want to go. You can't make me." Donald winced to hear his childish whine and feel his eyes brim with tears. He turned his back on his father.

"I'm not trying to drive you away, son, but this is a good opportunity and you must take it."

Donald risked a glance before offering the only argument he had left. "I want to talk to Mama," he said, his voice catching. He wished she would be his ally, but she'd likely side with his father. Now it was Papa who was looking at the carpet. Faded and threadbare in places, it was an easier sight than his own tear-filled eyes.

"We've discussed it. She agrees with me that it's for the best, Donny."

CHAPTER 2: 1861, CHIPPAWA, CANADA WEST

And I say it is as great to be a woman as to be a man

Angus hooted as he grabbed Jessie by the waist and swung her up onto a snow bank. "Keep out of my way, Horsie," he said, mocking her. It was her bad luck the shortest path to school passed by Angus's house. Hardened to teasing, her eyes narrowed to the breadth of a bat wing as he taunted her with that horrid nickname.

Since a child, she'd been fascinated by and fearless with animals, especially horses. Before she could ride, she'd created imaginary ponies she trotted to school while holding invisible reins. This led to mocking from her classmates. "Horsie, I hope you clean up after yourself. Horsie, don't break a leg or you know what'll happen. Horsie, did you bring oats for lunch?" For the most part, Jessie tolerated the ridicule, but she distanced herself from the others. Only Donny had not used that name, and now that she was sixteen, her classmates had forgotten, except this brute. Angus made sure to grab her attention by any means. No doubt he hoped to impress her by lifting her up effortlessly to the top of the snow bank.

Angus hooted at her obvious fury as he grabbed a handful of moist snow. Before he could pack it into a ball and aim it at her, Jessie leapt from the bank and lunged into his side, her elbow jabbing his ribs and eliciting a surprised grunt. In an instant, the boy was spread-eagled on the snowy path with Jessie astride his back and gripping his hair. Although stronger, he was no taller, and certainly not as fierce, she thought.

"Who's the horse now? Giddy up," she said, hitting his backside with her free hand.

Joey and another boy walked by, whispering and laughing. They waited further down the path to see what would transpire next. When Jessie jumped off, Angus stared up at her in disbelief, his cheeks red. Both sets, Jessie thought, smirking.

"You're as prickly as a burdock bush, Jessie MacKay. And you're no lady."

Jessie shrugged. "Sticks and stones." Angus, covered head to foot with snow, looked to be the loser in this skirmish. "All you need is a carrot for your nose," she said, enjoying the boy's irritation.

When she reached the school house, the door was still closed, and she stamped her feet to keep them warm. Donny was talking with the older boys near the back gate. As usual, his shirt and jacket were crisp and spotless, and unlike the other growing boys, his trousers were the proper length. For a long time, she thought his parents had insisted his appearance be so smart, but she now knew that it was Donny's doing. Why fine clothing so captivated him escaped her.

Beneath her heavy shawl, she wore a simple dark gray dress, protected by a brown pinafore, messy with ink stains and now frosted with a bit of snow. She cared not a fig for fine clothes or the latest fashions, although Donny said stylish clothes made him feel important. She found it more satisfying to be strong and able to overpower anyone who thought to tease her, and she'd been given plenty of opportunity to practice her skills. Wearing fine clothes would make it difficult to fight.

As the bell rang and they walked into the school, she waited until Donny hung his coat beside the other wool jackets that held the shape of their owner's shoulders. Then she grabbed his arm and whispered,

"What did your father say about your report card?" His arm stiffened and she could almost smell his anger.

"He's sending me to apprentice in pharmacy. I have to go to Fergus after the harvest."

"What? You agreed?" He frowned at her disbelief, his face growing as dark as a snow front. Fergus was miles away to the west, past the canal and the road to York. She would never be able to ride that far. Donny's face reflected his misery, but she felt her own keen sense of disappointment at the thought of losing her best friend. It annoyed her that being a girl limited her choices in life, but Donny's disappointment made her realize boys had their own problems.

Every day after school, she stole to the barn to work with her father, much to the annoyance of her mother who expected her to help with the cooking and the endless and tedious sewing and mending. For years, she had dreamed of being a farrier and horse doctor like her father, but he wouldn't hear of it. "Being a farrier is no job for a woman, Jessie," he told her whenever she asked. But she was not easily discouraged, and she continued to press him and to learn what she could by watching. Eventually her father had relented and let her stitch up the smaller wounds and trim hooves for shoes. At first, he refused to allow her near the forge, but she asked if she might make a small hook for her door, or a trivet for the table, and one thing led to another. Soon, she was better at fancy iron work than her father, although she yearned to form and fit shoes. She loved the smell of the forge and the heat of the steam on a cold winter's day.

When Miss Armstrong's teaching voice rose in its characteristic cadence, Jessie turned her attention to her favourite class, geography. Often there would be pictures of strange natives and temples in far away places like Siam. She saw Donny staring out the window, oblivious to the lesson, as usual. He was watching a rider approach the school gate, dismount, and secure his jet-black horse to the fence. Jessie studied the well-proportioned lines of the medium-sized stallion. She knew the breed had been developed in Quebec, and she noted with annoyance that its tail had been cruelly docked. A knock on the door preceded the entry of the stranger. He spoke briefly to Miss Armstrong who appeared to be expecting him. Then he took a wide stance in front of the class and cleared his voice.

"Good morning students. My name is Mr. Swanson, and I am the recruitment agent for the Great Western Railway headquartered in Hamilton. I would like to address the students who will be graduating this spring." He paused as if to gauge their reactions, and when the class responded with excited murmurs, he looked as pumped up as a new father.

"Class, quiet, now," Miss Armstrong said in a resounding voice that never failed to command attention. Mr. Swanson's proper British accent and fancy attire amused Jessie. She noted the soft shiny leather of his kid gloves and boots and decided he had not practiced much railroad work himself.

"The Great Western Railway is inviting the graduating students in the Niagara area to apply for employment. For the boys, we offer positions as railway construction men, porters, and delivery men. For the exceptional students, there are training opportunities in metalwork, trains operations, and accounting." He droned on for a while regarding the importance of these positions, and then looked expectantly around the classroom. "Do any of you have questions for me?"

Jessie suspected the work involved considerable manual labour. Her father said there were too few mechanics for the railroad, and people were brought over from England to work on the Western line. The good jobs would be taken by those with experience, not young Canadian graduates with inferior educations. One of the boys in the class asked about wages, and the amount sounded low to Jessie. She suspected farming would be more lucrative if you could work productive land. The training jobs would not even pay a wage for six months. Joey asked whether he could learn to run the steam locomotive. This led to snickers from his classmates. Joey had trouble tying his shoe laces. Then Jessie raised her hand.

"Could women do the jobs you mentioned?"

"These jobs require physical strength that women do not possess," Mr. Swanson said, but Jessie recognized an appraising look when she saw one. The excuse he'd given left Jessie smirking and made Mr. Swanson fidget. It was obvious she was taller than many of the boys in their graduating year. More snickers from the back of the room caused Miss Armstrong to raise her commanding voice to quell them. Before he left, Mr. Swanson removed several application forms from a smart leather briefcase and left them with Miss Armstrong.

When the bell rang at the end of class, Jessie said two words to Donny, "Fine horse."

"Fine clothes," he replied.

Jessie's father was working beneath the overhang next to their barn. A large dray horse tied to the post favoured a hind foot missing a shoe. Her father's face was bright pink, and sweat from his forehead sizzled like bacon when it dripped onto the hot forge. With his right arm, he worked air into the coals using the leather bellows. His left hand clasped the steel tongs holding the shoe, and she watched the shoe turn red–hot and the edges soften in the coals. He moved to the waiting horse and pressed it briefly onto the raised hoof to obtain a faint imprint. He then transferred the shoe to the anvil, quickly grabbing a heavy hammer to shape it properly. The acrid smell of burning hoof made the horse snort, and the clang of cold metal against with the hot shoe startled the animal again. As her father lowered the finished shoe into the water, a cloud of steam rose up, and Jessie's silhouette appeared in the fog he had created.

"There ye are, lassie," he said. "I could ha' used your help with the hoof knife."

Jessie knew she was not the son he wanted, but then neither was her brother. Thomas had no interest in the farm, but she was strong and willing. Besides, horses took to her quickly, and she was good at trimming the hoof, leaving it level, and never damaging the quick. Papa trusted her to clean small wounds, apply salves, and change dressings. She knew she was capable of doing what he did, and somehow, she would make it happen. She shook off her annoyance.

"A man from Great Western Railway invited us to apply for work today," she said, explaining her delay in returning home from school.

Her father glanced at her as he moved back to the horse. "Any jobs for women?"

Jessie shrugged, and her father only nodded. They'd discussed what she might do when she finished her schooling, or at least, Jessie had talked and her father had listened and then given her his usual answer. "No one will bring their animals to a woman, Jessie." Only this time he added, "But your mother would be happy with your help in the house, until you find a beau and marry."

Jessie snorted. "I'm as likely to find a beau I can tolerate as a woman farrier in Chippawa." But she blushed when her mind turned to Donny. She dreamed of starting up a practice with Donny, only now he was being forced to take another path. "Papa, don't you think Donny's bright enough to be a veterinarian?"

"Not all bright students do well at school work." This was not the first time the topic had arisen, nor the first time her father had tried to tell her Donny was different from other boys.

"I know Donny works hard at school, although he pretends he doesn't." Did that make him slow, she wondered. He didn't seem slow to her, and his memory was awfully good.

"Some people have a unique way of solving problems, and I suspect Donald has a mind like that," her father continued. "He's quick to understand, and when I show him something, he does not need to be told twice. Remember that badger you found two years ago with the arrow through its leg muscle, and Donald thought to push it through rather than pull it out? That was good thinking and it was less damaging to the badger."

"Dr. Forbes is sending him away to train as a pharmacist."

"Pharmacy is a good profession, Jessie. Perhaps that's the right choice for him."

"You wouldn't say that if you'd seen his face." She ran her hand gently over the horse's muzzle, getting a small snuffle in response. "I was wondering, Papa, if you might take him on as an apprentice?" Jessie realized her plan was transparent to her father who knew Donald was her only true friend.

"I couldn't afford to pay the lad, Jessie. We have trouble covering our debts as is."

"But he'll have no expenses if he lives at home."

Her father was quiet for a moment. "Send Donald to talk to me. We will see if something might come of it." Jessie hugged her father and a broad smile lit up her face.

She was still smiling when she entered the house. Her mother, normally glum, greeted her with an uncharacteristic grin of her own.

"Your brother and his wife are coming for a visit."

She waived a letter at Jessie who smiled weakly in return. She'd last seen Thomas and Louise at their wedding in York two years earlier. Her brother had moved up in the world, and it was plain from his infrequent letters and visits that he had little interest in the goings-on in Chippawa. But her mother had never been able to find fault in Thomas. In her mother's eyes, Jessie was a poor substitute for her older brother.

"Louise has given birth to a baby boy. Imagine that. He never said a word in his letters."

They were lucky to see a few lines from him every few months, thought Jessie. Her mother looked flushed and Jessie wondered if it arose from excitement at being a grandmother or embarrassment at not being told sooner of the pregnancy and birth. "Will they be bringing the baby?" Jessie asked. That would be the best part of the visit, she thought.

"He says Benjamin is now old enough to travel. They've named the boy after Louise's father."

Jessie took this all in. She wanted to ask how old the baby should be for it to travel, and why the baby was named after Louise's father and not Thomas's, but when she saw the fleeting appearance of disappointment on her mother's face, she bit her tongue. "I'll prepare Thomas's old room."

Thomas and Louise arrived mid-afternoon two days later. Neither was noticeably travel weary from the steamboat ride across Lake Ontario to Port Dalhousie and the train down to Chippawa. Jessie and her mother invited them into the house, but Thomas excused himself from the company of the women and left to find his father in the barn.

A pewter bowl filled with oranges, apples and a few sprigs of fragrant pine needles lent a festive mood and scent to their table, and the aroma of freshly-baked bread and roasting chicken wafted in from the kitchen. Louise wasted no time in passing the baby to Jessie and dropping down, uninvited, into her father's big chair.

"You cannot believe how exhausted I feel," Louise said with a sigh loud enough to split kindling. "Travelling with a newborn is not for the faint of heart, and I have not yet recovered from the trials of pregnancy and childbirth. The pain is quite impossible to describe."

Jessie was astounded that Louise was directing these remarks to her mother, as if she had not borne three of her own, one stillborn. But Louise didn't stop for a breath, prattling on as if she were the first woman to give birth. "How women collect the strength of will to produce more than one child I do not know. And now I have no time to rest, there is so much to do with the care and feeding of Benjamin, and that on top of all my other duties to my husband and my home and directing our maid who would like nothing better than to sleep all day in the pantry. My energy is being sapped from me daily, and I doubt I will be able to cope much longer without help."

Jessie realized her jaw had dropped as she stood listening to her sister-in-law's diatribe. Louise was dressed in the latest fashions with not a single hair out of place. She did not have the appearance of one drained by horrible hardship. Jessie felt sorry for her mother who sat still as an owl with a dazed look on her face. She was certain Louise, in spite of being "sapped", had sufficient energy to continue ranting for an hour or more.

Jessie stared into Benjamin's blue eyes held in a placid face framed by a halo of dark fuzz. The baby's blanket felt wet, and when Jessie mentioned it, Louise whipped out a cotton square from her satchel and waved it at her. Jessie carried the baby into her brother's room to change the diaper, having observed it done by a visiting neighbour.

She removed the white dress with braiding that extended well beyond his small body and pulled off the undershirt beneath. The knit diaper cover was wet as well, and she removed the soiled cotton square, using the dry corners to wipe the baby's red bottom. After folding the fresh square into a triangle, she threaded a basting needle to quickly secure the diaper in position. Smiling to herself, she thought that taking care of a baby required less skill than railroad engineering or even shoeing a horse, but the odour was much worse. Benjamin was fast asleep by the time she had finished rinsing the soiled square. She placed pillows around him and returned to lean in the doorway of the front room.

Louise was still whining about the difficulties in keeping a house in the latest style and entertaining her husband's friends while taking care of a baby. Jessie recalled the day Thomas had first introduced her to his family in Chippawa three years ago. Louise had acted like a little princess, making Jessie iron her clothes, only slightly crushed in her travel satchel. She'd asked her mother-in-law if she would serve her Ceylon tea, saying that she could drink no other. She quickly returned from a walk with Thomas to view the barn, complaining of the dirt and bad smells of the animals. Thomas was obviously smitten with a woman who clung to his arm like a fancy doll. That grovelling devotion annoyed Jessie more than anything else. Louise was admittedly pretty, but so was a nice-looking horse, and you could train a horse.

She left the house to find Thomas. Whatever her father and Thomas were discussing, they stopped abruptly when she approached. Thomas smiled at her and displayed a mouth full of large white teeth. He'd advanced to top salesman for a new clothing factory in York, and Jessie imagined how those flashing teeth could be put to good use by cajoling people into parting with their money.

"Ah, you are the very topic of our discussion, Jessie," Thomas said. "Louise and I would like to invite you to move to York and live with us, to take care of wee Benjamin. You would have room and board of course." Thomas glanced at her father and added, "But we could not provide wages. You are part of our family after all." His teeth were sending the message she was a very fortunate girl to have this singular opportunity. Concern was mixed with annoyance on Papa's face, and her heart skipped a beat.

"I've only recently been told of your baby, Thomas," she replied calmly. "I wish I'd known earlier, but I've made other plans for my future." Jessie was not adept at fabricating stories, and one of her father's bushy eyebrows lifted in surprise at her answer. She blushed.

"What other plans?" her brother asked, his shiny teeth retreating into a mouth that snapped shut in disappointment.

"Why, marriage, of course," Jessie said. It was the first thing that popped into her head. "You don't suppose you are the only one interested in marriage, do you?"

"Has someone asked you to marry him?" Thomas eyes were now bulging. "Why haven't I been told?"

"You said nothing of your baby, so why should you be informed of my plans?" Jessie could hear her voice rising in indignation, but she didn't care. She glared at Thomas who looked incredulous that someone might want to marry her, but at least he seemed to know her well enough to turn away and return to the house. After Thomas was out of sight, Jessie smiled sheepishly at her father.

"Now lassie, what man are ye planning to marry? You're barely sixteen. Think of what your Mother will be telling Thomas right now."

Jessie looked down at her shoes, anger still coursing through her. "I'm sorry Papa, but Thomas and Louise can move south of the border if they want a slave. Besides, I didn't say *when* I was getting married." Her father clucked his tongue but said nothing.

When she returned to the house, Thomas declined to speak or even look at her. Clearly, her Mother had set him straight concerning the possibility of any forthcoming nuptials. Jessie felt her mother's angry eyes drilling into her, but she had no intention of apologizing. Nothing would make her accept Thomas's offer.

"Jessie, I'd like you to reconsider your brother's request," her mother said, her disappointment and anger filling the space between her words.

"I'm sorry, Mother, but I have no interest in taking care of a baby in York."

"Benjamin is not any baby. It's Thomas's son."

"Exactly, Mother, it's his child, not mine. If they want a nurse, they should hire one."

"It *is* about the wage," Louise said. "I'm sorry, but we can't afford to pay you. I would think you'd be happy to settle for room and board."

"Why?" Jessie asked and felt her mother cringe.

"Because you are my sister," Thomas said. "Don't you want to help us?"

"Louise is quite capable of taking care of one tiny baby, Thomas," Jessie said.

"This is pointless," Louise said, "I think we can catch the late boat back to York if we hurry, Thomas." She began to pack up Benjamin's bag.

"You should stay the night so my parents can spend time with Benjamin," Jessie said.

"Perhaps you should have considered that before you declined our invitation," Thomas said, his annoyed tone a good match to Jessie's.

"How are these two things related?" Jessie asked, thinking Thomas looked a bit like Angus after she'd pushed him to the ground.

"Jessie is right, Thomas," Mrs. MacKay said. "Louise is weary and should rest before she returns to York."

"Please don't concern yourselves with my welfare," Louise said, eyes flaring and lips pursed. "I'm anxious to get back to my own home where I know I will rest more comfortably."

For several weeks after her brother's visit, Jessie and her mother maintained a cold silence sandwiched between occasional heated arguments. Jessie could not recall a single kind word passing between them.

"I never thought I'd give birth to a selfish daughter," her mother said.

"I never thought I'd be considered free labour by my brother."

"That's not fair, Jessie. Louise is not strong like you, and she can't cope with the baby."

"I suspect it was Thomas' idea, not hers. She would cope well enough without a man telling her she cannot."

Her father kept clear of these arguments, and Jessie spent as much time in the barn as possible. This did not stop her mother from needling her regarding the state of her clothing that was forever requiring cleaning or mending. She was told to wear her hair up nicely and not flying around in a loose and untidy fashion. Her manners at the table were under constant scrutiny, and even her laugh, on the rare occasion when that occurred at home, was described as unattractive and more like a guffaw. But what hurt her the most was that her father would not defend her, especially when her mother stopped her from doing her favourite things.

"I will not have you going into that barn every day after school," Mrs. MacKay said.

"But Papa needs my help," Jessie said. "I prepare the hooves for him."

"He has no right to ask you, and this work has likely ruined your chances of attracting a suitor. Don't think I haven't heard what is said about you in the village. They say Jessie MacKay acts more like a boy than a girl, that she fights like a boy and rides like a boy."

"I don't see why that's so terrible," Jessie said, but she was deeply hurt when her mother insinuated that no one would want to marry her. Did Donny think of her more as a boy too? When she'd suggested that Donny ask her father for an apprenticeship position, he hadn't seemed interested. Then she stupidly accused him of not really wanting to be a veterinarian at all, and he said she shouldn't tease him when it was out of his reach. She'd asked him whether it was because of his poor grades, the lack of tuition, or his father's poor opinion of veterinary medicine. The hurt look she received in reply made her regret her outspokenness, and not for the first time. Now he'd avoided her for weeks. The thought ran through her mind, albeit briefly, that moving to York to live with Thomas and Louise might be more tolerable than staying in Chippawa.

One afternoon, Miss Armstrong asked the class if any of the senior girls would be willing to work at the newly opened Welland Hotel. The Hotel was located in the town of St. Catharines where recuperative mineral waters were touted for bathing and drinking. The Welland was hiring employees for their new "Spa," a name Miss Armstrong said was adopted from a town in Belgium that first promoted the use of healing mineral waters. Jessie had no idea what a spa employee might do. When questioned further on the position, Miss Armstrong could provide little information except that employees would learn the trade and develop the necessary skills. "And no, it will not require bottling mineral water," she replied when Joey had asked. Everyone knew of St. Catharines' special water in little glass bottles. They laughed at Joey's question and shook their heads in wonder at rich people who would pay good money for bottled water.

Miss Armstrong said some thought the mineral waters in St. Catharines could cure gout and rheumatism, and visitors would often take in the waters to treat a chronic illness or simply to recuperate from the tedious sea voyage from abroad before they visited Niagara Falls. Later, when Jessie asked her father what he thought of St. Catharines' water, he'd shrugged and said, "Lassie, if you believe you are doing something good for your body, often you will begin to feel better."

Jessie approached Miss Armstrong after class to tell her she was interested in applying for a position at the Welland Hotel. Her teacher's eyebrows lifted at this statement.

"I imagined you to be happy on the farm, Jessica, and if not there, you are among the hardest-working students in the class and have many choices available. You are very good with the younger children and should consider teaching. To be truthful, I find it difficult to think of you being content working as a hotel employee."

"You said many of the patrons at the Welland Hotel are elderly and in need of rest and recuperation. I thought I might find satisfaction in helping them." Although this was a truthful response, Jessie did not mention she planned to save her salary to open her own farrier business.

"I suspect the majority of the people who are fit to make the trip are healthy enough," Miss Armstrong said, her lips pursed. "They simply enjoy being pampered, as would we all. But perhaps you will find it an interesting and rewarding occupation."

Jessie realized that Miss Armstrong had reservations, but she was unsure whether they were concerns with the position or her suitability for it. Nonetheless, her teacher agreed to help her submit an application along with her recommendation, and Jessie felt a small glow of optimism for the first time in a long while.

When the school year ended in May, Jessie found herself on her first adventure away from home, traveling up the Welland canal in a barge to St. Catharines. It pleased her to be leaving Chippawa before Donny, and she imagined him missing her. Their goodbyes had been brusque and uncomfortable. "I bet you'll hate it there," Donny had said. His words would have hurt more had Jessie not realized he was voicing his own fears over leaving home.

She carried a small bag containing a few clothes, having been told she would be provided with uniforms when she arrived. The barge passed green fields and new factories that belched black smoke. Then the noon horn blew and people flooded out of factories as if anxious to be outside, if only for a few precious minutes. Workers along the canal were busy repairing and expanding the waterway and adjacent roads, replacing wooden supports with stronger stone walls. The men moved at a much faster pace than those in Chippawa. It occurred to her that Thomas had adopted this frantic pace and she felt a trace of compassion for him until she realized that she too was headed towards town.

After disembarking at St. Catharines wharf, she followed the written directions provided in her letter of employment. She studied the crude map marked with landmarks and roads leading across the city, checking them off mentally as she walked three miles to the hotel. Tree-lined avenues framed beautiful brick and wood-sided two or three-story houses, much grander than any in Chippawa although not so grand as some in York. She peered into the front gardens, amazed at the effort that went into creating beauty rather than harvests. The showy gardens reminded her of Donny's love of fine but often impractical clothes which would likely disintegrate in a good downpour. Clouds overtook the sun, and the light sprinkle of rain that accompanied the clouds leached away a little of her confidence. Not yet gone a day, she felt a longing for the comforting familiarity of home.

The sun came out again as she passed a school house, and she stopped for a moment, entranced by the scene. Branches of an old lilac tree bent over a corner of the school yard and fought for space among the children who played beneath it. Petals covered the ground in a purple haze stirred up by several pairs of small scuffed shoes. A bright-faced child had collected dozens of blossoms and was sitting cross-legged on the ground giggling as she tossed them into the air by lifting her pinafore apron. Jessie drank in a great breath of the sweet aroma and smiled as she looked upwards, her mood brightening with the sky.

When she stood on York Street opposite the hotel, she felt both excited and intimidated. The grand entry was flanked by stone pillars as high as a two-story house, with rows of potted trees trimmed in the shape of perfect balls. Two men in red livery attended the horses and baggage, and there was a flurry of activity in front of two huge doors leading into the lobby. She followed her instructions to walk to the back of the hotel. Standing in the open kitchen door, she was impressed by the constant activity. She managed to go unnoticed until a small boy in a great hurry pushed past her, and she knocked over a broom resting precariously against the door frame.

"Out of the way, Miss. We got work to do."

"Ah, you must be the new girl we've been expecting," said a young woman her age. She was wearing a spotless starched white apron over a smart navy dress. "I'm Morag McLean. Leave your bag there, and I'll take you up to see Miss Claire. She'll help you with lodgings and uniforms." Jessie followed Morag up three flights of back stairs to a cramped office. She faced a small older woman whose rotund body strained the seams of her own navy dress. A laugh and a sharp clap rewarded Jessie's smile.

"You must be Jessica MacKay. I hope you'll use that wonderful smile of yours on our patrons. It's the tonic they'll need to put them in good spirits."

The next weeks passed in a blur. Although Jessie was kept busy all day and half the evening, she managed to find time to write several letters. The substance of the arguments she'd had with her mother slowly faded from her memory, but she would not admit she yearned to return home. Instead, she'd convey amusing stories regarding the Welland Hotel, the fancy patrons, her roommates in the loft of a building behind the hotel, and her uniform. At first, she wondered how she would keep her uniform in the immaculate condition Miss Claire demanded. When she complained to Morag, her roommate opened her closet to reveal a half dozen starched white aprons. "I go through two or three a day. There's no way to keep clean unless you sit in the lobby all day."

"I was only given two aprons." Jessie said.

"Did you ask for more? They'll give them if you ask."

Soon Jessie was following her example, and Miss Clare rewarded her with a gaze of approval.

"You look very attractive and professional in that uniform, Jessica," Miss Claire said, her jowls wobbling.

Jessie had brushed aside the compliment, but she had wondered for a moment what Donny might think if he saw her. Her dark blonde hair was pinned up to reveal a slender neck. Her angular shape took on a more feminine form beneath the starched apron with a frill on the bottom and the crinoline beneath her skirt. She believed her complexion was her best feature. Unlike girls who had spots, her skin was clear. The sun had given it a healthy bronze glow that other girls shunned, but Jessie felt it was foolish not to enjoy being out in nature for fear of losing a pasty white complexion. Two of the boys working at the hotel had asked her out for walks on her free half-Sundays, but she had no interest in their silly jokes and coarse behaviour. Neither boy could hold a candle to Donny Forbes.

Jessie spent her much of her time escorting female patrons to various baths or rooms for massages, and she would accompany the more fit patrons on leisurely walks along the canal or fine city parks. She would help unpack and pack their luggage, arrange for cleaning of clothes, consult on menu preferences, and deal with the front desk at their time of departure.

Walks were meant to stimulate appetites for the grand food many considered to be one of the chief attractions of the Welland Hotel.

Jessie had not been able to personally confirm the excellence of the meals, but they did not appeal to her when viewed from afar: tiny mounds of mashed vegetables with little pieces of poached fish or chicken and sprigs of inedible greenery for garnish. Patrons drank only spa water or tea made with the water. On her free afternoon, she would wander around the bustling town, exploring the gardens and woods. When she asked a man working at the bottling plant if he knew what was responsible for the healing properties of St. Catharines' water, the answer she received was less than satisfying.

"It's them minerals. Not like in your regular water, which has only water. Minerals is good for your organs."

She managed to keep a straight face at his response. She suspected her father was right. The exercise and simple diet lacking rich foods or strong drink had more to do with recuperation than St. Catharines' miraculous spring water.

Two short months later, she found herself training the new spa employees and escorting the "special" ladies on their daily activities. The special ones were often quite infirm and required help getting into and out of their wheeled chairs and mineral baths. Jessie was both strong and patient, and she realized those two attributes were generally lacking in the other female employees. The girls commiserated with her when she was assigned to the "old crows", but Jessie didn't mind helping the elderly. They were often more pleasant and appreciative in spite of, or perhaps because of, their infirmities. Old Mrs. Ferguson, who said immediately upon meeting Jessie said, "Call me Ginger," was a favourite. She had been a repeat visitor at Welland Hotel since it opened.

"I'd like to stay here till I die," she said in confidence to Jessie, "but the price is quite dear and my son expects his inheritance."

Jessie felt her heart shiver. She lifted Ginger's frail body from the bed to the wheeled chair. "Never mind tomorrow, think what a wonderful day we'll have. I'm taking you to a luxurious hot mineral bath to restore your energy. Then you'll have a ride around Montebello Park before lunch. After lunch, you can have a nap or attend a reading in the library. I understand there is a poet stopping by from York this afternoon, a Mr. Macintyre." The frown that appeared on Ginger's face told Jessie it would be a nap after lunch.

Later, Jessie passed by the library and listened for a moment to a strange poem concerning the wonders of cheese, delivered in a heavy Scottish brogue. The patrons appeared to be enjoying it thoroughly and clapped with enthusiasm after each stanza. As she headed across the lobby, she was surprised to see Thomas and Louise enter the front door, accompanied by a bellboy laden with their luggage.

"Jessica!" Thomas shouted out her name and she could see Louise grab his arm in embarrassment at his outburst. Several people turned to stare at her. She walked over to her brother, masking her dismay.

"Thomas and Louise. What a surprise to see you here. Where is little Ben?"

"We left him at home with the maid." Louise said, sounding her usual pompous self, Jessie thought. She realized she would have been the one left at home had she agreed to go to York. "Your mother wrote you were working here, and we decided on the spur of the moment to visit the hotel for a little weekend of rest. We've heard so much of the spa, but the autumn leaves alone are worth the trip." She simpered and added in a conspiratorial manner, "Although I hear the Springbank Hotel is much nicer." Jessie felt annoyed when this statement was delivered, no doubt what Louise had intended.

"I expect you'll enjoy your stay at the Welland. I understand the meals are excellent," Jessie said, managing to hide her irritation. Her face felt frozen, but she realized she was more confident and controlled when speaking with Louise after her experience with the hotel patrons, several of whom could be quite difficult. "It's a pity I won't be able to spend much time with you as I will be occupied with our regular guests."

"No, we've been assured we will have your full attention while we're here," Louise said, gushing. Jessie felt the smile freeze on her face.

"I'll let Robin show you to your room, and we'll see each other after you're settled." Jessie turned away without another word and left them standing in the lobby.

Ginger asked her what was wrong as Jessie helped her dress for dinner that evening. She hadn't learned to hide her annoyance as well as she thought. "My brother and his wife arrived unexpectedly from York this afternoon," Jessie said.

"And this is the cause for your distracted mood?" Ginger asked gently.

"They were annoyed with me when I refused to take care of their baby," Jessie said.

"You don't like babies?" Ginger asked.

Jessie smiled. "Taking care of someone else's baby should bring compensation, shouldn't it?"

"Ah. Your brother thought you would be honoured."

Jessie nodded. "I can deal with Thomas, but his wife, Louise, is very demanding and selfish. Perhaps telling you of their wedding will give you an idea. Their wedding reception was held in York at a very fancy hotel. My parents were required to pay for their own stay in the hotel, not being invited to lodge with Louise's parents or to stay in the house that their son purchased with money given to him in part by my father. When I asked Thomas why he had not invited our parents to stay with him, he said Louise had need of the room for her aunt and uncle who had traveled from Montreal to attend their wedding. Thomas did invite me to stay in their attic room, but later I realized I was expected to help with the cleaning and cooking. I did

34

not even have the opportunity to attend the wedding ceremony as Louise insisted at the last minute I oversee the arrangements for the wedding reception saying she could not trust the hired help. They left on a European holiday without even a thank-you."

Ginger commiserated with her, and after lifting Ginger into the wheeled chair and arranging her dress, Jessie said, "You look lovely," and enjoyed the blush of response that brought colour to Ginger's time-worn face.

"Why do you suppose they are visiting this hotel?"

"I suspect they are planning to make full use of my services and enjoy every minute while they run me ragged. My schedule has been revised by the manager to accommodate their wishes for the next few days."

"Ah," Ginger said. "I'll miss your company, then."

"I see no way to avoid it." Jessie grimaced at the thought of listening to Louise talk nonstop for two days. She imagined Thomas would be beside himself with boredom and his temper would flare.

"Hmm. Perhaps we can think up something to occupy their time, rather than yours." Ginger said.

"I've considered arranging for a bout of indigestion," said Jessie.

"Yours or theirs?" Ginger laughed and then paused. "I suppose a trip to the Falls in a slow carriage is out of the question?"

"You can be assured my brother will have seen everything he considers worth visiting in the Niagara region," Jessie agreed.

"Then perhaps we can invite your friend for a visit? Donald, isn't it?" Ginger wiggled her fingers together seeming to enjoy the subterfuge. Jessie had mentioned Donny to her roommates as well as Ginger, although for reasons she couldn't explain, she had felt the need to exaggerate concerning the nature of their relationship. Thankfully, so far, there had been no need to admit that Donny Forbes regarded her as a friend, but no more. Nonetheless, Jessie hooted at Ginger's suggestion.

"What a splendid idea! Donald could accompany us and make it difficult for Louise to order me around. If only I had enough money to pay for his travel and accommodations. Imagine their faces when they hear my boyfriend has arrived for a surprise visit. That would ruin their game."

Ginger grabbed Jessie's hands. "Jessie, my dear, I am happy to pay for his expenses for the pleasure it will bring me. Please let me do this. And say to Donald that it is your doing, of course."

"Ginger, you are truly generous, but accepting gifts from patrons is grounds for dismissal." Jessie was quietly thankful that strict rules of conduct for employees relieved her from the need to produce an actual boyfriend. They were silent for a few moments but then Jessie's face brightened. "I have another idea," Jessie said. "It's not as much fun as your suggestion, but it should dampen their spirits and perhaps send them home sooner than they'd planned." She knew the smile she flashed at Ginger was a bit wicked. "I will need your help though."

Jessie explained her plan and Ginger suggested they recruit two more of the regular patrons to take part in their "play." A few minutes later in the dining room, Jessie introduced Ginger to her brother and his wife who were seated. They looked surprised when Jessie suggested a hotel patron who was traveling alone would very much enjoy their company and would be able to tell them about the hotel amenities. Louise shrugged one shoulder, and as soon as Thomas mumbled "Of course." Jessie manoeuvred Ginger's chair to the table and arranged for another place setting. She regretted leaving the dining room. Before coming down for dinner, she and Ginger had discussed what might happen during the meal, and they both laughed so hard Jessie knew she would miss a very special performance.

"I plan to discuss, while we eat of course, the diseases that bring people to the spa," Ginger had said. "I will give special attention to the skin diseases that create pustules and papules, fissures, cysts, and ulcers. They'll be well-prepared for their soak in the spa pool tomorrow morning, you can be sure."

"You are a devil, Ginger, but if you can keep Louise from getting a word in, I will be especially impressed," Jessie said. Patrons with any open or obvious skin lesions were forbidden entry to the spa pool, but her brother and his wife would not know that.

Ginger agreed to direct her friend, George Killam, to their table for breakfast, suggesting George could impart his knowledge of spa history with them. George pretended to be an expert on ancient Roman baths, although what he said was largely nonsense. He also liked to affect senility and did a remarkably good job. Once told he would need to be prepared to out-talk Louise, George would take up the challenge. Then, Major Teddy would be asked to join the MacKays for their midday meal. The Major liked a glass or two of ale before lunch and he could be counted on to recount stories of the 1837 rebellion, over and over again. Few could survive a lunch with him without experiencing indigestion. Jessie smiled as she headed for the boarding house. She had suddenly developed a good appetite.

The next day, Jessie had planned to take a walk with her brother and his wife after their midday meal, but when she met them outside the dining room, Thomas and Louise announced they were leaving early. Jessie managed to look surprised as Louise described their ordeals at meals.

"One old bore after another latched on to us at our meals. We are now suffering from headaches and indigestion," Louise said.

"I don't suppose you had anything to do with choosing our meal companions?" Thomas said, his eyes mere slits and his gleaming teeth well concealed.

"I did introduce you to Ginger, and it was very kind of you to agree to entertain a lonely old lady."

"Entertain her? I should say not," Louise exclaimed. "That woman should be banned from the dining room."

Jessie waved gaily as the carriage rolled away. She had enough time before lunch to write a letter to Donny. She was anxious to tell him Louise had "foamed like Niagara" before they sped off in the carriage.

CHAPTER 3: 1861, FERGUS, CANADA WEST

A child as well as a man, stuff'd with the stuff that
is coarse and stuff'd with the stuff that is fine

The accident happened as Donald tried to maneuver a heavy barrel of molasses off a rickety hand cart. He'd meant to move the barrel beneath the counter, but as he rolled it from the cart, it dropped down onto an edge, split a stave, and drove a sharp piece of wood deep into the side of his left hand. The molasses and his blood rode out together in a sticky dark stream. He struggled to upend the barrel in an effort to prevent wasting more of the sweet syrup. When he pulled the wood shard from his palm, he yelped, and a wiry old man clutching a cotton rag was soon by his side. For a moment, Donald thought Mr. Strathmore might use the rag to wipe up the spill on the floor, but he pressed it to Donald's injured hand instead.

"It's a good thing it's molasses, my boy. It acts as an antiseptic, don't you know," Mr. Strathmore's smile revealed a gap of missing teeth along one side of his mouth that made him look slightly demented. Donald thought him a very old man to be in charge of a store. He was often forgetful and not particularly good at training his clerks.

"I've heard that letting the blood flow a bit will cleanse the wound." Donald said, gritting his teeth from the throbbing pain. That was one of the few things his father and Jessie's father had agreed upon.

"That'll do fine for a small cut, but it's more important to staunch strong bleeding, and you'll need to press hard to do that," Mr. Strathmore said. "You're looking pale, Donald. Sit down on that box for a moment."

Tom, the other clerk, stood gawking at them from the front of the store. If he hadn't been with a customer, Tom would have been there like a goose to grain to enjoy all the gore. Pain only bothered Tom when it was his own.

Mr. Strathmore returned with a piece of clean cotton to wrap around his hand. "Now, see you don't go getting that hand wet, and do clean up this mess as well as you can with your good hand," Mr. Strathmore said, toddling off.

The Fergus Dispensary and General Store closed to the public at six o'clock, but that meant Donald must sweep up and restock the shelves. Usually he could complete the task by eight-thirty, but not tonight. It had been a week since his accident, yet he was expected to complete as much work with one good hand as two.

A small triangular piece of wood had worked its way out that morning, taking with it a chunk of the flesh from the base of his smallest finger. Now the area felt as raw and painful as a tooth in need of pulling. He had written to his mother detailing the treatment with poultices a local doctor had prescribed. He thought his father might have made a comment and was disappointed to hear nothing. He couldn't stop aching for Chippawa. It was difficult to find much to admire in Fergus, and he missed his friends, especially Jessie. At the rate he was going, he knew he would be refilling shelves till well past ten o'clock.

It occurred to him anyone looking in through the large display window could read his mood from his slumped shoulders and sad face, and he made an effort not to look as dispirited as he felt. Although he was meant to be learning pharmacy, he spent his time restocking tools, nails, and feed as well as replenishing the dry goods. Twenty-five-pound bags of sugar, flour and oatmeal were levered awkwardly onto the lower shelves, and he must replace any missing jars of molasses and honey. When he reached the shelf with tea, coffee and spices, he unscrewed the jar with cinnamon bark and enjoyed a whiff. It reminded him of his mother's puddings and elicited a sigh. The other spices held no interest, and the smell of cloves reminded him of a painful toothache.

The pharmacy, once the largest part of the store, was now dwindling as Mr. Strathmore had recently decided to advertise as a general store. The drugs were handled exclusively by Mr. Strathmore who took it upon himself to replace the various patent medicines and elixirs sold each day. Donald was anxious to learn more about the medicines, but he was kept busy with tedious duties. When he'd complained that he was not learning pharmacy, presumably the reason for his apprenticeship, Mr. Strathmore had answered, "There is little new to learn, Forbes. It seems to me nothing useful has been discovered since I was your age. Physicians still put faith in blood-letting, purgatives and emetics."

"But you carry many patent medicines, sir. Surely those are new," Donald had argued. He couldn't believe there had been no changes over the man's lifetime.

"New bottles for old remedies, I'm afraid, and they promise much more than they deliver. Now if you want to learn something new, I have a book here you should study. I call it my herbarium." He brought out a large book tucked beneath the apothecary counter, and he opened it as reverently as he would a bible. The book contained colourful hand-painted images of medicinal plants with their roots, leaves, flowers, and berries illustrated in impressive albeit fading detail. Donald saw notes and maps in the margins which indicated where to find the plants locally.

"Our native tribes value many of these herbs, don't you know. Here is goldenseal, very useful for inflammation, and slippery elm for diarrhea. Bloodroot is good for skin problems."

"Do you collect all these plants yourself, sir?

"I no longer have the energy to hunt for them and prepare the extracts, and much of the nearby land on which they grew is now cleared and cultivated for grain. Besides, I find it more profitable to sell other items in the store, clothing for instance."

"But how did you know how to collect the right plant, sir? They all look the same to me."

"That's why you must study each plant carefully, Forbes. You must learn the particular appearance, how it changes through the seasons, where it grows, which parts of the plant to use, and of course, how to make the proper extract. When I was your age, I found this all quite fascinating, but it has lost its lustre for me now. Perhaps it helped that I had a young native girl to show me the location of these plants and their use." Donald watched the old man's eye haze over with the memory. "Bright Flower, I called her," he murmured. "She was enamoured of my cologne."

"Do you mean fragrance?" Donald was surprised since the men he knew shunned scent. Mr. Strathmore laughed at the confused look on his face.

"Years ago, I mixed cologne right in this shop and I found a ready local market for my efforts with the ladies of the town, don't you know. After preparing it, my clothes sported the fragrance, and Bright Flower was very taken with the aroma. I have not bothered to prepare it for many years, but perhaps you could learn this recipe from me. I doubt many other pharmacists would give you lessons in preparing scents." Donald could readily agree on that point, and they spent an aroma-filled afternoon mixing oils of lemon, jasmine, cloves, and Bergamot with oil of roses, alcohol and water.

"Who shall we sell these to?" Donald asked. For a brief moment, he imagined making his fortune with original new scents.

"I doubt there's a local market, what with French ones in competition these days, but perhaps you could send a bottle to your mother or girlfriend?"

Donald declined, suspecting his parents would not be pleased he was spending his time preparing something they considered frivolous, and he would never consider sending a bottle to Jessie since he could imagine her response: "All this potion is good for is attracting flies, and we have horse manure for that."

When he told Mr. Strathmore the women in his life were of a more practical nature, his employer brightened and said, "Perhaps we should make bed bug poison together next week? *Vini rectificatus* and camphor, don't you know."

When he had time after work, Donald would carefully copy a page or two from Mr. Strathmore's herbarium together with the description of the plant uses. Finding specific plants in the fields and woods around town was more difficult than he'd imagined. He was often unsure whether he'd located the correct plant, there being no Bright Flower to guide him.

Mr. Strathmore had suggested using the aroma of plants and their sap as a distinguishing feature, apparently an idea he'd gleaned from his native muse. But when Mr. Strathmore had failed to appreciate the distinctive aroma of each plant, Bright Flower had told him his nose had not received proper training as a child. "As I understand what she was trying to tell me, only my eyes and mouth really know the strawberry, but my nose cannot recall its smell without the strawberry present to stimulate the recollection. Do you agree that our minds cannot bring forth the memory of an aroma the way they can produce an image or a taste? Perhaps we are deficient in this regard in comparison with our native brethren."

Donald squashed the stems of various plants to smell the sap, but few offered a distinctive aroma that was adequately described using his limited library of scents. As Mr. Strathmore had predicted, with exceptions like citrus and resin, he was unable to use odour as a distinguishing feature.

On occasional free evenings, he would walk to the "Little Falls" in the center of town. The sound of the flowing water was only a weak echo of Niagara Falls and caused him to ache for home. He longed to ride the new horse, play cricket, or fish for walleye in the Niagara River. Mama replied to all of his letters and had recently written the new filly had thrown his friend Willie when he tried to ride her. "Serves him right," he had thought to himself, "I should be the one to ride Ruby." But what he longed for most of all was not the pony, or the place, but his family. Feeling his wounded hand, he realized the people who cared deeply for his welfare were no longer close by to reassure him.

It was past ten o'clock when Donald hung up his apron and prepared to turn off the gas lamps, but before he could do so, his fellow clerk Tom poked his head in the front door. Donald shared a room with Tom at Mr. Strathmore's home. His roommate was tall and gangly, easy to like, and with an endless supply of energy and tall tales of his exploits. His eyebrows were particularly bushy, and he liked to wiggle one up over the other and make people laugh. But now he looked tired as he swayed in the door frame, a stupid grin covering his face.

"What are you still doin' here?" Tom said, slurring his words. "You sure missed a good party down at the little falls."

A good party usually meant the clerks from the other stores got together to plan their strategies for wooing women, often describing the women as wild game they might have hunted. "Lucy is older and smarter than the others. She will take more effort to win over," Tom had said one time, rubbing his chin in an effort to look wise. Donald rarely contributed to the conversations as he had little experience to offer. But he listened carefully when they described their various exploits, most of which Donald suspected had never taken place. Even so, his eyes would widen when they mentioned the size of women's breasts or hips and discuss who they would prefer to bed. These were not women of easy virtue, he understood, but girls or women they saw on occasion in the store. When he asked whether the women they had taken to bed expected an offer of marriage, they had laughed.

"I know women who can be cajoled into giving their favours without having to announce the bans," Tom snickered.

Donald had been taken aback and it must have shown on his face. Tom told him later that it wasn't unusual for women to ache for sex the way men did. "The problem," Tom said, "is in recognizing the ones who might be willing to enjoy love-making. Taking them to the fair, feeding them a good dinner, or buying them trinkets are always useful tactics in winning favours," Tom advised, "and dressing well, of course, since you are selling yourself, the same way we sell goods in the store."

None of Tom's words of wisdom told him how he should converse with women. He didn't enjoy the games Tom was so adept at playing, such as teasing and flirting, although he admired his friend's easy ways with the women who entered their store, even the ones old enough to be his mother. He wished he felt more comfortable in the presence of the fairer sex, as Tom called all of them regardless of their physical attributes, and he wanted to offer them more entertainment than his own limited conversation. His Papa had never confided his experience with women, although he'd overheard Aunt Eliza tell his mother that Papa would have had many opportunities for encounters with wayward women on his travels to various ports. Maybe he could have discussed these questions with Jessie, but the idea of asking her made him uncomfortable, and he worried she would be critical of his motives. Besides, he knew she hated to be teased in the way Tom teased women, and she saw little point in idle banter.

Seeing Tom in that drunken state annoyed Donald. Tom had not offered to help clean the store but instead had enjoyed himself at the party, no doubt with a bunch of rowdies drinking illicit liquor. He couldn't really complain because the two of them had agreed that, rather than both staying late, they would alternate evenings and that way enjoy a greater measure of time away from the store.

"It takes a lot longer to do this work with one hand," Donald complained as he waved his bandaged one in the air. "Besides, I don't have the money to waste on liquor."

Tom always had pocket money and was well-dressed, a source of envy for Donald. Tom said stylish clothes were more important than being handsome when attracting the fairer sex. Donald had replied having plenty of folding money was more important than both.

"You'd have the money if you take that job in Ingersoll with me. It pays more than the pittance we get here, and the town is much livelier. Anyway, I'm home to sleep off this head." Tom pulled the door closed, leaving Donald wondering how he might leave Fergus and return home.

The way out of his situation came sooner than Donald anticipated. Two weeks later, his hand had not healed properly, and in the last two days it had become swollen and more painful. Mr. Strathmore was concerned he was running a fever as well, and he told Donald to take a week off work to go home where his father could oversee his recovery.

When he arrived home, his mother took one look at his hand and called for his father. Papa frowned at his appearance and mentioned the loss of weight. Donald replied that his mother's cooking had been sorely missed, but he knew his face was pale and damp and he felt oddly embarrassed by his illness, seeing it a sign of weakness or poor hygiene . The wound had been on the mend, but now it was clearly inflamed and there were areas of tissue decay and a few red streaks his father pointed out to him.

"Do you see these lines, son? These are not a good sign, but I think we've caught the infection in time. Another couple of days and you would have lost that little finger. As it is, I will need to scrape the wound to remove the decayed tissue." Donald knew from his demeanor it would be a painful procedure. He nodded solemnly but said nothing. "You'll have a scar here, son, but it's not as bad as my own. Did I tell you how I got my scar?"

Donald had heard the story many times and it was one of his favourites. "Tell me again Papa, while you work." He thought it would take his mind from the pain. He watched his father prepare the tools he would need.

"I was Assistant Surgeon on the Comet, sailing out of Portsmouth in August. The year was 1844. That was my fourth posting, and I was looking forward to luxurious accommodations which meant sharing my quarters with only one other. I had my surgical implements aligned on the lid of my trunk, much as I am doing here, awaiting cleaning and organizing, when my cabin mate rushed into the room carrying a live chicken. The second mate was a tall man and couldn't clear the beams. He filled the small room without trying. As I hastily made to move out of his way, I banged into the tray on top of my trunk causing a scalpel to leap up and drop down to become embedded in my thigh."

When Donald's father had first told him this story, he was so drawn into the tale that he'd cried out in surprise when his father illustrated his words by banging his fist on Donald's thigh. But this time, his father kept talking as he scraped away at his hand. Donald bit down on his lip and pushed his face into the pillow. He felt his eyes fill with tears.

"My yelp and the second mate's surprise were enough to free the chicken. It flapped to the ceiling, then fell down onto the handle of the scalpel causing it to tear down through my flesh a good five inches. The mate caught the chicken, and when he looked at my leg, he had the nerve to tell me I had my first patient."

His father shook his head as he recalled the scene, and he picked up a threaded needle. "Now, I'm known for my speedy sewing skills, and the wound wasn't deep. But I have to admit my needlework wasn't as precise as usual, so I have a unique scar, as you know. Of course, I never let that mate forget the incident, and I rode him at every opportunity. The only good thing to come of it was a chicken dinner, because once I sewed up the wound, I went to capture the creature and end its miserable life prematurely.

The mate said I had no sense of humour, and he was right on that occasion. When I tried to ascertain why he was bringing a chicken into our cabin in the first place, he gave me a far-fetched story about a prank, but against whom, I never knew, and neither did the chicken. When I returned to shore five months later, your mother asked me how I got the scar, and I felt obliged to concoct a more honourable explanation. I told her I had received an injury when boarding a slaver off Bermuda." At this point, his father looked over to his mother and they exchanged a smile.

"I doubted she believed me as she knows I normally remain below decks during those forays. I thought I had convinced her my skills were too valuable to risk in a fight." As he tied the final knot, he chuckled, "A little scar is good for the soul," concluding his tale and snipping the thread at the same time. His mother shook her head sadly and continued to squeeze Donald's other hand.

"Thank you for the story, Papa," Donald said, as he dropped off to sleep. He had cried out only once.

When he awoke, his mother was still beside him. He asked for a drink of water.

"Is the pain manageable, son?" she asked, eyes filled with concern. She lifted his head from the pillow and held the cup to his lips.

Donald sipped, "A little better than before, I think." He tried to flex his hand and grimaced. His mother felt his forehead, and when her face relaxed, Donald knew his fever had abated. "Please thank Papa for me."

Donald could hear his mother talking with Papa in the kitchen below his room. "I don't know why Strathmore was not on top of this. It was a nasty wound and he has taken responsibility for these boys. Donald could have lost his hand," his father said in his angry voice.

"At least he had the sense to send him home to you," his mother responded. She was banging bowls while, and Donald imagined she was preparing a pudding. "Will he have the full use of his hand?" she asked.

"He should," his father said, in a quieter voice. "There was minimal necrosis, and now the wound is debrided and properly dressed. You should have seen the state of the bandage he was wearing." There was a long pause. "I cannot send him back there," his father said. "From Donald's letters, it sounds as if Strathmore has only a tiny pharmacy these days, and he will not be able to provide suitable training."

Donald smiled. His fervent wish was that his father would let him remain in Chippawa, and he dropped into a sleep filled with comforting dreams. When he awoke, he could smell the pudding with a hint of strawberry preserves.

Staying in Chippawa was not to be, and while Donald recovered that winter, his father wrote to colleagues who might have a vacant position for an apprentice. He was slow to receive replies. With time on his hands after his chores were done, Donald visited Jessie's father at his farm a half mile up Lyons Creek. When he found the farrier, he was bending over an inflamed hoof of a large horse tethered at the side of his barn.

"There ye are, lad," Mr. MacKay said in his strong Highland brogue. "I've been wondering when I'd be seeing you." He stepped back from the horse and watched him lower his foot gingerly to the floor. "I heard ye had a wounded hand," he said looking down with concern at Donald's bandaged left hand.

"It's on the mend," Donald smiled back at the small man. He often wondered how Mr. MacKay could handle the large animals, being so slight himself, no bigger than Jessie really. Yet he exuded confidence and had a gentle but determined way with the animals.

"I am happy to hear that," Mr. MacKay smiled, nodding at the wound. "You know Jessie is working at a hotel in St. Catharines," he offered, bristly eyebrows raised. "She asks after you in her letters," he added.

Donald felt himself squirm since he had replied to her only once. Her letters told him she was learning a great deal, and he had decided she must have little opportunity to feel homesick or to miss seeing him. He had nothing but complaints concerning his own apprenticeship, and after sending her one letter, he found he had nothing more of interest to communicate. "She's written to me, but I wasn't here to see Jessie, sir. I was hoping you could teach me a little of animal medicine." He studied the large horse favouring his sore foot, wondering what would be done for the animal. "Jessie told me I should speak to you if I had interest."

"That was months ago. I thought ye'd given up on the idea."

"I didn't have much choice then," Donald said.

"And you do now?"

Donald shrugged, and Mr. MacKay paused a moment to consider his request. "Surely, Donald, I'm willing to teach ye how to treat sick animals, but I wonder how your father would view such training?" There was another long silence.

"I'll ask him." Donald said, omitting to say that when he'd asked his father a year ago whether he might apprentice with Mr. MacKay, he had had refused outright, saying Mr. MacKay had not attended an accredited school. He believed those lacked scientific training favoured treatments based on magic and superstition. Although Donald knew this was not the case for Mr. MacKay, he found it difficult to defend the man when Papa was so certain in his mind. He'd never even told Jessie he'd asked his father's permission and been refused. He was tired of arguing with her and losing those arguments.

"Perhaps that would be best," Mr. MacKay agreed. "I could use your help lad, but I will not be able to pay you."

"You will not regret this." But as he said this, a shadow fell across Donald's face as he wondered what he would tell his father. He would say nothing, that's what. He would tell his father he was visiting Jessie. He turned to the horse, rubbing its muzzle.

"This is Maxwell from the Kirkpatrick farm," said Mr. MacKay. A nasty bruise on his foot has now developed into an abscess that must be drained. First we must clean his foot of the muck he's been standing in."

Donald lifted the heavy foot and placed it into a bucket of soapy water, setting to work gently digging out the dirt around a painful looking protrusion.

"Will you bleed him?"

"Bleeding's a worthless procedure that only serves to weaken the animal."

Donald would not be telling *that* to his father. He had seen his father's records of his work as ship's surgeon. Bloodletting occupied much of his time aboard ships.

"What you need to know is that animals suffer like humans from bad air, bad water and inadequate feed. First, you must ensure that those are not the cause of the problem or contributing to the cause. A good farmer knows these things because his animals are his livelihood, and common sense tells him to treat them well. In the cities, it can be another matter entirely."

"If I study my father's books, would that help me to administer to sick animals?"

"Perhaps, but treating animals is more difficult than treating humans because animals cannot describe their symptoms."

As the days rushed by, Donald would have liked to discuss his new knowledge with his father, but he could not face the anger he felt sure to provoke.

One afternoon, as Donald was helping Mr. MacKay treat a particularly nasty bite on the rump of a stallion, his father appeared unexpectedly at the door.

"Mrs. MacKay said I could find you here, Donald," his father said, brows furrowed and face blotchy red. I stopped by to ask you to accompany me to town to pick up a few supplies, but Jessie is not here, and you appear to be engaged in work in this barn"

"Papa, I wanted to learn something new," Donald said, sensing his palms moisten.

"I have seen very little of you in the last two months. You do a few chores in the morning and disappear for the rest of the day." He paused and glanced briefly at Mr. MacKay. "Have you been here treating sick animals here all this time?

"Sometimes," Donald admitted, his eyes straying to the barn door. He thought, but did not say, sometimes they would go to other farms to treat the animals. He could see his father's face was now maroon, and a long pause ensued. Mr. MacKay wisely kept his mouth shut.

"I might as well tell you I've had a letter from Mr. Caldwell in Ingersoll. He's willing to take you on as an apprentice, and you will start in two weeks." His father nodded curtly to Mr. MacKay, turned on his heel, and left the barn.

Donald sighed. "I'm sorry, Mr. MacKay. My father is annoyed I didn't tell him I was here with you, but you can see he wouldn't have approved."

"That much is evident, but perhaps you should tell him this work we are doing is important to you. He is your father and will wish for you to be happy, whatever path you choose."

Donald shrugged. It was obvious his father considered it his duty to choose a proper path for him. Not for the first time, he thought Jessie was lucky to be a woman.

CHAPTER 4: 1862, INGERSOLL, CANADA WEST

I discover myself on the verge of a usual mistake

Donald wished he'd never left Fergus. His new master, Mr. Caldwell, was a difficult man, and he blamed his friend Tom for not warning him of this situation. Tom found employment elsewhere in town after spending only a few days with Mr. Caldwell. While Tom was right that Mr. Caldwell's dispensary in Ingersoll was twice the size of the one in Fergus, it employed only two apprentices and a clerk. The clerk, Winston, was much older than Donald. He was a downtrodden and humourless soul, rarely showing any liveliness or even a smile at Donald's attempts to engage him in conversation. The other apprentice arranged things so Donald and Winston did most of the work. The increase in salary hardly made up for the worsened working conditions.

Although the area of the store devoted to the pharmacy was more spacious than the one in Fergus, Mr. Caldwell, like his previous employer, had expanded his pharmacy into a general store, and his interest in pharmacy, like Mr. Strathmore's, had waned. However, he maintained a close relation with an apothecary–surgeon, Doctor Hoyt, who formulated the various prescriptions but had little time to train shop clerks. When Donald asked Doctor Hoyt whether he might pass on some of his knowledge of pharmacy, he was told he would do better to attend one of the new schools in England that emphasized chemistry and formulations. "It's becoming a profession in its own right in England, and, mark my words, only those trained at the right schools will be preparing formulations in future. If you intend on taking this path, training as a store clerk will not take you where you wish to go."

Donald could appreciate the truth in what Doctor Hoyt said, and it depressed him. The little he had learned of herbs and extractions made him eager to know more, but he would need proper training, and that cost money. He considered becoming a drug salesman. These men frequently called upon Mr. Caldwell, all pumped up with themselves and dressed in flamboyant styles, but Mr. Caldwell gave little attention to salesmen who promoted expensive and untested potions unlikely to be prescribed by the town's conservative medical men. He had only to imagine his father's face were he to tell him he was considering becoming a salesman of elixirs.

Mr. Caldwell supplied room and board out of Donald's wages, and Donald was expected to be on hand night and day to attend to the business. One night when Donald returned only a few minutes after his nine o'clock curfew, Mr. Caldwell was waiting for him in his tiny foyer.

"You're late, Forbes. You have made me wait for you in order to lock the door. When you are late, I am inconvenienced, so do not let this happen again or I may not allow you to leave the house in the evenings."

Donald was dumbfounded that his employer considered it reasonable to treat him in this manner. He imagined a drink or two would have helped Mr. Caldwell to relax, as it did his father, but his employer was a teetotaller and a "staunch Presbyterian", his definition of which included avoiding doing anything considered entertaining. When he had first arrived in Ingersoll, Donald had hopes the situation here might be different. After all, Mr. Caldwell believed in the importance of appearances. "I expect you to attend church each Sunday, and sit in my pew," he had said. "You will dress appropriately and not in your weekday clothes. Buy yourself a good frock coat, Forbes. Clothing says a great deal about a person."

Donald could not argue with that opinion. More than anything, he wished to wear stylish clothes like those worn by many of the customers who frequented their store. He knew how important it was to dress sharply, and if he hoped to move up in the world, he would need to look the part. But more than that, he loved the look and feel of the fine wools, linens and silks sold at their store, and he detested the appearance and texture of the rough heavy cottons and coarse woollens that made up his own wardrobe. Yet his parents expected him to wear his clothes until they looked as if they'd been to a party attended by moths. Had he worn fine clothes, he imagined the few pretty girls who came into the shop would notice him and would stop for a few words. He daydreamed of an imaginary young beauty entering the store. The bell above the door would tinkle, and she would say, "Good morning, Mr. Forbes. My, how stylish you look in that attractive gray frock coat. Could I impose upon you to show me all of your latest imported fabrics?"

It didn't help that the cost of a well-tailored stylish coat was much dearer than his father was willing to pay for his own garments. He had written to his parents twice to request money, but he'd received only enough to buy a pair of inexpensive boots. His mother gave her usual admonishment to take better care of his belongings. Doctor Hoyt had generously lent him several dollars towards the purchase of a new frock coat in black wool with a subtle gray stripe. When, unexpectedly, Doctor Hoyt needed the money returned, Donald wrote to his father to ask him for the sum as soon as possible. His father sent the money along with another strong rebuke.

Donald was determined to learn more regarding dispensing of medicines, and eventually he was able to convince Mr. Caldwell to allow him to work in the pharmacy with Doctor Hoyt for two afternoons a week. Doctor Hoyt shared his dislike of Mr. Caldwell whom he called an old maid and Donald had named "Coldwall". Having someone willing to train him improved his mood to such an extent that it elicited a comment from miserable Winston. "You act as though you'd been offered extra payment for your efforts."

Donald was taught how to prepare tablets, weigh chemicals accurately, and perform necessary calculations for preparing mixtures of chemicals. Doctor Hoyt was patient with him, correcting his errors and showing him simple ways to do the calculations.

"There is no shortcut to becoming a good pharmacist, Forbes. As with all things, whether you are a cricket player or a musician, the answer is practice. I know it's difficult, but you will never become good at anything unless you repeat it, over and over."

Donald expected his life might change when Doctor Hoyt was offered a position in Hamilton. The kind doctor had promised him a position as clerk, saying, "Don't worry, Forbes. As soon as I am established and a vacancy becomes available, you shall have an offer to join me."

Donald savoured the fantasy of a large store in the centre of the city of Hamilton where women were prettier and better dressed, and the fabrics offered in the store were more exquisite and costly. But only two months later, he was disappointed to hear that Doctor Hoyt had lost his position there, the circumstances of his dismissal vague. Now Donald would have no choice but to complete his two years apprenticeship, and he doubted he would have the patience to tolerate his situation for another year.

His opinion of Ingersoll changed when Donald met Elizabeth at the summer fete. He'd noticed her when she visited the store, and he would nod to her even when not serving her himself. The first time she nodded back, he found himself blushing like a girl. Now, sitting together on hay bales in a horse drawn wagon at the fete, he had an opportunity to introduce himself.

Elizabeth was attractive and stylish, with long red hair that she tossed often and to good effect. Donald could not take his eyes from her or keep from staring into large green eyes fringed by impossibly long lashes. Unlike many of the girls who entered the store, she did not feel a compulsion to fill a comfortable silence with meaningless prattle.

"Now we have a chance to meet outside your store," Elizabeth laughed. Donald thought the sound of her voice was delightful. "I hear Mr. Caldwell is very demanding of his clerks."

"I doubt anyone would deny that," Donald said, glancing around to see who might be listening. "I look forward to finishing my apprenticeship and leaving here."

"And now that you have met me, do you still look forward to leaving?" Elizabeth pouted.

Donald realized she was teasing him, and Tom would describe her manners as "charming". Teasing was something girls apparently enjoyed, and he felt confused and awkward. Somehow, it didn't seem an honest way to behave, and when girls tried their charms on him at the store, he was flustered, the way he felt tonight. But the more he talked with Elizabeth, the more he found in common with her. When he told her he was almost eighteen, Elizabeth said she was a bit older and chastised him that ladies don't reveal their age and gentlemen shouldn't inquire. She was impressed Donald's father was a retired surgeon from Edinburgh. "My father owns the lumber mill," Elizabeth boasted. "My grandfather is from Scotland too. Don't you tire of hearing of the wonders of "the dear green place" and all its natural beauty? Grandfather is always mentioning the sound of bagpipes over hills purpled with heather."

"I don't hear many stories of Scotland, but I enjoy listening to tales of my father's adventures at sea." For a moment, Donald felt a wave of longing for home.

When they realized their mothers came from loyalist families who were forced to leave the United States after the War of Independence, Elizabeth was off again on a history lesson. "My grandmother tells me she was lowered down a well to avoid the Yankee raiders at Queenston Heights. Don't you think being dropped down a well would be a lot more dangerous than being captured by Americans? Granny was terrified at the time, but I would have galloped off on Tyrant. He's faster than any horse in the county, and the Yankees would never have caught us."

Donald admired the fire in her eyes and thought Jessie would enjoy her spirit. Elizabeth didn't seem bothered that women were supposed to be demure. "I've never ridden a really fast horse," he admitted.

"You can ride Tyrant whenever you wish," she offered, and the mischievous look in her eyes made him wonder how the horse had earned his name.

"The name of your horse reminds me of my employer, and he gives me very little time away from the store. He'd prefer that I had none at all. But I do have Sunday afternoons free, and a couple of hours on some evenings."

"Next Sunday afternoon, then? We could meet at the west side of the pond." She paused and tilted her head which Donald found curiously attractive. "Could we keep this arrangement between ourselves, Donald? I'd prefer my parents didn't learn of it."

"Would your parents be concerned if I were to ride Tyrant?"

"It's not that, but they expect me to spend my time with a suitable man."

"And I'm not suitable?" he said, smiling, but confused by her meaning.

"I knew you'd understand."

"I'm not sure I do."

"Do you have a sister?" When he nodded, she said, "Then you should understand how parents feel about their daughters spending time with someone they consider a poor prospect for marriage."

Donald was annoyed at being considered a poor prospect, and he felt his anger rising. "I don't plan to marry for a long time yet, and you're still too young."

"Perhaps I'm not as young as you think," she said, raising her eyebrows as if daring him to ask her age again.

Once or twice a week on the evenings Donald was not working late in the store, Elizabeth would leave her house, telling her mother she was visiting Tyrant or catching a breath of air. She would wait for Donald at the small park near the church where the spruce trees provided privacy. They would stroll down to the pond, holding hands when no one was around, searching for the Ingersoll "monster". Several years earlier, a few enterprising lads had stuffed a cow hide, partially submerged it in middle of the pond, and then convinced the rest of the county to visit the alligator monster. Donald was amazed to learn that hundreds had fallen for this silly prank. Even so, he found himself investigating the dark recesses of the lake.

Elizabeth took the lead in moving their relationship from holding hands to kissing. Pressing his lips to hers for the first time should have felt like a victory, and it would have been to Tom, but Donald felt uneasy remembering that he was unsuitable". Tom would have described Elizabeth as "a tasty morsel best left untouched". The sermon a week before had mentioned this very thing. Still, Donald yearned to take their relationship further, but he wondered how Elizabeth would interpret his advances. This concern turned out to be needless as Elizabeth did not pull away from his caresses, and in fact, she shared his enthusiasm.

One warm fall evening in the golden grass by the lake, they found themselves in a passionate embrace neither was willing to end. There was an awkward moment while Donald fumbled with Elizabeth's bodice and skirt, and in the excitement of his efforts, he could not contain himself. Tom had talked of this problem in derogatory terms and called it "sending out the troops before the battle begins." Elizabeth smiled at his embarrassment as he clutched his damp groin.

"I think you have found me too thrilling," she laughed quickly as she adjusted her clothing, "and I believe I should feel flattered." He smirked, as if his overly-eager response did not matter to him, and he happily agreed that her beauty was to blame. But ever changeable, she followed this with a caution. "We are being foolhardy, Donald, and this should not happen again. There can be unintended consequences of sexual congress." For a moment, she sounded like a scolding mother.

She patted his face and pursed her lips when he tried to reach for her again. For the first time, she struck him as older and far more in control of her passions than he was. After that evening, she found excuses to meet less frequently, and would only allow him to kiss her on the cheek. Donald found himself confused and embarrassed by this turn of events, and he wondered if he had lost her interest, or worse yet, her respect. It took him a while to work up his courage to inquire.

"Have I done something to offend or annoy you? I thought you enjoyed my company?"

"You know I do, but you should also be aware that this relationship was doomed from the start." Donald thought she was being overly dramatic, but then, she often was.

"While I am here, I want to see you as often as possible." he argued, thinking he wanted her embraces but not all the talking that seemed to go with it. "I don't understand why we can't be together more often."

Elizabeth sighed audibly and spoke slowly, as if to a small boy. "I've told you before. I fear becoming more attached than we are at present, and I don't want anyone to know we are seeing each other."

It was clear to him Elizabeth was resolved, and it made him angry she could so easily distance herself from him. Then again, how could he criticize her motives when his own affection for her was confused with gratitude for her attentions?

On one of the evenings when Elizabeth was unable to meet him, he attended a gathering in Ingersoll at the invitation of a clerk in another store. Jake introduced him to the game of five card draw poker that was taking place in a back room of a shabby hotel. Donald took quickly to the game, appreciating its challenges and enjoying the thrill of the win. He knew the luck of the draw was important, but it was the art of bluffing that appealed to him. He found he was good at reading emotions and he believed he was able to keep his face free of emotions. Jake had convinced him the game was a way to meet influential people, and more important, to make additional pocket money. His early successes led him to think he had talent for card playing.

Soon he began to attend the poker game on a weekly basis, and he watched his earnings eaten up by his losses. He would justify his losses by invoking bad luck, and he found it difficult to stop playing even when he ran low on ready cash. An old fellow took him aside after they'd played one evening and offered him words of advice.

"I see you rearranging your cards when you play. That's a certain give-away to the other players. You are telling them when you're trying to fill a straight or working with a pair."

"Must I leave them all jumbled in my hand?"

"Is that so hard for you? And another thing, do you know the chances of drawing two or three of a kind, or filling an inside straight? If you're determined to win at this game, you will need to learn the odds or you will lose."

"But this is a game of chance," Donald argued. "Why should I know the odds?"

"Because that fellow knows the odds." The old man said, pointing to the smartly dressed salesman who organized the weekly card games. "Smart wins over luck most of the time, and that man is happy to win most of the time. Green lads like you are greedy and want a big pot right away. Instead, you all end up losing what little you've got."

Donald found it too difficult to work out the odds for all the combinations and to keep them in his head. It took all the enjoyment out of the game for him. A low point came when he could not cover his losses, and the man running the poker evenings told him he must talk to Jake, the clerk who had introduced him to the game.

"Got yourself into trouble, did you?" Jake asked. Jake was wall-eyed and Donald thought it made him look stupid until he realized he was the one who had ignored the advice he'd been given.

"You work behind the dispensary counter, don't you?" Jake said.

"Sometimes I restock and sell patent medicines."

"Then you'll have to take opium from the dispensary to cover your debt. I'll tell you how much you will need to weigh out."

"We keep only laudanum and morphine sulphate. They'll miss it if I take any." Donald was shocked at the suggestion.

"Don't worry, it's been done before," Jake said, smirking at Donald's discomfort. "Take the morphine powder and replace the weight you take with the same amount of corn starch."

"You've done this before?" Donald said, but got a shrug in return. "Was this your plan all along? Get the gullible store clerk into debt and then he'll steal for you?" At that moment, he badly wanted to throttle Jake.

"Nothing says you've got to steal. You can sell something, or ask your parents for the money, but just so you know, you've got only a week to repay your debt."

Sick with fear and anger, Donald wished he could talk to Jessie, although he doubted he could bring himself to tell her how stupid he'd been. He tried to imagine what she'd do, but his remorse only fuelled his old feelings of inadequacy. He'd already borrowed as much as he could against his salary, there were no possessions of any worth to sell, and he could never ask his parents to pay his gambling debt.

The night he convinced himself to steal the morphine, Donald had eaten little for three days. His hands were shaking so badly the powdery substance lifted into the air as he tried to spoon it into a bottle, and the metal of the spoon clattered loudly against the glass edge. He came close to tipping over the bottle in the process.

After replacing what he had removed with an equal weight of corn starch, he cleaned up the ghostly residue of his crime. There was a short-lived sense of relief when he handed the bottle to Jake the next day, but that same week, Mr. Caldwell dismissed the other apprentice who had been caught filling his private flask with alcohol from the dispensary. Donald lived under the constant threat his own theft would be discovered. Distressed by this situation, he vowed never to play poker again. Even the sight of a deck of playing cards would make him clench his jaw.

His lesson was learned at a high price. Having borrowed against his wages, Donald worked diligently for several weeks, forgoing parties and the purchase of a new shirt he craved He couldn't afford to entertain, and his easy manner with customers changed to a dour countenance, much like Winston's. For a brief time, he tried to take a greater interest in his work, but he found it difficult to concentrate and wondered if he would ever move ahead in life. Elizabeth commented on his grouchy behaviour, but he refused to confess his situation, blaming "Coldwall" for his anger. This led to their argument.

"You could stop complaining and find another position in town."

"Not without a reference, and he would never provide one."

"My father may have work for you at his mill. They always need men to feed logs into the blades."

Donald stared at her for several moments, realizing for the first time she had no interest in his profession or whether he moved ahead in the world. He asked quietly, "Would you still want me if I lost both hands to the blade?"

Elizabeth's eyes widened, and at least she had the sense to blush at his question. "I'm sorry if you feel offended by my suggestion. I meant only to keep you here longer."

"Much as I admire you, Elizabeth, I am not here for your amusement."

"As far as I can tell, you are not here for anyone's amusement, including your own."

At that point, she stomped away and refused to speak to him for two weeks. He offered his apologies by sending a bouquet of flowers he could ill afford. The next day she entered the store and apologized so sweetly that Donald could only kiss her, narrowly avoiding being caught by Mr. Caldwell.

CHAPTER 5: 1862, ST. CATHARINES, CANADA WEST

There is that in me...I do not know what it is...but I know it is in me.

Jessie felt little guilt when Thomas and Louise shortened their stay at the hotel, but now she was angry as she read her mother's letter aloud to Ginger. Thomas lost no time in telling tell her parents how disappointed he was with his weekend at the Welland Hotel, and he was considering lodging a complaint with the management.

"We should have considered that possibility," Ginger said, shaking her head. "But it won't reflect badly on you, dear. I'll make sure of that. What did your mother say concerning you?"

"Oddly enough, she seems far less angry with me than with Thomas and Louise. She says, 'I hold no blame for you in this, as I know Thomas and Louise often expect too much from you and might look for an opportunity to find fault.' I'm sure my mother will persuade Thomas not to lodge a formal complaint, if only to avoid risking my position here."

A few months later, at the quiet summer drew to a close, Ginger asked her why her friend Donald hadn't been to visit. "I know other girls on staff have beaus who visit them regularly."

It was true Morag had a boyfriend who worked in one of the factories by the canal, and she had asked Jessie on more than one occasion if she and her beau might speak privately for an hour or two in the attic room they shared. Jessie would go for a walk, but she was not naïve, and she knew why boys visited girls. "Donald regards me as a friend, and we are both too busy with our work to make visits."

"Friendship is the basis for a lasting relationship. You said you share many things in common, such as a love of animals, and I see you write often to him," Ginger said.

"That's not enough." Not enough to make Donny want to visit me, or even write back, she thought.

"Are you talking of romantic love?"

"I suppose so. Donald seems angry so much of the time, at least when I'm with him. I think his anger may keep him from caring deeply for anyone."

"Do you know why he is angry?"

"I used to believe it was because he wanted to do one thing and his father made him to do another, but now I'm not so sure. He doesn't seem to know what he wants from life, or perhaps he is unable to meet his own expectations. I can see from his letters he isn't happy with his current situation."

"Perhaps he would benefit from a discussion of his problems with his good friend?" Ginger winked.

"Do you think I should invite him here?" Jessie looked doubtful.

"A surprise visit to see him might be best."

"A visit?" Jessie pondered. "I would like to see the shop where he works and perhaps meet his employer whom he describes as a dreadful man," Jessie said, having stopped herself in time from saying 'dreadful old woman'. "You think surprizing him there is best?"

"I suspect he would urge you not to visit. If he is not happy, he would not want to inflict that upon you. Still, a chance to tell you his problems may be what the boy needs."

"I have free afternoons saved up, so perhaps I can take time from my work to make the trip."

"Truthfully, I have an ulterior motive. You know I live in Port Burwell? You would do me a great favour if you would accompany me home in October, and that will allow you to take a short stage-coach ride from there to Ingersoll on our new road. You are welcome to stay with me overnight on both ends of your visit. That would give you a good half-day in Ingersoll. I've explored this possibility with the hotel management and I have their approval to "borrow" you."

"I see you've been plotting again." Jessie said, laughing. "And as usual, you have a good plan. I would be delighted to accompany you."

Jessie and Ginger traveled down the Welland Canal to Port Colborne where they boarded the steam ship that stopped in Port Burwell. Ginger's home on Lake Erie was beautiful but remote from the village. After an overnight stay, Ginger's son drove Jessie in a pony cart to the stage coach depot where she could travel to Ingersoll. The coach, painted bright red, wore splotches of mud from the October rains. The new gravel roads were less costly to maintain than the old plank roads in Chippawa, but she had been warned of the potholes. By noon, she was in Ingersoll, her lower back complaining.

She had no difficulty locating the General Store with the large picture window filled to overflowing with dry goods, as Donny had described in his first letter. There had been a half-hearted effort to decorate the window for Thanksgiving with bedraggled turkey feathers. When she entered the store, a small bell announced her arrival, but before she had a chance to look around, an older, dejected-looking clerk approached her. Jessie smiled, recognizing Winston from the description in one of Donny's rare letters.

"Good morning, Madam," he said sombrely. "And what may I help you with today. We have lovely new fabrics as well as ready-made dresses and hats. Or perhaps you desire an elixir or beauty aide." Jessie could detect not an inkling of enthusiasm, but the man knew his merchandize, and he whisked her over to the women's section, all the while extolling the qualities of his products.

"This is my first visit to your store," Jessie admitted. "I have no interest in viewing clothing today." Winston insisted on giving her the full tour, including a demonstration of their new pedal sewing machine, but he stopped talking abruptly when a man who was undoubtedly the store owner, walked by, his manner imperious.

"Excuse me please," Winston apologized. "There is a regular customer needing assistance."

This gave Jessie the opportunity to study the store on her own. She was disappointed in the size of the pharmacy area, since this was presumably the reason Donny had chosen to apprentice here. It displayed only a few patent medicines on one narrow shelf, and the counter area was quite small. She waited until Winston was free so she could ask him where she might find Mr. Forbes. Before that happened, Donny appeared from a back room in the company of a beautiful woman with flowing red hair a lovely blue dress. Jessie was standing behind the rack of ready-made clothes. Her jaw dropped when Donny looked around surreptitiously, failed to see her, and then kissed the woman full on the lips. He disappeared into a back room as the woman left the store.

Jessie stood frozen for a moment, and then followed the woman outside, but when she looked down the street, the woman was flicking the reins and driving away in a small trap pulled by an impressive thoroughbred mare. She was apparently a woman of position in town.

Jessie walked quickly back to the relay station and sat down on the bench, trying to collect her thoughts. She knew she shouldn't be surprised Donny had found a girlfriend. After all, he was young and attractive, actually very attractive, she realized. But he was carrying on with that woman right in the store where that nasty employer could catch him. She wondered if they might be engaged to be married, or at least seriously considering marriage. That would explain his forward behaviour, she thought. Suddenly, she felt a deep sense of loss followed quickly by a spark of anger. Was she angry with the woman or Donny, she wondered?

She sat for a long time on the bench, becoming more and more annoyed with herself as time passed. Should she could go back and find Donny and pretend she hadn't seen the woman, or should she return to Port Burwell? Ginger had convinced her that her motive for seeing Donny was to help him with his problems. Now she wasn't sure he had any problems, in fact, quite the opposite. The decision was made for her when the stage coach and a light rain arrived at the same moment. She stepped up into the coach.

When she arrived back in Port Burwell, Jessie could not hide her disappointment. As soon as she saw Ginger's calculating eyes, she knew there was no point in fabricating a story and saying how pleased Donny had been to see her.

"There are many worthy young men without red-haired girlfriends," Ginger said, having listened to her story. She passed her a cup of sweet tea. "Besides, there is nothing to say that Donald is committed to this woman."

"But she was so beautiful and confident."

"So are you, my dear."

Jessie doubted the truth of this. Had she been as confident, she could have faced Donny in his store. Had she been as beautiful, Donny might have kissed her the way he'd kissed that woman.

Time passed quickly at the Welland Hotel. Jessie was promoted to Assistant Manager in charge of booking reservations and billing. She was flattered that management thought her competent, but she missed her daily interactions with the hotel patrons, and she could not imagine herself content as hotel manager were she to stay long enough to move up to that position. Nothing had changed her poor opinion of city life, and she still dreamed of finding work as a farrier. When she received the letter from her parents, her mood brightened immediately, and she realized how unhappy she had become.

"Morag, I'm going home to be a farrier," she said smiling as she showed her letter to her roommate. Jessie's parents were planning a move to Galt, precipitated by the arrival of a new blacksmith who had settled in Chippawa and had attracted away many of her father's clients. Jessie suspected the new blacksmith had more conventional views on animal welfare that would be more popular with the conservative Chippawa villagers. But fortune smiled on her father because the major of Galt invited him to move his business there and guaranteed more work than he was conducting at present.

"I thought women couldn't be horse doctors," Morag said.

"We'll see about that. My father will need my help now."

"I still don't understand why you would trade your position here to hammer iron shoes onto dangerous horse hooves."

"When you put it that way, it does sound a little mad," Jessie laughed. There's lot more to it than shoeing horses, Morag. We care for them when they are ill or wounded, and horses are wonderful, beautiful creatures, each one different and special in its own way. They are never cruel unless driven to it, which is more than I can say for many people. It's also the way of life. If you could spend time in the countryside, you would understand what I mean. I miss the freedom, the fresh air, and the birds and flowers. I will never become accustomed to living in a city with its clamour and odours."

"Stop, please," Morag pleaded, laughing. "I only wish you would be that enthusiastic with boys."

On more than once occasion, Morag had insisted Jessie join her and her beau on an outing with a male friend. These outings had not been successful. Jessie was impatient and did not know how to carry on a conversation with the men that did not end up with her criticizing their motives and behaviour. When Morag extracted the information that Jessie had her heart set on a boy who was interested in another woman, her friend was more sympathetic.

Excited to join the new venture, Jessie was concerned her parents, and especially her mother, did not intend for her to work at the forge. The letter from her father was not explicit on that point. Perhaps they expected her to apply herself to bookings and accounts only. They had written there would be sufficient work to pay her a salary, but only after the first year or two when their debts were paid. Jessie tried to read between the lines. Would her father be willing to let her work with the animals? Even the possibility lightened her heart.

She began a letter to her father asking for more information and another letter to Donny to let him know her plans. Would he even care to hear she was moving to Galt to work as a farrier? Perhaps he would feel jealous she was accomplishing her dream. It never entered her mind he might think her unrelenting and single-minded in her goals.

CHAPTER 6: 1863, INGERSOLL, CANADA WEST

Under Niagara, the cataract falling like a veil over
my countenance

As the snow deepened, winter's chill settled into the new year like an unwanted relative. Donald's mood darkened. Nothing was going the way he had hoped. He disliked the work, Mr. Caldwell's constant criticisms, and Elizabeth's reluctance to meet with him. His debts had not been paid up so he could not enjoy his few evenings away from the store. Then he met George Kemshall at church. George worked as a senior store clerk with his friend Tom, but he had plans to enrol in the new veterinary course offered in York. Donald experienced pangs of jealousy as George expounded on his ambitions.

"The school is not well organized as yet," George said, "The fellows in charge at the old Agricultural Hall are top-rank, but the government won't give them a penny, so they must demand a steep tuition to cover their costs. I've been saving up for three years, and my clothes are practically falling to tatters."

Donald had noted his clothing first thing they met. It was neat but threadbare, and Donald suspected that Tom would have had little time for George since he was not "selling himself" properly. In fact, Tom had never even mentioned George to him, or told him of his ambitions to become a veterinarian.

"What do you know of the academic requirements?" Donald asked.

"I've heard tell they'll accept anyone who can muster the ready cash. I find that a bit worrisome because it will lower standards."

It wasn't the least bit troublesome to Donald. Although he hadn't mentioned it to Mr. MacKay, he had strong doubts he would ever be accepted to veterinary college because of his poor school grades. Now it seemed his fears might be unfounded. "I'm interested in the profession, but my father is a surgeon and he's convinced it's a waste of time to doctor animals."

"It doesn't surprise me he'd say that, if he's a surgeon," George said but didn't elaborate further. Donald nodded, knowing his father would place veterinarians well below nurses and farmers in terms of value to society.

"Do you know what lectures they plan to offer?" Donald asked.

"I've got the curriculum in my room, if you're interested. There's anatomy and physiology of course, and breeding and feeding of animals. Also, chemistry, and laboratory dissections, but I'm not too thrilled with the chemistry part." The two men spent an enjoyable evening talking, and George promised to write Donald and tell him how he found the courses and professors.

George left Ingersoll two weeks later, and as promised, a letter arrived shortly thereafter. He exuded excitement and satisfaction with the school and advised Donald he should start saving his money for the tuition before the amount increased. But in spite of his efforts, most of Donald's money continued go to paying down his debts, buying clothes, and taking outings with Elizabeth.

On the few evenings he spent with Elizabeth, Donald was expected to return to Mr. Caldwell's home by nine o'clock, but as the days lengthened into spring, he failed on two occasions to return until past ten o'clock. Each time he missed curfew, Mr. Caldwell would work himself into a passion and scold Donald soundly when he arrived late at his house.

"This is the third time you have been out past curfew this month, Forbes. You must be in by nine or I will begin docking your pay."

"None of the clerks in other stores must be in before ten o'clock," argued Donald who could not understand the fuss.

"This is my regulation and I will have it so," Mr. Caldwell said, his weak jaw clenched and his face plum-coloured. Watching him, Donald secretly hoped he would suffer a fit. He suspected Mr. Caldwell may have discovered he was seeing Elizabeth, although he had not mentioned their liaison to anyone, not even Tom.

He continued to defy his employer in this and other small matters such as sleeping late on Sunday mornings and missing church. The next Donald heard was that Mr. Caldwell, in an obvious fit of anger, had written to his father to complain that Donald had flouted the rules. Donald's father had replied by return post to Mr. Caldwell, apparently apologizing for his son's poor behaviour and enclosing a note to be given to Donald.

When Mr. Caldwell handed him the letter from his father, Donald's face darkened as he read the few short sentences. Papa expected to see him home shortly, and he was disappointed to hear his son had failed in his apprenticeship. His father's letter came as a shock. "My father says he expects me home and believes I have been dismissed. I thought we had agreed I would stay on until the end of the year?"

"Your father may have over-reacted to my letter," Mr. Caldwell said, looking more annoyed than satisfied. Donald suspected Mr. Caldwell had hoped for support from Papa in demanding Donald abide by his regulations. Instead, Papa had assumed Donald's behaviour had led to his dismissal. Donald was flooded with disappointment but managed to hold his tongue. He wanted to tell Mr. Caldwell he was the one to over-react by sending his father a letter in the first place, but he needed to know where he stood.

"Will I be staying or not?" he pressed. He dreaded facing his father after a second failure, so in a more conciliatory tone, he added, "I would like to give it another try if you would be willing."

Mr. Caldwell took his time in answering. "It's no good, Forbes. I have been as patient with you as I can. You will finish with me by the end of this week. I can give you this week's salary and money for your journey home, but that is all."

Donald was livid. He had been advanced money to his pay for clothes, but he still owed three dollars for his boots, so he would have little money in his pocket when he returned home. He could not imagine why he would be let go for being a few minutes late. "You are a mean person to be so hard on me," Donald shouted at him. "Everyone says you are a hard man." As he stomped from the shop, Elizabeth's surprised face stared up at him. He had not seen her enter the store, and his cheeks, red with anger, darkened in embarrassment. He did not stop to speak to her, and the bell over the door chimed loudly as he left, as if cheering his departure.

Tom offered Donald a blanket on the floor of his lodgings for a few nights while he decided what to do next, but when Tom was at work, Donald found his stash of home brew and helped himself. The alcohol fuelled his depression, and when he could no longer face himself when sober, he remained inebriated for several days running. Tom would have put a stop to this had his friend not succumbed to the fever that was making the rounds of the villages. Donald knew he should stay and act as nurse to Tom, but in his foul mood, he could feel sympathy for no one but himself.

He moved to a small room above a nearby tavern where he cleaned floors and counters for his keep during the day and indulged his misery by developing a taste for the local brew at night. His self-pity made him a poor companion, and no one approached his corner in the bar. One night, he listened with interest when a loud patron despaired of his brother in the Southern states of America who had been called up on the army draft to fight in their civil war.

"The North will start conscription soon, mark my words. I don't know why they haven't done so yet."

"Good, I say. More jobs will open up for us north of the border, with all their young men gone to war," another fellow said, and there was a lively discussion concerning what the draft could mean for men in the Niagara area, including possible increases in wages to prevent workers from heading south. Donald realized he might find a job more easily in America because he was safe from the army draft. He'd liked the Americans he'd met. They had a less stodgy outlook on life and seemed more willing to take a chance. Perhaps someone would take a chance on him.

After a few days, Donald had worked his way through his small amount of money and credit, and he wrote to his father saying he'd become ill. Receiving a letter in reply but no money, he wrote again to his parents threatening to do something desperate. He received ten dollars by return post, and a short note from his father telling him to return home as soon as he was fit to travel. He could not bring himself to face Elizabeth before he left.

Donald arrived home by coach two days later. It was a beautiful spring morning, but he took little pleasure in seeing his small village. He was pale and his clothes fit loosely since he had been subsisting largely on beer and self-pity. His mother sighed as she reached out to help her son with his trunk. He kissed her perfunctorily, asking after her health.

"I'm fine, Donald. Rhoda and I missed coming down with the fever this year. But your father has dropped a stone with the illness."

"He could stand to lose weight, I'd warrant." His mother looked at him sharply as they hoisted his trunk into the back of the buggy.

Donald rubbed Ruby's muzzle before taking the reins for the short trip home. Neither of them spoke.

As Ruby neared home and her pace increased, Donald viewed the farm house through critical eyes. It was smaller than he remembered, and shabbier. The house could use a coat of paint, and he heard prominent squeaks as he mounted the stairs to the porch. "The old place needs work," he commented to his mother.

"Money for upkeep goes where it's needed first," his mother said, looking hurt. Donald felt a twinge of regret at his criticism and tried to make up for it by saying how tidy the house looked, but to his disappointment, Rhoda and his father were not there to greet him.

"Rhoda is at school and your father has business in town," his mother said when Donald inquired. "I suspect you will want to wash up before they arrive home for dinner," she added. Donald had not been able to wash properly for more than a week. After bathing, he put on fresh clothes and only then became aware of the odour of stale beer that permeated his traveling clothes.

He heard his father returning home as he dressed, and he was astonished when he saw him. Papa looked shrunken and much older. "Mama said you were ill. Have you fully recovered from the fever?"

"It takes longer to recover strength when you are older. You don't appear to be in the peak of health yourself." His father studied him carefully and Donald felt a wave of guilt.

"My fever wasn't so bad," he said, flushing at the lie. "Tom was much worse off. Papa, I'm sorry it didn't work out with Mr. Caldwell." He wasn't sorry one bit to be away from that man, and the thought of him made his jaw clench.

"You can imagine my disappointment to receive that kind of letter from him. He implied you couldn't follow simple instructions."

"It was to do with his curfew, Papa, and he was very unreasonable."

"It doesn't seem likely being late for curfew was the only problem." Donald was surprised at his father's restrained tone. The scolding he'd anticipated didn't materialize, and Donald wondered if illness had sapped his father's spirit. Instead of feeling relieved at receiving a mild reprimand, he felt worse than if he had been severely rebuked. Dinner that evening was a quiet affair. Even Rhoda, normally exuberant and anxious to relate the local village gossip, was subdued. They ate quickly and Mama didn't offer a pudding.

In the following days, there was no further talk concerning Ingersoll. Although this should have pleased Donald, it deepened his feelings of guilt and failure. He tried to understand the situation that had led him to lose his apprenticeship, turn to drink, abandon his sick friend, and fail to say goodbye to Elizabeth. His growing guilt fed his misery. When his mother tried to discuss his plans for the future, he evaded her questions. He was forced into physical activity only when it was time to plant grain. As he worked with the horse and plow, his melancholy slowly began to lift.

Once the fields were planted, he had time for long walks in the countryside. He became aware of the beauty of the bright green spring leaves and the reflections of the clouds and trees in the calm water of the pond near their farm. He studied the small animals beginning to raise their young and listened to the birds announce their arrival from the south. But he made a point to avoid the town. The deafening sound of the falls would draw him to the river's edge to ponder the power of the Niagara River as it spilled over the rocky escarpment. Old white cedars greeted him, and as he watched the cormorants and herons flying effortlessly, his outlook gradually improved. He found himself walking one sunny day to the MacKay farm.

"I heard you were back in town," Mr. MacKay said. The small man was occupied with a large mortar and pestle, pounding green leaves.

"It didn't go well in Ingersoll." Donald suspected the gossip would have spread through the village, so there was no use prevaricating. He sat down on the edge of the trough, feeling uncomfortable.

Mr. MacKay looked up, and bright eyes beneath wild eyebrows studied him. "Could you help me with this poultice Donald? I have a touch of rheumatism in this wrist and it's painful for me to pound."

Donald took over mashing the leaves. "What is this?

"Thistle, or you may call it burdock. You've undoubtedly seen it growing here. The settlers brought it in and it has taken hold in this land."

"I know it, and I try to avoid it when I can," Donald recalled the nasty burrs from the tall plant that stuck to his clothing or the coat of his horse.

"The plant has beneficial properties, too. A poultice of the young leaves speeds healing. The leaves and seeds are useful for burns, aches and such.

Donald listened to the story of the thistle as he pounded the root. He relaxed and watched the pale green syrup accumulate in the cup. When finished, Mr. MacKay asked him to apply the poultice to a seeping wound on the fetlock of a horse waiting patiently in the barn. Donald recognized the animal immediately.

"What's Ruby doing here?"

"I suspect you are really asking why your father allowed the filly to be brought here. It was your sister Rhoda who brought her to me, and I doubt your father knows."

"Ah," Donald said, pleased Rhoda acknowledged Mr. MacKay's talents, but concerned his father would be upset if he learned of it. They worked quietly to apply the poultice and wrap the leg. He had hoped to ask advice from Mr. MacKay, and when they finished, he faced him. "I must leave Chippawa again. I will look for a position in New York State this time."

"Your father approves?" Mr. MacKay said.

"He'd prefer I didn't work south of the border, but he seems to approve of the plan." His father expressed satisfaction that he'd taken the initiative in looking for his next position.

"And you? Do you look forward to leaving Canada?"

Donald considered the question. He was reluctant to leave home when he first went to Fergus, but now he found reasons to want to try something different. "I'm looking forward to living in a big town, in a different country."

"It is good to experience something of the world when you are young. Your own father was lucky in that regard, employed by the Navy. But do not forget, your home will always be important and special in your life. You should not discard it too easily." Donald wondered whether Mr. MacKay was thinking of his own son, Thomas, who rarely visited his parents.

"My father is right that I must establish myself and I can't do that here."

"What of your dream of becoming a veterinarian? Is that now something of the past?"

Donald felt himself sinking again and he shrugged his shoulders. "Perhaps it was a foolish idea." When Mr. MacKay looked surprised, Donald realized he had sounded critical of his profession. "I don't mean it's foolish to treat animals, but how would I pay for the education, and where would I find work?"

"Did you not consider saving a part of your wages?"

"There's little enough for my keep as it is," Donald said, realizing how much money his parents still contributed to his living expenses.

"Then perhaps you can do so when you have finished your apprenticeship and have secured a permanent position?"

"Perhaps," Donald sighed audibly. He did not believe he would have the discipline to save money or to hold a dream for so long.

As if reading his thoughts, Mr. MacKay said quietly, "It is good to work towards a goal, but do not expect your dreams to materialize without sacrifices."

Donald thought of the sacrifices he'd made. His father said things that came easily were often not worth the having. Still, his poor school reports and recent failures weighed heavily on him. He knew he would never be a surgeon, and becoming a veterinarian could be beyond his capabilities even if finances were not a problem.

"You have a true affinity for animals, Donald. You understand what is needed and your fingers are nimble. You would do well as a veterinarian, if your heart is in it."

Donald brightened a little. "Do you think so?"

"Of course, and why not? Is it so very different from what your father and grandfather have done?"

Donald shrugged. "My father would say so."

"This is your life, Donald, not your father's. Remember that, will ye lad?"

His words made Donald think of Jessie. She had always wanted to be a farrier, but when he heard she'd taken a position in St. Catharines, he thought she'd outgrown the idea. Donald was surprised when he received a letter from her saying she was managing to save money from her salary with the thought of opening her own farrier business.

"Jessie has written. She is doing well, it seems." Donald said. He wondered if her father knew of her plans.

"The lass does well at whatever she puts her mind to, but she still talks of becoming a horse doctor." He shook his head. "When she gets an idea in her head, no one can shake it loose."

"Is that so bad? You've told me I should work towards a goal." Donald said.

"Goals for women are different than goals for men." He looked up at Donald sharply and paused, as if considering his words carefully. "She always asks after you in her letters. Do you not write to her?"

"I am a poor letter writer." Donald thought of the many times he had started a letter to Jessie but failed to finish it, or if he did, to send her only a few brief sentences. Sometimes, as he related a silly story, he could imagine her voice in his head, and it was often critical. He would rewrite the story until the voice approved, but it was too much work. "She must wonder if I am still working in Ingersoll."

"She knows you're home now. There are others who write to her, even if ye don't."

Donald nodded solemnly. It would be even more difficult to face her if she knew his second apprenticeship had ended in failure. "Remember when we were children, and Jessie and I planned to open an animal hospital?"

"There are animal hospitals in Europe now, but none here that I know of. They will be built, in time."

"Perhaps not in time for me," Donald said. "Or Jessie. My father believes no one would pay good money to have their pets doctored, but have you seen how city people fawn over their little lap dogs? I believe people would eagerly pay to save the life of a well-loved pet."

"I agree with you, but you must try to understand your father's position too. It would take you as long to become practiced at animal medicine as human medicine. There would be less prestige and less monetary reward."

"I think I prefer sick animals to sick people," Donald said, though he wondered if that were true.

"I won't give you an argument on that. But tell me, what of the pharmacy work? That is something of great interest to me as well. What have ye managed to learn?"

"Not as much as I'd hoped. I believe you have taught me more. These days, general stores supply bottles of patent medicine and do not formulate much of their own. There are worm powders and elixirs of many types, but as I notice the same people buying them many times over, I doubt they can be very effective. There is laudanum of course, and several disinfectants, but little you haven't mentioned. I did discover a useful herbal book with pictures of the medicinal plants and now to prepare extracts. One needs to find the plants of course, and I suspected many of the old jars with remnants in our stores had lost much of their potency."

"The Chippawa introduced me to their healing herbs. Often they are effective for both animals and people." He brought down a small case of bottles and they spent a happy hour looking at his samples and discussing how to prepare the extracts.

Donald could not leave without questioning the MacKay's plans to move to Galt.

"I expected Jessie might have told you. There will be more business for us there. I have found a suitable property, although the house and barn have seen better days and will require my attention. I plan to travel there next week."

"Jessie is excited to be coming home to help in the business."

"I do feel guilty taking her away from an excellent position in St. Catharines. I suspect they wish her to stay on, but you will know as well as I that her heart's not in that work. She has gained experience with the billing and accounts, and that will be useful in our new venture."

Donald wondered if Mr. MacKay thought Jessie would be content with paper work. "Jessie doesn't let much stand in her way," he said. Mr. MacKay looked at him with amusement but only nodded.

Over the next month, Donald mailed application letters to three pharmacies in New York, and he received a positive response from Newark, a town near Rochester. Mr. Smith, the store owner, said he'd be willing to wait for him to begin work after the fall harvest. It was after he accepted that Donald overheard a conversation in the General store in Chippawa that had him thinking again of enlisting.

As the fellow in Ingersoll had predicted, the northern army had instituted a draft. One of the locals was telling of a cousin in New York whose name showed up on the first draft list. To avoid going to war, that fellow had borrowed three hundred dollars from his relatives and paid to have his name removed from the list.

"I gave him part of that money and so did my Pa and his Pa, but he hasn't paid us back. Now they've got him on the list a second time, he's that unlucky, and there's nothing for him but to join the army this time. If he'd hired a replacement with the first three hundred dollars, he wouldn't be in this fix," the man said, turning to Donald to explain. "Once you give them a replacement, you can't be drafted again. You know son, you could be a replacement. There's good money in it and the Army pays you a salary too."

That conversation planted the seed of a new idea in Donald's head.

CHAPTER 7: 1863, CHIPPAWA, CANADA WEST

*Loafe with me on the grass, loose the stop from
your throat*

J essie said her farewells to the Welland hotel staff who clustered around the kitchen door. They'd held a goodbye tea party for her, and Miss Claire promised to welcome her back whenever she tired of horses and country living. Morag embraced her, letting her know, once again, she was a fool to leave, but that she secretly envied any woman who could be happy without a man. Jessie shook her head. She had always believed that a woman was in charge of her own happiness and had no one else to blame if it eluded her.

"Just when I'd begun to enjoy the ancients," Morag whispered, referring to their older hotel guests, "now I must step in and do the books. I have you to thank for that."

"And the increase in salary that goes along with it." Jessie smiled. They hugged solemnly and promised to write.

As soon as she arrived home, Jessie's mother surprised her by apologizing immediately. "I want you to know how proud I am of you, dear, and I'm sorry for how poorly I treated you before you left. To be truthful, I was worried for your future, but now I realize you are quite capable of supporting yourself. I hope you'll forgive a mother's concern."

Happy to accept her apology, Jessie wondered at her mother's change of mind. Had her success in St. Catharines and her change in appearance had something to do with this new attitude? Both her parents spoke less often of Thomas, perhaps because he had given them no help in their upcoming move. When asked if he would arrange for advertisements for their new business, Thomas had replied he was far too busy. Fortunately, Jessie had learned how to prepare notices for various functions at the hotel, and she was able to do part of the work herself. She also had contacts within a firm in St. Catharines that agreed to prepare their flyers. It seemed Thomas' pedestal had cracked and Jessie stood taller by comparison. She waited as long as she could before voicing the question that was burning on her tongue.

"Have you had news of Donny?"

"I'm not sure what that boy will do now, Jessie. I understand he had been behaving strangely since he returned from Ingersoll. Donald visited your father a few weeks ago, but I was not privy to what they discussed."

Jessie was annoyed it was her parents, not Donny, who had informed her he was back in Chippawa, and she'd heard gossip that he'd been sent home under a cloud. Her mother's comment concerning strange behaviour was upsetting too, and as soon as she could, she rode over to the Forbes farm.

Jessie envied Anne Forbes her talent for making a home feel warm and inviting. There were no little china figurines, forlorn yellowed ferns, or knick-knacks like those that cluttered her parents home, and the colors of the curtains, carpets and furniture covers were vibrant. A spoiled old calico cat rubbed up against her legs, and she stooped to scratch her silky orange ears. When she stood up, Donny was staring at her curiously.

"Hello Jessie," he said. "You look different."

"Different?" In fact, she thought Donald looked changed. His clothing was immaculate and in the latest style as always, but he had lost weight and even his face looked pinched.

"I mean, you look nice. Your dress is very attractive," Donald said, smoothing his hand over his own cambric shirt and inviting her to sit down on a comfortable old rocker while he sat opposite.

Jessie wore a green dress purchased in St. Catharines before she left. She made sure the dressmaker removed the superfluous ruffles and bows popular with many women but viewed by Jessie as mere decoration. A small spoon bonnet sat on the back of her head, framing her face and hair. The sleeves of the dress and the skirt billowed out, emphasizing her small waist, and soft ankle boots, laced long the side, completed the outfit. She was told she was dressed in the latest fashion, so she was not surprised her outfit met with Donny's approval. He had not seen her in a hooped skirt before either, and although she considered hoops to be silly, she wore them today. She had to admit, hoops were far cooler in this hot weather than wearing stifling layers of petticoats. She had even practiced sitting down properly to prevent the hoops from flying up towards her face.

"My father says you will be leaving soon for Newark," she began. "Would you like to ride with me tomorrow and perhaps take a swim in the river? We could exchange experiences of city life."

"I've had experiences," he said. "Unfortunately, few are worth recounting."

Donald's bitter tone and apparent listlessness came as a shock. She wondered if this was something that happened as a boy matured and felt the weight of decisions concerning his future. Perhaps his recent experiences were to blame for his manner, and she wanted to hear more, especially regarding a certain red-haired woman. Instead, he changed the subject.

"You've done well at the hotel, and I enjoyed hearing stories of your friend, Ginger."

"I'll miss her and several others, but I'm glad to be back in Chippawa. City life has little appeal for me."

"Don't you find the pace too slow here?"

"That's one of the things I enjoy best. People in cities fill much of their time with nonsense, if you ask me." When she saw the smile at the corner of Donald's lips, she decided not to elaborate.

"I will admit I've enjoyed the countryside more this year than any time I can remember," he said. "I see things in nature I'd ignored before or did not appreciate when I was younger."

"City folk would laugh if they heard us. They believe a little park with sculpted shrubs and a few roses is all they care to experience of nature." Jessie thought of her sister-in-law, Louise, who had informed her parents she regretted hearing that Jessie had to return to live in the *country*.

"Let them laugh," Donald said, and he smiled for the first time that afternoon. "They don't know what they're missing. Only yesterday I was out walking across the Dewitt property and saw a vixen chased by her kits. I expected to hear a horn and hounds baying in the distance. Then the mother froze suddenly and leapt up and down, her jaw snapping vigorously. She kept this up until the kits, missing her attention, turned back to discover what she was up to. It dawned on me she was snapping at grasshoppers. The kits tried to copy her but failed miserably, and I could hear their yips of frustration across the field. I started to laugh at the scene, and of course they heard me and vanished in an instant."

Jessie smiled as she imagined the scene. "The Dewitts live far from here. Why didn't you ride Ruby?"

"Walking gives me more freedom," he said, avoiding her eyes. "Sometimes I like to be alone with my thoughts."

Jessie wondered what was bothering Donald but was reluctant to ask him directly. It was true Ruby would not go unnoticed by their neighbours. She imagined Donald would feel it necessary to stop and talk with each neighbour. "A ride would be a nice change," he said.

"Should we meet tomorrow at noon at the little stone bridge over the Lyons stream?" She had chosen a convenient place between their two farms.

The next day, Jessie waited for Donny for over an hour, wondering whether he had forgotten their planned outing. The cool air of the morning vanished when the high clouds dissipated, and the heat was building but still bearable beneath the mulberry trees. She'd brought fresh bread, cheese and winter-softened apples to eat while they rode, and she was tempted to unwrap the parcel and nibble. When Donny appeared on Ruby, the shimmer of anger accompanying him seemed poised to flare.

"I'm sorry Jessie. I was talking to Papa and time vanished."

"At least you remembered me," Jessie smiled and watched his face brighten in response. Quick to rise to anger, Donald was also quick to release it. It was one of his best qualities, she thought. "Let's ride down by the water first. I'd like to see what the beavers have been building."

They followed the rough roads around the farms and fields, commenting on the changes they observed. Jessie realized these changes were not new to Donny who apparently had been tramping over the countryside since his return from Ingersoll. She enjoyed listening to his insights into their neighbours' lives. His father was a good storyteller and observer of life, so she expected it came naturally to him.

"Every time I walk by the Weaver's, I have to stop and admire the bottles Mrs. Weaver has put up for the winter. She keeps herself busy canning the world, one vegetable at a time. And that front door over on James O'Dell's house? I have seen it painted a different colour each time I walked by— first blue, then green, and now that terrible bright yellow. I imagine his wife reading a journal article describing the current fashionable shades of paint and sending poor James to do up the doors and window frames again."

Jessie laughed. "And did you imagine what the inside of their house might look like then?"

"Stripes, of course," Donald replied. They both laughed and Ruby shied at the noise.

When they reached the area where the beavers had previously built their dams, the Lyons stream was flowing freely and there was no evidence of their activity.

"The lodges are gone. They've taken them all," Jessie said, scowling.

"There will be more beaver hats in England, no doubt," Donald said.

"I'd heard the villagers had agreed to protect the few beaver we have left."

"You forget the villagers are the ones whose trees are chewed up and whose farm land disappears under water when the beavers have their way," Donald said. "I'm surprised there are any left in the Niagara area."

"I hope settlers in the west will not be so short-sighted," she said, but realized if city folk didn't care a fig for nature, there was little hope of that.

It was four o'clock by the time they reached the swimming area along the Chippawa Creek. There were several bathers cooling off, and most respected the unpredictable current in the creek to remain near the shore. Jessie headed behind the bushes to remove her outer garments. In the heat of the day, she'd regretted wearing her old flannel swimsuit beneath her riding pants, and the extra layer had soaked up the perspiration and clung to her skin in what her mother would consider a scandalous fashion.

Anxious to cool off, she was wading quickly into the river before Donald had secured Ruby. "You're slow as molasses," she chided him from the water. Donald smiled and ran down the bank. He was wearing shapeless gray wool bathing pants that clung to him. His arms and legs were well-muscled, and she felt a surge of appetite that had nothing to do with hunger for the bread and cheese in her saddle bag. Could he be looking at her with similar interest? He chose that moment to turn away.

"Is something wrong?" she asked, dropping lower in the water.

"I forgot there was a strong current here."

They enjoyed floating in the cool water and watching the children play in the shallows. Someone had built a log raft and anchored it close to shore. It lured the children like fish to bait.

"Where have you been swimming?" Jessie asked.

"Ingersoll has a small lake. I swam there on Sunday afternoons, when the weather was fine."

"With friends?" She was thinking of the red-haired girl and imagining them swimming together.

"I was friendly with the other clerks. But you must have bathed at the Spa. What was that like?"

"The Spa was for the hotel patrons only, and I doubt that I missed much. It wouldn't have given me much pleasure to lie in a large tub filled with aching old bodies." She wasn't being totally truthful. Although the spa water held no appeal, she had enjoyed spending time with the elderly patrons who shared interesting anecdotes and life lessons.

"What about boyfriends?" Donny said, now floating on his back so she wasn't able to see his eyes. "Is there someone special?"

"I didn't meet anyone who interested me in that way." Jessie said. It annoyed her that she saw herself as self-assured, yet she struggled to tell Donny how she felt about him. He should be the one to approach her first, and she'd not be reduced to using feminine wiles, assuming she could manage to conjure some up. Besides, she didn't think Donny would respond well to being teased or manipulated. She knew she wouldn't.

"I had a girlfriend," Donald announced, looking proud, if only for an instant. "Her name was Elizabeth." Then he frowned and rolled away.

"Tell me about her?" Jessie said, biting her tongue not to inquire about hair colour.

"Why do you want to know?" Donald seemed puzzled rather than annoyed.

"I'm curious about your friends. Do you miss her?" Jessie felt her face flush as she pictured the afternoon she had seen him with Elizabeth, assuming that was the woman she saw.

"Not really. Besides, I'll never see her again."

"You could if you wanted to. Ingersoll isn't the end of the world." She was secretly relieved Donny had no plans to see the woman again.

"Don't tell me what to do," Donald snapped back. He waded to the shore and scrambled up the bank.

Jessie watched the anger flare up in him and wondered at its source. Was it because he was let go from his position? Had something awful happened between Donald and Elizabeth? She followed him to the pebbled shore and sat down quietly on the blanket beside him.

"Can't you tell me what's bothering you?" she asked. "You used to tell me your problems."

"We were children then. My problems were little ones."

"I've listened to big problems now." Hotel patrons told her she was a good listener, but she was often amazed by their experiences and wondered how people managed to complicate their lives so badly.

"I'm angry with myself, Jess," he sighed. "I've made bad choices and I don't seem to have much luck. I want to forget Ingersoll. There was no future for me there."

"Isn't the important thing whether you enjoyed the work?"

"My employer said I didn't keep track of things to his liking. Sometimes I forgot to do things, not on purpose, but there was too much to remember."

"If that's all, there's a simple fix. Get yourself a little notebook and write things down. I did that at the hotel so I'd remember who was arriving and when they'd be leaving, and when to see to orders or do the accounts. No one can remember it all."

"But I don't want to work in a store selling notions."

"I'm not planning to spend all my time taking care of the books for our business either. My father must allow me to work with the animals, and if not, I will start my own farrier business. I've saved part of my wages, Donny, and I hoped you could too so we could work together."

"You've always known what you wanted, and I envy you. All I know is that I want to become a lot more than what I am now."

"Have you spoken to your father?"

Donald didn't reply, and Jessie remained still, hoping he would say more about Elizabeth. They lay back on the grass eating the apples and cheese she'd brought. Silence with Donny was always comfortable. She enjoyed the feel of the cooling breeze over her wet bathing outfit and the sounds of children laughing in the shallows.

"I feel like a small boy, sometimes," Donald said "It's as if Miss Armstrong or my father appear everywhere I go to tell me I'm not trying hard enough, or I'm not smart enough."

"I'd like to help," Jessie said quietly.

"Elizabeth treated me like a child. At first, I thought she liked me. Then I wasn't so sure, and somehow, she made me feel less of a man."

"I've heard women make light of men. I think that can happen when there is isn't enough respect." Did he love Elizabeth, she wondered?

As if hearing her unspoken question, Donald replied. "She made sure I couldn't care for her from the start, told me I wasn't 'suitable material' for matrimony."

"Did that disappoint you?" Jessie couldn't imagine Donald would even consider marriage during an apprenticeship, but perhaps he had been lonely.

"Not really, but I wanted her respect and I lost that too."

"How did you lose her respect?" Jessie couldn't believe Donny would force himself on a woman, but the idea flitted, unbidden, across her mind. She kept very still.

"I never said goodbye properly. She saw me shouting at my employer when he dismissed me. I was so embarrassed, I couldn't face her after that."

Suddenly, the river seemed so quiet, the children gone home, Jessie realized. She relaxed, knowing Donny had perhaps offended Elizabeth by not saying goodbye, but nothing more, nothing worse. It was all so easily remedied.

"Why not write to her and explain what happened."

"It's too late now."

"It's never too late to set things straight. She may feel badly you didn't like her well enough to say goodbye. It doesn't have to be a long letter. Tell her you are glad to have known her and you regret that you did not say goodbye before you left."

Donald sat up and leaned over her, and her heart beat faster. "You always have a solution to my problems, Jessie. You're a good friend."

Then he lay back down and asked a strange question. "Do you think of yourself as brave?"

Jessie pondered a minute. "The way I see it there are two kinds of brave. Reckless brave and practical brave. I like to think of myself as having the second type."

"What is practical brave?"

"That's when you weigh the options and it works in your favour to be brave. In some ways, it's harder because you've had a chance to consider the risks, and your choice may be dangerous, but you do it anyway. Say for example someone gets caught in the current out there, and it looks like they'll drown. A reckless brave person might jump in without thinking, but he really shouldn't because if he's not a strong swimmer, he's likely to fail at saving the person and may drown himself. Practical brave is someone who realizes his limitations but still tries anyway. This person is more thoughtful and may improve the odds by using a boat or a rope or finding others to help."

"Sometimes there's no time to think, only time to act."

"True, but maybe the practical brave person has considered how he might behave in different situations. It would be like planning ahead," Jessie said. She sat up and began gathering up the remnants of their food.

"Premeditated bravery," Donald laughed. "I guess that still counts." He turned an inquisitive gaze on her. "Jessie, why weren't you interested in the boys in St. Catharines?"

"I've told you already." She wanted to say more, but the words remained tucked securely under her tongue. Perhaps she didn't want to risk losing her best friend by putting pressure on him to be more to her than he was willing to be, or maybe she couldn't face his rejection. Instead she changed the topic. "Why did you ask me about bravery?"

"Because I'm considering enlisting in the Northern Army."

Jessie stood up in shock. "Why would you ever consider anything so foolish?" Her words were out before she could consider them, and they sounded harsh even to her ears.

"The bounty money, for one thing. It's a lot, and once you join up, they pay you a decent wage." His face had darkened, but she couldn't stop the questions flowing from her lips.

"But you're learning a trade now. What will the army teach you? How to kill people?" She glared at him and his face flushed.

"I was hoping to become a hospital steward and maybe save lives. I wasn't considering joining the infantry."

"But stewards need training, and someone to give them a reference. What if you have to fight? I can't believe you're even considering this, Donny. Haven't you been reading the newspapers? Don't you know what happened in Gettysburg? More than twenty thousand soldiers died in one battle." Jessie's wondered if her face was a red as Donny's until she realized he wasn't angry. He looked embarrassed and disappointed.

"I thought you'd understand," he said quietly. They were both standing now, staring out at the river, feeling the setting sun on their backs.

"Understand what? You still haven't explained why you want to do this. If it's the money, you'll be earning a good wage in a few years. Why hurry?"

"I don't like being a clerk. I'm not learning anything interesting."

"Then become a veterinarian. Isn't that what you want?"

"You know why I can't. But if I join the Northern Army, I can use the bounty money to pay the tuition after the war."

Jessie suddenly understood his plan, and she could appreciate the attraction for him. The bounty money would solve his problems. "But it's such a big risk. I don't want you to get hurt." As soon she said this, she could see Donny relax. He looked at her curiously.

"Is that why you were so angry?" he asked.

"Of course! What did you think? We were discussing reckless bravery and that's what it sounded like to me. Now I see enlisting could provide the money for schooling, and it's worth the risk to you. All I ask is you give your new job a chance before you join the army."

Donny gave her a brief hug. "Thanks Jess. Your opinion means a lot to me."

They dressed and spoke little on the ride back. Jessie hated the idea of Donny entering the war, but what more could she say? She could hardly criticize him when she'd left the security of a high-salaried position to do the work she loved.

"Let me know when you plan a visit to Chippawa, and I'll try to arrange a visit at the same time," she said.

Donald nodded, "Please say goodbye to your father for me. Tell him I hope his new business is a great success."

"It's my business, too, Donny."

"Of course, and you know I envy you and wish you luck." She did know, just by that wistful look on his face.

She felt his eyes on her as she headed down the road. He called out, "Jessie, don't forget me." She turned in her saddle and saw him waving and smiling, their argument forgotten.

"Don't forget me either," she shouted back, and without thinking, she blew him a kiss. Premeditated bravery, she thought.

CHAPTER 8: 1863, NEWARK, NEW YORK

The day getting ready for me when I shall do as much good as the best

Donald leaned against the doorway of his bedroom watching his mother pack his clothes into a wood-framed trunk. The outside of the trunk was patched in several places, and he wondered if it would withstand the rigors of the journey and rough handling during the station change. He would be heading south by steam train tomorrow, across the border into New York. Rhoda said she envied him the journey to a different country, even if it was only a hundred miles east as the crow flies. She'd asked him about the new sleeping cars. "Imagine sleeping in your own bed on a moving train." He'd shrugged. The trip was a short one and would not involve any sleeping.

"Should I include these books?" his mother asked. She was concerned he might be charged duty should he plan on selling any of his belongings. "Surely the used clothing of a young boy with an offer of a job in hand wouldn't be scrutinized too carefully," she muttered when he didn't reply. Even so, she exchanged the bronze picture frame with an old leather one. Donald didn't care.

"They are hard workers in America. And competitive," his mother muttered. "You say you like a challenge, and I expect you'll find one."

"At least he has experience and training to prepare him," Rhoda added from the doorway. He saw his mother nod in agreement, but she did not look comforted.

They'd avoided discussing the civil war. Several men from Canada West were now in the Northern Army, and a few had joined the southern cause, but Donny knew of no young men from Chippawa who had been persuaded to enlist. He suspected his mother found that reassuring, and he watched her fondly as she folded his flannel shirt and stuffed the heavy socks into the corners of the trunk. When she wasn't looking, he stuck a small memorandum book with a pencil in with his socks. Jessie had shown him her notebook with the dates on each page and a list of things to do, and it made good sense to him. Bored, he left his mother and Rhoda to meet with his father at the bank.

The evening meal was waiting when Donald returned with his father.

"The sum is not short," Doctor Forbes said, continuing an ongoing argument. "That amount is more than sufficient for your needs until you finish your apprenticeship."

"Papa, it will not be adequate. I will have things to purchase when I arrive, including boots and a coat for the shop. I will need money for my laundry and food on occasion."

"We keep sailing over the same waters with you, Donald." His father's face was now red. "Others manage with less than we provide for you."

"Times have changed since you were my age, Papa." Donald's voice rose in pitch. "It will not do for me to dress like a pauper if I wish to be accepted in good society, but never mind. I will manage on my own." When his disappointment and anger could no longer be contained, he said, "Who paid for your education, Papa?"

"My family was wealthy and could afford to pay. That is not our situation."

"Then perhaps I must join the Northern Army. I could make three or four hundred dollars by taking the place of a northerner called up on the draft."

"As usual, all you think of is the money. You do not seem to appreciate the danger involved in such a venture."

"I'm not afraid of war, even if others hide below decks." Donald tensed when he heard his mother gasp, but he continued to argue. "Papa, you are the one who fought against slavery and believe the northern states justified."

His father ignored him. It was a sore point between his parents that the British aristocracy were seen to side with the South. His mother's family had lived through the war of 1812, and she was less trusting of Yankee motives, saying that if the northern army won the war, there was good reason to expect them to continue further north and take Canada. However, one thing it seemed they could both agree on was that their son should not be part of this conflict.

"I wish you would put your arguments away until we have finished our supper," his mother said. She took Donald aside and whispered to him, "Do not continue on this way. Only a logical argument will sway your father."

"I'm not hungry," Donald said, leaving the kitchen abruptly, annoyed now at his mother as well as his father. They had no idea of the real world. The steam rising from the stove top distracted him only briefly. Even the sweet smell of the huckleberry pudding did nothing to improve his mood.

In his room, Donald pushed aside his trunk and sat down heavily on the bed. He could smell the spicy aroma of saffron. He had realized years ago that his mother would use the precious Spanish spice when she wanted to appease Papa after an argument. He suspected his father took it as an apology and enjoyed the flavour all the more for it.

He picked up the empty bronze picture frame, wishing he'd asked Jessie for a likeness he could carry with him. She was lovely, he thought, so unlike Elizabeth who flaunted her beauty. Jessie held herself in a more natural way, as if she were unaware of the effect she might have on a man. Any man would be lucky to marry her, yet she seemed to have no interest in them. When she was so capable in her own right, perhaps she had no need of a man to care for her. She certainly wouldn't want someone who had failed at a simple apprenticeship, not once but twice. He had meant it when he told her not to forget him, but would he ever become as accomplished as she was? He let the cloud of misery descend.

When Donald arrived at Newark late the next night, he was obliged to stay overnight at a hotel. He met Mr. Smith the following morning and gave a silent sigh of relief when he realized his new employer appeared both kind and reasonable. Mr. Smith had arranged for him to board in a house two blocks from the store, leading to another silent prayer of thanks that he would have no more annoying curfews to contend with. He immediately began a letter home detailing his trip to Newark, the beautiful trees in a city that was much smaller than he expected, and the description of the fancy goods sold in the stores. His real motive, however, was to request money to pay the tailor. He knew this would not please his parents, so he explained how he could not go to church in the same linen coat he wore in the shop. He added more weight to his argument by telling them Mr. Smith had offered him seating in his pew at his church. Donald blotted the ink and reconsidered what he had written. He simply must have more money for clothing, but he knew what his parents would think when they read his letter.

A week later, Donald tore open a telegram from his mother with the wire transfer. He could now pay off his boots, and he had seen a hat that would set off his new coat with style. Newark was much more aristocratic than Ingersoll, but his new outfit would set him above the others at his station. He examined himself in the hall mirror, noting with satisfaction the sophisticated profile he cut with his kid leather lace-up boots and smartly fitted tweed frock coat. He thought Elizabeth would have enjoyed parading with him through the park. A few weeks after he had sent a letter of apology for failing to say goodbye, he had received a letter back. Elizabeth was engaged to be married the next spring, and her parents had approved of the man. Donald imagined the fellow to be well-established in a profession. Cheese, no doubt, thought Donald, smiling when he recalled that the citizens of Ingersoll had recently boasted of having made the largest cheese wheel in the world. Elizabeth had not indicated how she regarded her fiancé, and Donald hoped she would be happy. He scanned his mother's letter rapidly. The news from home held little interest for him, and he found the endless discussion of the new fertilizers tiresome.

His position was an improvement over the last. He was now making seventy-five cents a day, and Mr. Smith had hired extra help for heavy lifting of barrels and wood for the stoves. He worked from six in the morning to often nine at night, and he did not like his duties so well as those in Fergus or even Ingersoll. He maintained the lists of items shelved and sold in the ledger book, displayed the wares and took payment from the customers. Mr. Smith kept a close eye on him in the store.

"You must learn how to work smarter, Forbes. Our profits depend on people buying our merchandise. This is a result of two things, and two things only. The first is the quality of the merchandise, which is my concern. The second is the belief by our customers that their lives will not be complete without our merchandise, and that is your responsibility." When Donald asked how he would accomplish that, Mr. Smith said, "You sell them the idea, Forbes. Remember, without a firm belief they need something, they will not purchase."

It was not long before Donald realized Mr. Smith's idea of working smarter had more to do with working faster, talking faster, and moving merchandize faster. He struggled to keep up with the other clerk.

"You are doing well, Donald, and I am especially impressed with your knowledge of fabrics, but I believe you can do better yet. You should know all the details of your merchandise, and it's not enough to explain to our customers the features of our sewing machines. You must say how they are superior to all other sewing machines."

"I will try sir, but I had hoped to work more often in the dispensary, to improve my skills at pharmacy."

"Your skills in pharmacy are adequate. It is your business skills that concern me. A successful pharmacist needs to know the business end."

Donald didn't care to know the business end or talk customers into buying things they didn't want or need, but it was true that Mr. Smith had little to teach him about pharmacy. He was annoyed when customers seemed content to purchase bottled patent medicines. His father would scoff at them, saying they were full of nothing more than alcohol. He thought it ironic that Mr. Smith was a member of a temperance society and believed drinking was sinful, and yet the patent medicines he sold were full of alcohol. Mr. Smith had made efforts, largely unsuccessful, to indoctrinate his clerks into teetotalism.

Eager to make friends, Donald attended a party hosted by two of the clerks at another store. He knew he would be expected to bring liquor, and the other clerks were happy when he appeared at their door with a bottle of local whisky. He did not care much for strong liquor and preferred beer or the sweet wines from the Niagara region.

But he saw how the fluid could enliven a party, and he often worried for the women who were present when liquor was drunk to excess. His painful memories of Ingersoll were associated with drinking beer to excess, so now he drank moderately.

The Christmas season came and went, offering little solace. He received letters and a parcel of baked goods from Mama, and a book describing the new veterinary science from Jessie who, as usual, urged him to write more often. She talked with excitement and pride about her work in Galt, but it did nothing but make him envious and long to quit his position.

When he learned there was a veterinarian in Newark who attended the same church, Donald introduced himself and told him of his desire to take up the same career but his inability to pay for the schooling. Mr. Caruthers was sympathetic and confided he had found himself in a similar situation a few years ago. He was fortunate when an established veterinarian agreed to pay his tuition in exchange for four years work as his assistant after his graduation.

"You agreed to become indentured?" Donald said in such obvious disbelief that it elicited a smile from Mr. Caruthers.

"In a way, perhaps, but I knew the man well and trusted him to be as fair with me as I would be with him. It worked to my benefit, and it was the only way for me to achieve my goals."

Donald nodded and considered the possibility, briefly, but becoming a replacement in the Northern Army had much more appeal. For a few months work in the army, he would have enough to pay his tuition and be owing to no one.

The idea was still in his head when Mr. Smith called Donald into his office late in January. He informed him his business was not prospering and didn't warrant him keeping two clerks. He offered to provide Donald with an excellent reference. Donald could see Mr. Smith was sincere as he delivered this speech. He also knew sales had dropped noticeably in the last few months, in large part due to the war but also competition from other stores. Still, he was disappointed he was not the clerk chosen to remain. For the first time, he thought he could stand this job, and he had even begun to save some of his wages, but fate apparently had other plans.

"Dick has more experience, and he is recently married," he said, as if reading his mind. He patted him on the back, telling him he would do what he could to find another position in town.

"I will be sorry to leave," Donald said, even if his answer was only partly truthful. "I've been thinking of joining the Northern Army, so perhaps this is what I will do."

"Are you sure about this, Donald? The news we have of the war is not good. Many believed it would be over by now, but it seems the two armies are well-matched in abilities if not numbers. You should consider yourself fortunate you are not eligible for the draft."

"I'd hoped I might work as a steward or orderly in the army. I understand that pharmacy clerks can be taken on for the hospital work."

"If that is your decision, I can help you. I am friends with Doctor Vorster, a surgeon with a New York infantry regiment. I will write to him and ask if he will take you on as a hospital steward. With your experience and a father who is a surgeon, I expect he will agree. With the right placement, you could develop hospital skills to complement your pharmacy knowledge. Then you should have an easy time finding a position in a dispensary or hospital when the war is over."

Donald smiled broadly, wishing his parents and Jessie could see the positive side of his decision, but he failed to tell Mr. Smith he planned on accepting money for signing up in place of a drafted man. Had he done so, he might not have been cheated.

The drafted man he agreed to replace had offered him three hundred dollars, the going rate for a replacement. They had arranged to meet at the recruitment office where the man handed in his draft notice and presented Donald as his replacement. Once the forms were filled in and signed, he was to receive the money. However, he was handed only one hundred dollars in cash and a bank draft for the remainder. "I don't travel with that much cash, and neither should you," the man had said when Donald complained. "When you are stationed at your camp, you will be able to cash the draft there."

"I want the cash now. Accompany me to the bank and we'll cash the check," Donald said, fearing the bank draft might be worthless.

"You can't do that, Forbes. You've signed up. You can't leave here without permission. I'll go to the bank and bring the cash back if you want."

"You're not leaving with that paper. How do I know you'll bring the money back to me?"

"Keep the cheque. That's a better option anyway, as I said."

The man disappeared, and Donald realized he'd likely been duped. Why hadn't he asked to see the cash before he'd signed? If the draft was no good, he'd come back for the man and his money after the war was over. At any rate, he had no time to brood because his train was boarding.

The army training barracks were located in the small town of Elvira. The odour emanating from the barn-like barracks made Donald question why anyone would build space for thousands of men next to swampy land with poor drainage. Despite the cold air, he was quickly sickened by the smell of the men and their filth. He laid his coat and bag on the empty bunk closest to the door, but a gray-haired man motioned him over.

"You'll get used to the stench in no time," the old recruit whispered, "but you'll never keep warm near that door."

When asked where he hailed from, Donald said Newark, having decided it was best not to mention he was from Canada. The conversations he'd overheard on the train made him realize that bounty men were not popular, especially the 'jumpers' who took the money and deserted only to join up again and claim more bounty money. He'd never considered doing that, and it made him angry to think of men profiting from the war until it struck him he was one of them. When the men in the neighbouring bunks caught sight of the addresses on his letters home, they accused him of taking money from Americans.

"Replacements are as bad as the bounty jumpers," one fellow complained. "You don't give a damn about the war, only the money."

"That's not true. My father fought against slavery for many years. Our land is against slavery," Donald said. His father had explained to him that the war started because the southern states were in fear of losing their way of life. It was a subtlety lost on Donald.

"I don't see your whole country down here fighting with us, do you?"

The accusations hurt him because he knew the private was right. If it hadn't been for the bounty money, he wouldn't be sitting in these accursed barracks. There were two hundred men packed into the hall, and the general ruckus was worse than any chicken coop. The food was rotten enough to make the men sick, although the liquor they consumed could be mostly to blame. The place reeked like a distillery until a couple of them spewed their dinner on the floor. Listening to their childish conversations made him uncomfortable and sad. The boys were so happy to be off the farm, they were practically bursting with excitement.

"Ma says I'm to see as much as I can, 'cause when I get back to the farm, all I'll see is the back end of a mule as I plough the fields."

They talked as if they planned to enjoy every minute, especially the fighting. It didn't matter that none of them knew how to handle a rifle, and the drill sergeant didn't provide them with bullets for practice since that was considered a waste of ammunition. They'd aim their rifles at each other and shout, "Bang, got you!" They were all new to war, and Donald realized no one with real experience was bothering to dampen their enthusiasm.

"This war will be over by the summer. Everybody says so. It's on to Richmond to show those rebs what we're made of, and then back on home."

How many times had he heard that? For Donald, the only good thing to happen during that first week was his new uniform. He was issued with the standard dark blue wool pants and private's jacket, complete with brass buttons. One of the recruits was handy with a needle and would alter uniforms for a fee. Donald paid for his services and was very pleased with the results. Still, he was envious of the officers who wore satin sashes and red tasselled sabres when in full dress. He would have preferred a fedora to the flat-topped Yankee cap he was issued, and he wasn't impressed with the quality of the boots.

"My own boots show better workmanship than these," he complained to the sergeant.

"Tell that to the rebs. They'll be eager to take 'em from you," the sergeant said, smirking. "Of course, they'll shoot you first."

A week after he arrived, he received a letter from Doctor Vorster letting him know he'd been accepted as a hospital attendant with the 111th New York Volunteers. The sergeant claimed Donald's rifle and bayonet and let him off drilling five hours a day. Donald asked the tailor lad to sew on the green armbands with gold braid and the entwined snake emblem that set him apart as a hospital steward. No one could tell him what the snake was supposed to signify, but he got spiteful comments about the colour of the hospital flag being yellow, and the snake being meant to keep the rebels from firing at him.

"That's mighty nice of them. We can all wear a magic yellow snake and jus' march up to those rebs and chop 'em down. They won't fire a shot," an older recruit said.

"He ain't got no rifle or hadn't you noticed. I suspect that has more to do with avoiding getting fired at than any magic snake."

"You don't have a weapon?" one boy asked. "You must be mighty brave to go out there without a gun or a sword."

"He's not going out there, dummy. He stays behind the lines, and when you get shot, you got to get to him."

"Don't be so sure of that. I've seen hospital tents lit up with cannon shell and stray shot," said the old recruit. "The battle doesn't always stay where you put it."

All this talk made Donald realize he had little idea of what lay ahead. He'd imagined working in a hospital away from the front, but the regiments had their own small tent hospitals, and he would march with the troops to the battle grounds. He wondered how close to the action he would get. If the wounded men had to reach the tent on the arm of a friend, it could be no more than a half mile, and he suspected that was well within cannon ball range and even the range of a sharpshooter. He needed to find someone wearing the green armband and to learn more, but when he asked at each of the other buildings, there were no other hospital attendants or stewards. A sergeant eventually took pity on him.

"The hospital stewards are in Washington, and they will be sent out to the field hospitals from there. You enlisted as a private and since you've now got your letter to be a steward, you're doing things different. I'll see if I can get you sent on to your regiment because there's no point in staying here if you don't need field training."

"Donald thanked him and returned to the barracks feeling a mixed sense of relief and trepidation since he still had no idea what would be expected of him. He wished he could go home for a few days before he joined his regiment, but his hopes of getting a furlough were quickly dashed by the sergeant who told him he would need a senior officer to speak on his behalf. Before he'd even met the man, he was writing to Doctor Vorster to request a weekend leave.

CHAPTER 9, 1864, GALT, CANADA WEST

Both in and out of the game and watching and wondering at it

essie and her parents stood in a line, hands on hips, as they sized up their new property. The sun warmed their backs, but the air had gathered up the ground's chill. The barn stood below the house, a fresh coat of dark red paint covering the trim. The new forge oven was housed in a shed built on the leeward side under a high roof. Behind them stood a long single-story frame house, a merging of two earlier ones fashioned haphazardly by the previous owner. It straddled the top of a small hill and boasted a view of the Grand River snaking away in the distance.

"It's adequate, but that privy is too close to the well. What fool would put it there?" her father asked.

"The one who didn't want to walk fifty feet further in the middle of a cold winter's night, that's who," her mother replied.

"It must be moved," her father insisted.

"Perhaps we could move the house instead," Jessie suggested, drawing a smile from her father.

"I'd rather carry myself than the kitchen water, thank you," her mother harrumphed.

"That's settled then. We move the privy."

The business of shoeing and iron-work, as promised by the Galt city mayor, was burgeoning at the MacKay farm. When Jessie ordered a new forge hearth installed, and paid for it from her savings, her father's face beamed with pride. He allowed her to work the bellows and heat the first iron shoe. She took this to mean her parents were resigned to having her work alongside him. By the end of October, he reluctantly allowed her to take over doctoring the ailing animals that were brought to their farm while he concentrated on the forge work. It was not yet common knowledge she was acting as horse doctor and farrier, but that would happen in time. She eagerly anticipated the day when her father would take back his words that people would not bring their sick animals to a woman. Only her mother was unhappy, and it wasn't concerning the time she spent in the barn.

"I'm worried sick about our debt, Jessie. We have never owed so much money to the bank before." Jessie tried to console her, telling her they had paying customers and there was no cause for concern. "But your work is so physically demanding, my dear. I believed you would be busy with accounts, not hooves. I know you are entirely capable, but I can't seem to stop feeling anxious."

"I'm doing what I want to do, and I always leave plenty of time for our books." Jessie wrapped an arm around her mother's shoulders, amused that she was the one now providing reassurance.

"It's your decision, Jessie. If you're happy with it, then I must resign myself." She squeezed Jessie's arm. "Your muscles are as impressive as your father's now. How wonderful it must be to be strong." The wistful way she said this took Jessie by surprise. She realized her mother no longer felt responsible for her happiness, and that had made all the difference in their relationship.

A visit later that month from the manager of mortgages for the Galt Bank raised Jessie's curiosity. Robert Symes had been to their farm several times, ostensibly to check on his investment. He had expressed satisfaction with the changes they'd made to the property, including improvements to the kitchen and barn. Every month, her father deposited his earnings in the bank, and the amount was always well in excess of the interest owed on their loan. Jessie knew her father was beginning to feel concerned over the man's regular visits.

"Has Mr. Symes ever shown an interest in you, Jessie?" he asked her bluntly after the bank manager had visited for the second time that month.

"He's told me of his carriage horse more than once. It's a thoroughbred cross with a Cleveland Bay, I believe. He wonders whether the lungs are sound since the horse labours when pulling a full carriage. But the animal is coon-footed, so his poor performance is no surprise."

"You miss my point, lass. I think he is here so often because he's attracted to you, not to your knowledge of horses."

"Papa, that can't be so." The man was twice her age, and his breath was as laboured as his horse's. The idea made her laugh.

"What do you find so amusing, my dear?"

"He's here to check on his investment, Papa. Perhaps he wishes us to fail so he may collect his payment in a more rewarding manner."

"Jessie! Be kind. The man would likely propose marriage if you would give him half a chance. He is a bank manager, after all, and could offer you a comfortable life outside of the barn." But Jessie saw the glint of amusement in her father's eyes and she pushed his shoulder in feigned annoyance.

"I thought you had plans for me to marry Donny?"

"It was you with the plans, but you don't pine too badly for the lad."

"Papa, I don't want to be anywhere else, but this farm would be perfect if Donny were here with us."

"What does Donald think of this?"

"I've told him how happy I am here, and how much I enjoy the work we do, and I did ask him to consider joining us here. I'm sorry

Papa. I should have asked you first, but I doubted he would agree anyway."

"You're likely right. Donald may not believe he is needed here, and that boy can be as stubborn as you, Jessie. Perhaps in a few years, you might talk to him about starting a business together.

"A few years? Papa, will I have to put up with the breathless bank manager for a few years?"

"That bank manager and others. People in town are curious." One of the boys who moved here from Chippawa has asked after you, wondering if you'd married."

"Which boy?"

"Angus McDowell. Do you remember the lad from school?"

"That bully!" Her mother said no one would marry her because she was too much like a boy. What had happened to change that? When she asked her father, he told her to take a look in a mirror.

In February, Jessie received a letter she had hoped never to read. Donald had enlisted, and although he sounded excited and proud of himself to have received a bounty, knowing he was part of that dreaded conflict made her heart sink. At least he had obtained some assurances of a position as a hospital attendant. She showed the letter to her father.

"Could he end up in the infantry, Papa?"

"It's difficult to say, Jessie. He has the experience he'll need to become a steward. There can't be many boys who want to tend the sick and wounded and have pharmacy experience too."

"His parents won't be happy."

"Aye, that's certain. The Northern Army has the draft now, so the American boys must take part when they are called up. I hear there have been riots because the rich boys can buy their way out, yet Donald joins up even though it is not his war to fight. It is sure to bring disappointment to his family."

"He tells me he hopes to have three days at home before the spring campaign begins. I thought I could visit him in Chippawa, if you can spare me for a short period."

"We can manage. I expect he will be happy to see you, especially if you can act as a bulwark."

"A bulwark? Oh, between Donny and his parents, you mean." Her father nodded and screwed up his face as if he'd eaten something sour. Then they both smiled. He did look a bit like Doctor Forbes when he made that face.

Jessie took the train to Chippawa a few days later and walked the two miles from the station to the Forbes farm. It was blustery weather, too soon for spring, but also too soon for mud. Rhoda met her at the door and ushered her into the drawing room.

"I'm glad you brought your bag and you planned to stay over as you indicated in your letter. But Donny is not coming, so please tell them you are returning tonight to Galt. I'll explain later. Make yourself at home, and I'll get the tea." After Rhoda left, Doctor and Mrs. Forbes could be overheard arguing in the kitchen, his voice strident and hers subdued.

"Donald was too hasty," Doctor Forbes said. "Now look at what he's done. He's risking so much and has missed receiving his full bounty. He should have told Smith what he intended. Smith would have let him know swindling is rampant. I can assure you, men desperate to avoid the draft are not above cheating."

"But we knew the money was a great enticement, and he was not content being a store clerk. You of all people should understand why he did this. There was a pause, and then Mrs. Forbes added, "He still seems so very young and easily misled at times."

Rhoda returned with the tea tray, a guilty smile on her face. "As you heard, my parents are upset about Donny joining the Union Army."

"It's unfortunate news, although he has been considering it for a while," Jessie said, believing it should not have been a great surprise to his family. Donny hadn't told her about losing his replacement money, and she wondered how that had happened.

Doctor and Mrs. Forbes entered the drawing room to take Jessie's hands in greeting, but their argument continued as if Jessie were not present.

"I tell you, entering the war as a mercenary was a mistake," Doctor Forbes said.

"Really," Anne Forbes replied, giving him the full force of her cool gray eyes. "And weren't you paid for waring in Spain?"

Doctor Forbes grumbled. "That was a different thing entirely. I was employed by the Royal Navy and I went where I was ordered."

"Surely you did not expect to avoid war entirely." Jessie was amused that Doctor Forbes found it difficult to defend himself against his wife's logic. He changed tactics and relented.

"At least he should be out of the infantry, so he will avoid the worst. As a hospital steward, Donald might advance to assist in surgery, but he will experience hard times. There is no avoiding that."

Concern was evident on Mrs. Forbes face at this pronouncement, and no more was said on the subject. Doctor Forbes left quickly after greeting Jessie and asking after her health. Jessie suspected Doctor Forbes would prefer to see his wife angry than despairing.

"Jessie, dear," Anne Forbes said, taking her hands again. "Tell me how things are going in Galt? Are you all happily settled there?"

"We are pleased with our move although we miss the Falls and our friends here, of course. There is much work to advertise and to refit the house and barn, but we are well-settled and have many new customers." Jessie smiled as she felt pride in her work. "Donny said he might be able to get a furlough to travel home this weekend. I wondered if you'd heard from him." Mrs. Forbes eyed her carefully before she spoke.

"Only that he is in Elmira at an army training camp, and none too pleased with his accommodations. He threatened to enlist and now he has done so, without our approval."

"But if he becomes a steward, he should enjoy the work," Jessie said.

"Perhaps, but his position in Newark would have led to his becoming a pharmacist in due course, and with much less peril. Patience is not his strong suit, I fear," Mrs. Forbes said, allowing a large sigh to escape.

"I think impatience can be a good thing if it drives a person to try harder." Jessie said.

"Bless you, dear. You know the right thing to say to make me feel brighter."

"He said nothing of a visit home at this time?" Jessie said. Mrs. Forbes looked uncomfortable.

"He knew no one who could sign his papers for a furlough home. Apparently, one requires connections for that, and too many of these young boys might not return after a furlough, especially those who must cross back over the border."

Jessie tried to hide her disappointment. She chatted briefly of local news and turned to leave, saying she had time to catch the evening train back to Galt.

"But you have your bag here, dear. Why not stay the night?" Mrs. Forbes said. Jessie watched Rhoda's eyes widen and her finger wave "No".

"Thank you, but I'd better not leave Papa alone with all the work. It seemed a slim excuse when she'd planned to stay the night had Donny been there. Rhoda offered to walk with her as far as the school house.

"I have something important to tell you," Rhoda whispered as soon as they were past the gate. She pulled a telegram from her pocket, unfolded it, and offered it to Jessie. "It's from Donny. Mama didn't mention this to you, but I think you should know. Donny couldn't get a furlough, but he was given permission to stay in Elmira to say goodbye to his family before he leaves for his regiment tomorrow night. He asked if it would be possible for Mama and me to meet him at the Elmira train station this evening. I wanted to go, but you heard my parents arguing. They're still too angry to see him, and they won't allow me go either. Could you meet him, Jessie? He should see a friendly face before he enters the fray.

Jessie took the telegram and read it quickly. "Do you think I could get there this evening?"

"I checked the departure times, and there's a train leaving at six o'clock. You must change trains at Buffalo and Canandaigua, but you should be into the station by eleven tonight. Do you have your certificate of naturalization with you?"

"I always carry it with me."

"Good, and I brought my purse with me. You'll need extra money."

Jessie hugged her as she took the money. "Thank you. I'll pay you back as soon as I return. Rhoda, it's as if you were expecting me to go."

"To be truthful, I was planning to board the train myself, with or without my parent's consent. But this is a much better idea."

Pulling their heavy woolen shawls tightly around them, they walked quickly down the path towards town. As they reached the schoolhouse, the bell rang and a dozen children spilled from the building, almost knocking the two women over in their haste to escape. Miss Armstrong stood at the door, her arms compressing a generous torso. She waved at them, beckoning them over. "She'll want to see you, Jessie, not me," Rhoda said, retreating quickly. They hugged goodbye, and Jessie walked slowly up the path wishing her timing past the school house had been more propitious.

"Why Jessie MacKay, come in out of this bitter wind. Spring hasn't landed here yet."

The schoolroom felt like an old friend, and if memory served, it was as draughty as ever. They both migrated towards the stove in the center of the room, a few coals still gleaming to warm them.

"What brings you back to Chippawa?"

"I was visiting the Forbes family with hopes of seeing Donald," Jessie admitted, as she watched Miss Armstrong scrutinize her clothes and pinch the fabric.

"Hasn't our Donald enlisted in the Northern Army?"

"Ah, the village gossip still reaches everywhere," Jessie nodded. "Donald was hoping to obtain permission for a furlough before the Spring Campaign commences, but he was unsuccessful. I'm on my way back to the train station now." She was pleased how she'd managed to avoid an outright lie.

"Once, I had a plan to convince you to become a teacher. Had that idea ever crossed your mind?" Jessie laughed but stopped when she realized Miss Armstrong was serious. "And why not? You're bright and hardworking. I know you have ambition, and I've heard you were not anxious to care for babies."

"It's true I refused to be nurse maid to my brother's child, but not because I dislike babies."

"Then I'm sorry you missed seeing Donald." Jessie blushed under Miss Armstrong's penetrating gaze. Her old teacher looked like an owl with that long nose and piercing eyes magnified by large round glasses. "Don't worry, my dear. That dreadful war will soon be over, and your young man will return home."

The steam train to Galt pulled slowly out of the station as the southern bound train arrived, and the combined smoke from the two engines was suffocating. Jessie's parents were expecting her to remain the night in Chippawa, so she felt no need to tell them of her change in plans. She settled herself into the carriage, the seat back straight and unyielding, and she placed a small parcel of purchased bread and cheese beside her travel bag in the empty seat next to her. She felt excited to be traveling alone to see Donny, and she wondered how he would react when he saw her. Would he be very disappointed his family had not made the effort to see him, and would his surprise at seeing her lessen his sorrow?

The trip and station changes were uneventful but she felt an odd mixture of excitement and trepidation. As the train drew into the Elmira station, Jessie could not identify Donald on the platform, nor did she recognize him among those waiting in the station house. Even when he jumped up and waved, it took her a moment to realize the young man staring at her was Donny. She felt a sharp intake of breath at how handsome he was in his uniform. Even with his new beard, she recognized his piercing eyes, and watched him as he looked expectantly around the room.

"It's only me, I'm afraid," Jessie said, moving up to take his hand. "Rhoda told me you'd be waiting here, and she wanted to meet you but felt it was best I come alone." She could sense his disappointment even as he smiled. "This is all still new to them, Donny." They would need a chance to come to terms with it, she thought. "I had difficulty recognizing you with the beard and uniform."

Donald tugged at his chin. "They all wear them sooner or later, so I've been told, and I've had a head start. Mr. Smith let me wear a moustache at the store. He said it made me look older and more knowledgeable."

"Then you must be a genius, now," Jessie smiled. She wasn't sure she liked his beard, but she could see how it would be practical in the Army.

"I'm glad you're here, Jessie, but I hadn't thought about what to do if anyone showed up. I slept last night in a room above the restaurant next door. It's simple and inexpensive. Shall I see if I can arrange a room for you?"

She nodded, realizing she was exhausted from the day of travelling. When Donny picked up her bag and wrapped her arm around his, she wondered at the smile playing on his lips.

"I'll say you're my sister, shall I?"

"Are you concerned for my reputation?" That extracted a laugh, but he wasn't as amused when the Innkeeper told him all the rooms were taken and he would have to share his room with his sister.

"We'll look around town, I think," Donald replied, his face looking pink above the beard.

"It's nigh on midnight, son. Other places are closed, and we're only open because of being next door to the train station," the man replied, slowly lifting his eyes from the register. "Take it or leave it. It'll be an extra two bits a night if your sister stays."

"We'll take it," Jessie said, and was glad the man did not look up to see her blush.

The room was small and Spartan, but the old wood floors shone with care and the bed coverings were spotless. A faded water colour painting of the Falls hung above a bed that could fit a friendly couple in a pinch. Their single smoking oil lamp provided the only light. "I'll set myself down over here," Donald said hastily as he pulled a heavy patchwork quilt and small pillow from the bed. He sank down with his back to the wall as Jessie perched on the side of the bed. "I expect I will remember this floor as luxury when I'm out on the road," he said.

They discussed the army training barracks and what little Donald knew about the regiment he would join. Jessie told him about her visit to his home, omitting the argument between his parents but telling him about Miss Armstrong's idea that she should consider becoming a teacher.

"She appreciated how you handled all the bullies. You're a no-nonsense person, Jessie."

"I hope there's more to being a good teacher than threatening children."

"Being tough and smart is a good combination."

"I will take that as a complement," Jessie said. She looked down at her dress and frowned at the soil on the hem. Normally, she would have brushed it off at home and given her shoes a quick clean, but all they had in the room was a small washstand with a single ewer and bowl. "Is there more water?"

"I'll go downstairs and get some, if you want to use what's there first. I was told to throw the waste water out the back window. The privy is out the back door to the left. Do you want me to accompany you?"

"Thanks, but I can see it from here," Jessie said, looking out the back window at the small shack with a telltale quarter moon carved into the door. "Why don't you use this water, and I'll bring up another ewer on my way back." She poured the water into the bowl and headed downstairs with the empty pitcher.

By the time she returned, Donald had washed and was lying on his back under the quilt, arms under his head. She poured her water into the bowl, made a quick job cleaning her hands and face and finally wiping off the hem of her gown and her shoes as best she could. After dumping the water from the window, she turned to Donald. "Could you face the wall for a moment while I remove my dress?" He smiled and obliged. She'd have preferred to have removed her shift and corset as well, but she made do with loosening the stays and pulling her nightgown over her undergarments. She slipped between the sheets and told Donald she was decent.

"I'm glad you're here, Jess. I would have felt sorry for myself if no one had met me tonight, but I can't say I expected my parents to appear at the station."

"When you weren't at your home this afternoon, I was disappointed. I thought I might not see you for a long time. I was pleased when Rhoda told me you'd be here."

"Were they really that angry with me?"

"I could smell saffron," Jessie smiled when she heard Donald chuckle.

"Mama must have had words with Papa. I think she does that to deflect his anger from me."

"Like that tiny gosling with the wire wound around its foot. Remember?" The mother goose had rushed at them, trying to lure them away from her baby when they'd tried to capture it.

"I hope I'm not being compared to a goose," Donald said.

"A gosling," Jessie corrected.

"Are you angry with me, too?"

"I am disappointed you weren't able to remain at the pharmacy, that's all." She wanted to ask about the bounty money but knew Donny well enough to control her curiosity until he mentioned it.

"Jessie, I'm excited to join the war. I'll be a hospital steward, and that's far better than selling sewing machines and elixirs."

"You're sure to have adventures, if it's what you want."

"That's not it. I've always wanted to be a surgeon, and this is as close as I'm likely to get." Jessie winced when he made this admission.

"I thought you wanted to be a veterinarian?" She was glad he couldn't see her face freeze in surprize.

"That's what I decided to do when I realized I wouldn't become a surgeon. And being a veterinarian is a good career too. I love helping animals, but they're not people, are they?"

Jessie felt oddly betrayed. "Don't get your hopes up. I expect you'll be spending more time with bedpans than scalpels." She cringed at hearing the vinegar in her voice. Donny should be going to veterinary school so they could work together. Somehow, she'd misunderstood his motives all along, or maybe she hadn't been listening. Healing animals might be satisfying to him, but animals didn't show you respect when you saved their lives. He'd adopted more of his father's attitudes than he knew. Her dream of a business together was fading quickly, like the painting above their bed.

"Who knows what will happen," Donald continued, not affected in the least by her sour response. "Maybe I'll be anxious to be a veterinarian after this experience. Right now, I can't think beyond the next week or next month, and I'm not making any plans for the future until this war is over."

"Good. Then neither will I." Jessie said.

"What does that mean?"

"I was thinking how we'd planned to open an animal hospital."

"I thought you were happy with your life in Galt? Don't you hope to take over your father's business? Besides, I can't believe you're still thinking about an animal hospital." Jessie heard him laugh, as if he considered the idea childish, and she flushed with anger.

"I was thinking of a life with you, you blockhead." At that moment, the lamp sputtered out. It wasn't how she planned to tell him.

CHAPTER 10: 1864, CAMP ON DUMPLING MOUNTAIN, VIRGINIA

You shall listen to all sides and filter them from yourself

Donald lay in the darkened room wondering how to respond to Jessie. "Did you just call me a blockhead?" he whispered. When she didn't answer, he asked, "Can't we have a life together without the animal hospital?"

Jessie laughed, and the tension broke. "Of course, we can."

"Does that make you the blockhead?"

"Alright, I take it back." They lay quietly for a while. "Donny, are you sure you won't return home with me?"

"I knew you'd missed me as soon as I saw you at the station. Not every self-respecting girl would run away to meet a bearded man in a strange country and sleep in his bed." He imagined her smiling, and he stood up in the dark and groped his way to the edge of the bed. Taking her head in his hands, he kissed her firmly on the lips. He could feel Jessie's eager response as her arms entwined around his head. Her smile tasted as good as it looked. "I've signed up and can't go home now, but don't go getting attached to another fellow, Jessie MacKay. There's plenty of time to think of the future."

He needed to see her eyes and her smile to know what she was feeling. He wasn't sure what he felt, and there was no way he could consider a married life with anyone until he had established himself. Returning to the floor, he eventually heard the steady rhythm of her soft breathing and realized she was asleep. For the second time, he wondered if he had made a mistake by enlisting. The first time was after he failed to receive all his bounty money.

Startled awake by the racket made by a rooster perching on their window sill, Donald pretended to drop back to sleep while Jessie slipped on her dress. He watched her carry the pitcher downstairs, and then he rose and put on a clean shirt. He took the pitcher from her when she returned, poured it into the bowl, and headed downstairs to give her privacy while she washed. In spite of the cold winter weather, he was looking forward to wandering around the small town with her.

The restaurant downstairs provided cups of strong coffee and slabs of crusty bread with strawberry preserves. Leaving their bags with the station master, they checked the departure time for the afternoon train back up the Niagara peninsula and set out on a tour of the town. Donald took her to a nearby drug store and introduced Jessie to the owner he had met the previous afternoon. He said she was his girlfriend who had stopped to see him off to winter camp in Virginia. Jessie's broad smile told him he'd done the right thing not to introduce her as his sister.

The day passed quickly, but before they parted in the late afternoon, Jessie insisted on purchasing a tintype. Two young people who looked far too grim to be dreaming of a future together stared back at them from the plate. The seriousness of the picture made them both laugh. "You'd think we'd received some awful news." As he looked at the two faces, he was surprised to feel a tug of loss. They hadn't even said goodbye, and already he missed her. He'd made her a kind of commitment last night, although he hadn't explicitly asked her to marry her. He was still surprised to realize he could consider marrying his best friend, but he knew life would never be dull with

Jessie. At the train station, Donald kissed her again and promised to write. Jessie's eyebrows rose to express her doubt.

"If you haven't written me properly by now, being on the march is unlikely to improve your record." He could only shrug in agreement. The quizzical look on her face as the train pulled out made him wish he could read her thoughts.

He spent an anxious night on the train. When it pulled into Fredericksburg early the next morning, a wagon was waiting to take him to his regiment stationed a few miles from the small town of Culpepper. The wagon was decked out as a proper four-wheel ambulance, and although there was room on the front bench to sit with the driver, he was told, with a toothless smile, to make himself comfortable in the back. Every hole and rock in the road made itself known to his posterior at the speed they took. Corduroy roads, covered with planks of wood, were no better, and his spine was jarred repeatedly. By the time he arrived at camp, his tailbone was so sore he had trouble straightening up. The driver introduced him to Doctor Vorster who greeted him with a knowing smile as Donald slowly lowered himself down from the wagon bed.

The doctor was a small man, and as if to make up for his lack of height, he held himself as straight as a gate post. His eyes were busy taking Donald's measure as Donald's eyes were drawn to a prominent feature on he doctor's face. A moustache ran the full width of his head and then some, and it was so perfectly fashioned that Donald wondered, briefly, if it were real. When the doctor talked, the tips of the moustache waved, making Donald's own lips ride up in a smile.

"How did you enjoy being treated like a patient riding in that contraption?" Doctor Vorster asked as he took Donald's hand in a firm grasp.

Donald, rubbing his bruised backside, understood what he meant. "That wagon may cause more anguish than a bullet," he said.

"Now you know first-hand what it's like to travel in back, and that's your lesson for today. Anything you can do to reduce the pain of your patients will help them heal faster. Ambulances are a necessary evil, I'm afraid, and I'd much prefer to move the wounded by train or ship. Let's go into my tent and talk. I need to know how I can best make use of you."

Donald had the opportunity for no more than a quick assessment of the camp. Winter's cold still held tight to the land, and double-wide planks were in the process of being laid along the major lanes in preparation for the rain that would replace frozen ground with mud. He figured there were two hundred tents and a few wooden cabins set next to a large area of stumps. Doctor Vorster pointed out the hospital tent and a smaller one next to it for the stewards. The latrines weren't located far enough away to disguise the odour.

"You will be considered a hospital attendant for the 111th regiment until the hospital steward position becomes vacant next month."

"Is an attendant the same as an orderly?"

"I don't care what you call it, but we need people to help with the morning sick call, keep records of ailments, prepare medicines, and order supplies. Then there's patient treatment, changing dressings and the like, and patient care, which is administering drugs, feeding and removing their wastes. Duties change when we're on the move. We'll have a forward tent for stabilizing the wounded for transfer to the division hospital. You need to tell me what you've learned and what you're good at. I've found proficiency at a duty is often associated with aptitude and enjoyment."

"I'd like to help with the patients, the treatment especially, although I've only had experience with wounded animals," Donald said. Doctor Vorster raised his eyebrows at this disclosure, but said nothing, so Donald continued. "I do not particularly enjoy record keeping, but I can do too that since that's what I've been trained to do at the pharmacies where I apprenticed. I know a fair amount concerning drugs and the formulations of common medicines, so I can help there too."

"Good to hear. Mr. Smith sends a fine recommendation. I understand your father is a surgeon? Well Forbes, to be honest, anyone can keep records, but few are good with patients, so you will be valuable indeed if you can help the wounded men of our Regiment survive this accursed war. We have lost far too many to disease, and that pains me deeply."

"What diseases, sir?" Elmira had lots of boys who stood in line for sick call each morning. He'd wondered if they were truly sick or simply weary of endless marching.

"You can appreciate how crowded it is here. We have close to a thousand men in the 111th and upwards of twenty thousand men camped in this region alone. The young farm boys who have not had mumps and measles will catch those while here, and there is little we can do. But we can do something about dysentery and water borne diseases by keeping the latrines and animals away from our water supply and being careful with hygiene around the food supplies.

"I wage an never-ending battle to make sure that happens. In our own surgical tents, we must strive to remove all tissue, blood and excrement before it attracts flies and vermin. I warn you now. I will not tolerate a dirty tent, so we must all work together to achieve that goal. In the field during battle, keeping a clean tent is impossible, but in those situations, we can pick up and move daily and leave the rubbish behind us." Doctor Vorster slumped down on stool behind his desk and motioned Donald to take the opposite stool. "I don't mean to lecture you on your first day in camp, but it's been weighing on my mind as I send young boys north to the hospitals every day. Too many have died of disease before they carry a rifle into battle. That must stop or we risk losing this war."

Doctor Vorster pulled out a well-used book from a vest pocket and started making notes in small script. "Forbes, I'm assigning you to the forward surgical tent when we're on the road. You will assist in operations, in stabilizing patients for transfer, and attend to patient needs while they recover. In certain situations, you may be called upon to accompany the wounded men north to the division hospital or on to the Washington hospitals. During the times when there are no battles, you will attend morning sick call with me, formulate and distribute drugs, and help in ordering supplies."

"Are there wounded men in camp now?" Donald said, thinking that sniper fire or skirmishes might have produced a few victims.

"The only wounded man went north in the same ambulance that met you at the station." Donald felt sorry for the patient bouncing in the ambulance, and Vorster misinterpreted his expression. "Don't concern yourself. There will be plenty of opportunities to gain experience before we head into battle in the next month or two. Come now, I'll introduce you to our hospital steward."

Reginald Clarke, a pompous looking man in a blood-stained coat and greasy monocle, was more thorough than Doctor Vorster in winkling out Donald's experience. Lips pursed, Clarke nodded after Donald gave him an extended version of his pharmacy training. When he mentioned he wanted to help treat patients, the steward was less than enthusiastic. Donald suspected Clarke would prefer to take charge of such decisions.

"It will be a madhouse when the wounded start coming in from the front lines. You must be trained to do all that is needed. I'm sure Doctor Vorster has told you to keep the surgical tent clean? That's something you'll have to remain on top of, because I'll be occupied in surgery."

"Why is he so particular about cleanliness?"

"The doctor had his own brush with death when he cut himself with a scalpel that had been used on a patient with an infection. Ever since, he's maintained a clean tent. Me, now, I think rinsing with fresh blood is as good as cleaning with questionable water, but if you get anywhere near pus, then you must wash your hands and the knives thoroughly with carbolic soap and boiled water."

"I had a friend who told me similar things. He took care of horses."

"Horses!" Clarke shook his head. "We lose hundreds of mules and horses each week. Don't get me going on that. What we need is more of those veterinarians they have in Washington." Donald smiled, wishing his father and Jessie could have heard those words.

Clarke directed him to a tent filled to the canvas with surgical supplies. "Another man will join you this month, so enjoy your privacy while you can. We will take our meals and pick up the patient meals at the mess tent while we're here in camp. After we set out on the road, we'll be on biscuits and salt pork, and no one enjoys that. After you've eaten, I'll introduce you to our supply lists.

Even the possibility that he might be doing endless supply lists couldn't douse his excitement. He couldn't wait to write and tell Jessie he would be helping with the surgery. He felt sure his father would be impressed.

Walking to the mess tent, he realized the camp that had appeared well-organized from a distance was more disordered when viewed up close. Cook fires blocked the spaces between tents and the roughly-built wood cabins. Donald wondered if he would soon envy those cabins after a few cold nights under a billowing or dripping canvas tent.

Taking his plain meals in the mess tent, he listened as the men from his regiment who had survived Gettysburg teased the green recruits. They called them 'fresh fish' and made jokes at their expense instead of spending time preparing them for what lay ahead. Donald paid attention when he was advised to dig a moat around his tent to keep the melting snow and rain from his bed, and to hang his haversack from a peg instead of leaving it on the ground. He bought very little from the sutler's wagon, shaking his head at the steep prices of food and clothing, but after a few days, he purchased two fresh eggs. He lightly boiled and eagerly devoured them, thinking back on the dozens he had reluctantly gathered at home, never imagining how much he would yearn for their taste.

The regiment drilled daily for several hours while Donald attended morning sick call with the surgeons and helped treat the occasional wounded picket who was unlucky enough to cross the enemy's path. He was able to absorb a great deal of information in quick order because he learned through demonstration and practice, not from reading books or from notes on a blackboard. Doctor Vorster was an efficient surgeon who demanded excellence from his aides, and Reginald Clarke turned out to be a well-informed and patient teacher. Donald became familiar with all of the medicines he would need to organize or prepare, including silver nitrate to stanch blood flow, sulphur for skin ailments, iodine and alcohol as antiseptics, and opium and morphine for pain. He saw how the slow-moving lead bullets from a smooth-bored rifle caused less tissue damage while the Minié balls often cracked the bones making amputation necessary. He managed to impress Clarke with his skills with chloroform, and after watching Donald a few times, Clarke left him in charge of keeping patients unconscious during amputations and bullet extractions.

Donald enjoyed the opportunity to change bandages so he could study the details of wound healing. He became adept at injecting morphine with the new hypodermic needles. But most of his time was spent in caring for patients after their treatment. He was expected to feed the patients and ensure the hospital tent was as comfortable as possible as well as clean. Even these duties were satisfying.

For the first time, he began to develop confidence in his abilities, and he looked forward to new challenges. Morning sick call brought men who could not stand duty that day. Doctor Vorster taught him to recognize the shirkers and become hardened to their stories when there was no physical evidence to support their claims of bowel disturbances or painful rashes. These men would eventually stop appearing at sick call, making his job easier. The few patients wounded in skirmishes were generally the less severe cases, and when conscious, they were grateful for his attentions. No one kept track of his movements, but Donald found himself working harder than ever before, and without complaint. He had only to look at the resolve of the wounded and follow their stoic example.

Three weeks after he arrived, Donald was sent to meet a new hospital recruit and show him around camp. He recognized the man by his green armband, although his army uniform was disheveled. Simpson was standing with a dozen infantry recruits at orientation, a large, solid man with dark hair and tanned skin that seemed at odds with his light gray eyes. Jessie would have called them moose eyes. Instead of focusing on the Sergeant, the man's eyes slid this way and that as he took in the layout of the camp.

When Donald introduced himself, all he got was a monosyllabic "Yeah" and a reluctant offer of a large meaty hand that was too soft to have spent much time getting to know a farm or foundry.

"Were you drafted?" Donald asked.

"Nah, I volunteered when they promised I could work in a field hospital."

"Don't expect to get much respect from the men here. The infantry thinks we have it easy, and it's true that those relegated to ambulance duties are often unfit for much else. Stewards and hospital attendants get more respect, but we earn it. By the way, I should warn you to keep well away from the alcohol and opium supplies if you want to keep your position." Simpson raised his brows but said nothing. His morose demeanour might keep people at arm's length, and if that was his plan, it was effective.

They'd wandered towards the river and had reached the dense brush at the edge of the camp. "We keep latrines and horses away from the drinking water, so they're at the far side of camp, said Donald pointing towards the trees a quarter mile downstream. The kitchens are the opposite direction, and you may end up on kitchen duty when we have no patients. It's a long way to carry water, but I'm afraid they will make use of you any way they can."

"When do I get training? Any idiot can lug water."

"They'll be plenty of training, and you'll work with me as you learn the rules. But we're also expected to prepare, if necessary, and serve food to our patients." Simpson's attitude bothered Donald who knew that quiet patience was needed for tending the wounded. Moreover, if Simpson complained about toting water, he wouldn't be happy with handling bedpans or cleaning the tents. Donald felt himself frowning as he wondered how Simpson would behave when they saw action. "Much of what we do now is ordering medicines and bandages, and keeping track of patient numbers, camp diseases, and responses to treatment."

"I'm fine with all that."

They were walking on the banks of a lazily flowing stream oblivious to the war being waged close to its shores. There was a spot where the troops bathed around the bend, but with the weather so cold, it was not popular and the men gave no more than a quick splash to their arms and faces.

"Fancy a quick wash in the river before dinner? It looks like you could use one," Donald said, with an obvious reference to Simpson's dirty hands and face, but Simpson looked offended by the idea.

"River? Nah. I got a skin condition. Besides, I have to get settled." Simpson moved off rapidly leading Donald to wonder where he thought he was going.

By the time Donald had washed and returned to the tent, Simpson had made himself at home by setting his bag beside the empty cot and spreading two blankets over the thin cotton mattress.

"I didn't know we'd be sharing," Simpson said. "I was pointed to a tent, but it was the wrong one. I expect it was the surgeon's tent, but I tell you, I smelled something brutal in that tent, and it's been rotting there a long time."

"Doctor Vorster is a stickler for cleanliness. It must have been another tent you entered."

"Follow me. I'll show you, and I'll bet you it's the doc's tent."

Sure enough, Simpson led him to Doctor Vorster's tent where he slowly lifted the flap. An odour of decay emanated from the small space, and they both pulled back quickly from the entrance. They were startled by Reginald Clarke's voice behind them.

"You're wondering what that smell is, I'll wager," he said, a smile playing over his lips. When Donald and Simpson nodded, Clarke said, "There's something foul, alright. It's Limburger."

"When did he die?" Simpson asked.

"Not before he was eaten, I'd say," Clarke laughed, seeing their response. "Limburger's a cheese, you dolts. The Doc loves a good cheese, and not your ordinary cheddar, mind you. This one's sent to him from Europe."

"He eats something with a smell like that?" Simpson said.

"There have been suggestions his nose may not be in perfect working order, or perhaps the smell of the cheese disguises an odour he abhors more," Clarke said.

"Like the decay of putrefied flesh," Donald said when Simpson remained looking dumbfounded.

"He eats something with that smell?" Simpson repeated, shaking his head.

Donald led Simpson back to their quarters. "We're lucky to have such a large tent for the two of us, but the medical supplies are kept in here too because we keep track of them and we do the ordering. Not the interesting stuff, but bandages, suture thread, saw blades and such."

"Interesting stuff?" Simpson said. "Like cheese?"

"Opium, alcohol and anaesthetics which are kept in a locked wagon," Donald said, "The surgeons are in charge of those."

"Do we work together or in shifts?"

Donald considered the question and Vorster's caution concerning the pace of their work. "I suspect we will both work when there's work to be done and rest when we can. At least once the regiment starts moving south. Until we leave winter camp, we will both receive training from Doctor Vorster and Steward Clarke. I will show you what I've learned in the last two months, but you'll have to pick it up quickly. We could move out any day. In the meantime, grab that mess kit and follow me," Donald said, pointing to a plate, tin cup and fork on another crate.

Simpson knew the basics and seemed to have no trouble taking in new information, but he had a poor attitude. Donald despaired of teaching him to improve his care of the patients, which, to Donald's mind, was inadequate and often unfeeling. Simpson would wake the patients for a treatment that might be done as easily when they awakened naturally, and he would spare no time to listen to their concerns or help them with correspondence. When Donald recommended a different approach, he received a tolerant look from Simpson, as if patient comfort was none of his concern. Once, he watched Simpson with a dying patient who asked him if there was life after death. Simpson had shrugged and replied cruelly, "Sure, I'll still be alive when you're dead."

Their relationship outside of the surgical tent was less than amiable. Simpson remained distant from the medical staff, spending his off-duty time gambling with a group of rowdy young recruits. Donald did not enjoy the rough jokes Simpson repeated, and that made it easy to keep to his rule to avoid card games. Donald found Simpson uncaring and his moods unpredictable. In turn, Simpson belittled Donald's appearance and work ethic. "You must be a Mama's boy," he said when Donald received two letters from his mother in one week. Donald ignored him. He was too busy wondering why he'd received no letters from Jessie.

CHAPTER 11: 1864, GALT, CANADA WEST

Steep'd amid honey'd morphine

It was a windy night in early spring when Jessie heard her mother cry out her name. A smoky haze filled her room, and the acrid smell of burning timber grew stronger as she became fully conscious. She knew instinctively only a large fire could produce such an ominous whooshing sound, and when she opened the bedroom door, a menacing layer of heavy smoke slid in.

"Jessie, help," her mother cried again. Jessie pulled the heavy blanket from her bed, clutched it around her shoulders and mouth, and ran for her parent's room at the far end of the hall. Flames from the central kitchen were blocking her passage. As she turned to retrace her steps, the fire crept through the attic to emerge directly above her. Desperate to save her parents, she raced under the flames and back into her room. Coughing, her eyes watering fiercely, she lifted the window sash, dropped down to the frozen ground and ran as fast as her lungs would allow. Flames shot straight upwards from the roof above the kitchen, and there was a loud crack as a roof beam collapsed. Mercifully, the fire had not yet fully encompassed her parents' room on the other side of the kitchen.

Unable to push open their window, she grabbed a piece of firewood stacked nearby and smashed the glass. Using her blanket to brush aside the shards, she pulled herself up over the sill. Her mother, on hands and knees, moved towards her, but her father was nowhere in sight. She dropped down into the room, reached her mother, and began to half lift, half drag her towards the window. She was unaware that the inrush of fresh air had fueled the fire. A smouldering beam gave way above her and erupted in a burst of flames as it fell. Her mother's body took the brunt of the weight of the beam, and Jessie, sobbing in anger and frustration, wriggled furiously to release her own nightgown trapped beneath the burning timber. When her hair was set alight, she struggled to the window, grabbed the blanket to smother the flames, and leapt out into the night. Coughing uncontrollably, she ran from the house and doused her burned head and arms in the water trough. Losing consciousness was a blessing.

When Jessie awoke the first time, she heard a ticking clock and distant murmuring voices. Her mouth was as dry as newsprint, and her head and hands were swaddled in thick bandages. Waves of pain sent her in and out of consciousness. The second time she opened her eyes, a man with shirt sleeves rolled to his elbows was standing beside her bed, tapping on her knee.

"Awake now, Miss MacKay?" There was pain, but not as bad as before. She wondered where she was but lacked the will to enquire. The man, presumably the doctor, lifted her shoulders and she took a sip of water, but even swallowing was painful. She was not aware of the passage of time, or of the individuals who tended to her. Her bandages were changed, and she heard unfamiliar voices. Always she dreamed. She ran beside horses galloping over grass-covered fields. There was a wide azure river and she swam in it. As she floated in the water, her blond hair streamed out behind her like a long yellow wing.

"Miss MacKay, can you hear me? I'm Doctor Porter."

Jessie opened her eyes. The doctor was standing over her bed, smiling this time. "Where am I?" Her voice was weak and raspy, and it hurt to inhale.

"You're in the Galt Infirmary. You've been with us for five days. You received minor burns to both arms and one shoulder, but there are major burns to your hands and part of your scalp. He lifted up the corner of one bandage. "Your wounds are healing nicely."

"My parents?" she whispered impatiently.

"I'm sorry, but they both died in the fire." With those words, she felt untethered. A flash of a dream came back to her—no, not a dream, her mother in flames. She squeezed her eyes shut. The doctor was still talking. "—brother was here briefly, but he returned to York. We'll let him know you've regained consciousness." The loss of her parents made it difficult to breath, and tears spilled from her eyes. "Now, now, you must buck up, Miss MacKay. You're fortunate to be here, and you will heal, in time." Still smiling, he lifted her head to deliver a foul-tasting liquid, and she drifted back to her dreams.

An older woman wearing a white head scarf brought a bowl of broth and a spoon. "Try to hold the spoon, dearie," she said, placing the spoon between Jessie's hands that had been bound to resemble mittens. Jessie was unable to even grasp the spoon. "Never mind, dearie. We'll wait till the bandages are removed. Perhaps next week." The woman fed her the broth and afterwards, she removed a cotton cloth beneath her that smelled of urine. Jessie felt helpless and depressed, two emotions she had not experienced to any degree in her life. She set her mind to regaining a measure of independence as rapidly as possible.

When she next awoke, the pain was fierce. Desperate, she called out for help. The woman who had fed her the previous night came to her, patting her leg and telling her she was suffering from opium withdrawal. "They gave you a liberal amount for the burns, dearie. The doctor is cutting down the amount gradually, but you're bound to notice."

Jessie couldn't separate all the sources of pain: her wounds, the loss of her parents, their farm, and the withdrawal of the opium. Her heart ached to realize the loss of opium was more painful than any other. She desperately wanted her dreams, but she realized they were born of the drug. She badly needed Donny, but he was gone too.

One day, she woke to see her brother Thomas sitting beside her. His chair was facing the window and he appeared lost in thought. When he turned towards her, he jumped slightly in his chair.

"How do you feel?" he said. He glanced down at her hands, finally free of bandages. They lay on the top of the sheet, puffy with red welts and blisters surrounding areas where the tissue was still healing and starting to contract. His lips tightened.

"Better than I did a few days ago. I understand why people find opium so enjoyable." The doctor had insisted on massaging her hands and neck with oil to reduce skin contracture, and the pain was excruciating at first.

"You wouldn't continue to use that terrible drug, would you?" said Thomas, the disgust apparent on his features. Jessie doubted he had ever suffered pain of the sort she'd experienced.

"I needed it, Thomas." As she said this, Jessie realized that even if the physical pain was becoming bearable, the emotional pain was raw.

"The doctor tells me you will be discharged shortly. He's waiting for your hands and scalp to heal."

"He may be waiting a long time." Jessie was annoyed to hear anger and self-pity creep into her voice. She told herself she wouldn't complain, not when her parents had died and she'd survived. She was fortunate there wasn't more damage to her face. All her hair had been charred and was now trimmed close to her scalp. The fingers of both hands were so stiff she couldn't form a proper fist.

"We held the funeral service two weeks ago," Thomas said, looking down at his shoes. "I'm sorry you weren't there." Jessie considered the two meanings behind that sentence but kept still. "I had to sell the farm to cover the debts and to pay for your treatment. Unfortunately, there's nothing left." He was fidgeting now, as if there was more bad news to follow. "They say the fire started in the kitchen."

The stove, thought Jessie. Her mother hadn't been able to adjust to her new stove. She'd kept it going all night to save her the effort of starting it up in the morning, but overfilled, it ran hot, drying the wall board behind it. All it would take was the escape of a single, determined cinder.

"And there's one more thing." He was staring at her, and she imagined her swollen face hid any response she might reveal. "I'm moving with my family to England in two weeks. It's an excellent opportunity for me."

Jessie wondered if he were saying goodbye or planned to invite her to move with them. She suspected Louise would not permit that, but she would ask anyway. "I suppose it's too late for me to offer to care for Benjamin." She heard rather than saw him squirm. She would not make it easy for him. "Do you have any suggestions how I will live?"

"I have considered your situation. The doctor has been kind enough to discuss your disability with me. He believes you will regain full use of your hands, but the scars will make it difficult to find employment such as teaching or the work you were doing at the Hotel." Jessie wondered at his detached manner. Reserve, many would call it. She would call it indifference. He cleared his throat. "The doctor and I thought you could work as a domestic here in the hospital. The pay should be adequate for you to support yourself."

Tears filled Jessie's eyes. "Why are you here, Thomas? You have nothing to offer me." His eyebrows shot up but he said nothing. "Please leave now," she said more forcefully. She turned away from him and closed her eyes, squeezing out the pain and hungering for an opium dream.

Three weeks later, Jessie had rented a dismal room in a boarding house two blocks from the hospital. Once the swelling abated, and she could appreciate the full extent of her injuries, she realized many doors would be closed to her. The left side of her face was undamaged, but the skin on the right side close to her hairline was mottled in ugly red and white ridges that ran from the side of her head and down to her collar bone. There was no hair yet to hide the disfigurement. Aside from the area around the scar, sparse blonde strands grew as stubble over the rest of her head. The swelling in her hands and face was reduced, and her hands, although still scarred and stiff to move, responded well enough to her commands. The doctor told her to keep massaging her hands, but scrubbing and cleaning hospital floors made that recommendation pointless.

To earn money to live, she had accepted the position offered her. The doctor told her fewer people would stare at her at night. When she finished her work at dawn, she would cover her head with a scarf. She walked bent forward and looked at no one she passed on the streets. She ate all of her meals in her small room.

She found solace in reading poetry. She had admired the English poets, but one day she came across a book written by a new American poet, Walt Whitman. The little green book had a cover cleverly embossed with woven strands of grass. She was able to discern the pattern even with her damaged finger tips. On reading his stanzas, her solitude grew more bearable.

Hours continuing long, sore and heavy-hearted,
Hours of the dusk, when I withdraw to a lonesome and unfrequented spot, seating myself, leaning my face in my hands;
Hours sleepless, deep in the night, when I go forth, speeding swiftly the country roads, or through the city streets, or pacing miles and miles, stifling plaintive cries,

Hours discouraged, distracted, — For he, the one I cannot content myself without—soon I saw him content himself without me.

Had Donny heard about the fire? Her mind kept slipping down to lie helpless beneath the weight of the words that kept repeating: *You have nothing to offer him now, and it is for the best if he never hears from you again.* There was little news from the North as the spring campaign had not yet begun. Still, the numbers reported to be dying of illness alone were staggering. The thought of never seeing him again was another pain to endure.

One night while scrubbing the floor of one of the wards, she heard a deep voice call out to her. "Please. Could you give me a drink of water?"

Jessie brought the man a cup of water and placed her arm under his shoulders while he sipped. He was old, perhaps fifty she thought, pale and emaciated. His shoulder bones seemed sharp enough to cut through his thin cotton vest. As she was studying him, he was staring at her. He did not flinch when he saw her bright red scars. Instead, he thanked her for the drink and as she turned to leave, he spoke.

"Wait. What do they call you?"

"Jessie."

"Can you stay with me and talk for a while, Jessie? My name's Jack."

"I have another ward to clean." Was he desperate for company or frightened of dying? Perhaps both.

"When I first saw you, all I could see was the left side of your face. You looked beautiful."

"What do you think, now?" Jessie gripped the mop handle, her knuckles white.

"You look interesting. I like interesting."

"I like interesting too, but I would prefer to have my face and hands the way they were." She turned to leave, expecting she'd satisfied his dark curiosity, but he took her wrist in a weak grip.

"What?" she swiveled around and glared at him. Jack released her arm and sank down to the bed with a sigh. She felt a rush of remorse.

"Please, come back and talk to me tomorrow? They expect me to die soon, and I need something to look forward to, to keep me going. A visit from you, Jessie?"

Something in her broke when he said that. She'd been hiding a lie from herself, and Jack had voiced it. Her feelings of desperation slowly abated as she drew in a deep calming breath. With Jack's words had come the realization that she could recover—but only if she found, somewhere within herself, a reason to keep going.

"Alright, Jack. I'll find time for a visit tomorrow night." Perhaps she could offer him comfort, but she doubted he could help her.

She was wrong. Jack did help her. During the next two weeks, she talked about being lonely and abandoned to someone who shared those feelings. It was comforting to speak of her dreams and their loss to someone who had felt that pain. She found she could even laugh again. That happened one night when Jack first suggested she consider dressing like a man.

"Scars can make a man look mysterious," Jessie agreed. If I were a man, I would have more choices in life, like being a farrier." She had told him how she always wanted to tend horses, and how close she had come to realizing her dream before the fire.

"That's the ticket then," Jack said. "Dress like a man and behave like one. You're tall and strong. Your hands resemble a man's hands now. The scars on your scalp and neck will be taken as reason enough for lack of a beard."

"But how do I behave as a man?"

"I'm surprised to hear you ask such a question. You had a father and brother. You worked in a hotel. So, you tell me? How do men behave?

"They all behave differently."

"Of course, and that's a good thing too."

"Spitting, I suppose. Or scratching in public?"

"Let's choose admirable qualities to emulate."

"My brother imagined he knew everything worth knowing." Jessie sighed, wondering how Thomas would fare in England.

"I suppose that's more typical."

"Some men are bullies," she said, thinking of Angus.

"Not many. You can be a polite and respectful man, who does not spit or scratch, and does not demean women."

"My father was kind, but he thought women had a certain place in society, that women were weaker than men."

"Perhaps 'weak' is not quite accurate. He may have thought they needed protection, or they were not as physically or emotionally as strong as men."

"That sounds weak to me," Jessie replied.

"In that case, it should be easy for you to behave as a man." They both laughed.

"Let's not forget, I must be kind to children and animals," Jessie mocked.

"And enjoy beer, good food, and willing women."

The conversation that followed had them both laughing loud enough that the night nurse hushed them to silence. Jack made her realize it was her attitude, not her scars, that held her back, and it was in her power to build new dreams, perhaps even realize old ones. One night, she told him about Donald.

"Why haven't you mentioned him before?" Jack said gently. "Don't tell me. You find it difficult to see beyond your scars. You've lost your family and livelihood, so you think you have nothing to offer him. But, my dear, if this man cares for you, all this will mean nothing to him."

"Then why hasn't he found me?" Tears welled up and she willed them away. "I refuse to make him feel obligated in any way."

"You have every right to spill a few tears, considering what you've experienced. But you should contact your friend. Perhaps he has not been told of the fire. He deserves to know and to have a chance to offer you support. You should not make excuses to avoid *your* obligation to him." Jessie hadn't considered this, and she told him Donald had enlisted in the northern army and she didn't know where he was stationed.

"The army isn't at the end of the world," Jack said, reminding Jessie of something she'd once said to Donald. They both sat silently. "Besides, you could enlist, too."

Jessie laughed at his crazy idea. She could not bring herself to tell the Forbes family of her predicament. Donny was full of self-pity after he'd lost his position in Ingersoll, and she wouldn't allow herself to do that.

When Jack died peacefully, she shed the tears she'd stored inside since the fire. Unable to attend her parents' funeral, she attended Jack's small gathering. Alone at his grave, she promised him she would follow her dreams, even if that meant finding Donny and giving him the chance to reject her. But she wasn't ready for that, not yet.

CHAPTER 12: 1864, CAMP ON DUMPLING MOUNTAIN, VIRGINIA

I do not ask the wounded person how he feels, I myself become the wounded person.

Horses were scarce in the regiment, but Donald was expected to help locate the wounded and either treat them in the field or send out for the ambulance wagon. Doctor Vorster offered to lend Donald a feisty gelding he'd recently purchased. Bred for speed rather than strength, the gelding was proving to be a problem.

"I bought this beast at a good price thinking I could use him on the road, but I'm not sufficiently accomplished with horses and this one has a mind of its own," Doctor Vorster complained. "You say you like working with animals, Forbes. If you can do something with him, he's yours for the duration of the conflict."

Calvary horses often received army training, but this one refused to stand under fire. Even the noise and smells of the camp would turn the animal skittish. Donald was gentle with the horse, which he named Lancet, and they slowly established a rapport that allowed them to work as a team in the field. Simpson was annoyed not to have a horse, and one day he returned to camp leading a scrawny mule and saying he had traded for it. When Donald caught Simpson mistreating the animal, his own temper flared. The mule had several cuts on his withers where Simpson had hit him with a willow branch.

"If I catch you torturing that mule again, you'll wish you'd never stolen him," Donald said. The look on his face must have surprised Simpson who glared back at him but said nothing.

Donald treated Lancet as well as possible under the circumstances, including finding good grazing for his charge. Aside from the horse, Donald's most valuable possession was his leather saddle bag containing his medical supplies. Simpson's small opium tin was stolen the first week in camp, and after that they slept with their supplies under their pillows. They joked about how opium made them sleep better.

Although camp morale had been good when Donald had first arrived, there were the usual complaints concerning the sleeping accommodations in the damp and cold, and the quality, if not quantity, of the food they were served. While in camp, there was fresh beef, onions and bread, but they knew they would have to subsist on salt pork and biscuits once they left camp later that spring. His father had told him how scurvy was rampant in the navy, so Donald supplemented his diet with dandelion greens, much to the amusement of Simpson and the others who saw him munching on the weeds. "I see that horse has infected you with some strange appetites," Simpson mocked.

Every evening, weather permitting, he would walk to the lookout above Culpepper. He had finished reading a letter from his mother for the third time. She hadn't heard from Jessie either and said that a second letter to the MacKays had been returned. He worried about what had happened. Could they have moved again?

Interest in his appearance, so important to him before he joined the regiment, had waned. Now he paid little attention to the cut of his clothing, and he washed for hygiene, not vanity. What would his parents think of his appearance? It occurred to him that he should have a photograph taken. He did so and purchased two copies, planning to send one to Jessie, but the photograph came as a shock.

He was gaunt, and the uniform that was his pride for the first few weeks now hung on his frame like a coat on a hanger. Army food stayed his hunger only, and he had lost at least a stone. Still, there was something unexpected in the likeness. His face and posture made him appear relaxed, even contented, and the smile was an honest one. When Simpson saw the photograph, he snorted, "A face only a mother could love," so Donald mailed it on to his mother. He knew there was little he could do to calm his parents' anxiety, even if the only action his Regiment had seen so far was a few small skirmishes.

Men lined up outside the hospital tent and complained of suffering from camp diseases, particularly dysentery. Representatives of the Sanitary Commission told them repeatedly that reducing the filth of the camps would lower disease but getting this message through to the recruits was next to impossible. Young men, whose mothers or sisters had cleaned for them, rarely bothered to wash themselves or their clothes. Some foolishly drank water because it was convenient even if it was taken downstream from camp. Sick men recovered or they did not, and it was difficult to predict who would survive.

The first time he assisted Doctor Vorster in an operation to remove a limb, he was cautioned that the procedure may take getting used to. Donald was surprised at the warning. "I've seen operations before."

"On animals, I suppose, and no amputations I'd wager." Clarke said.

"You're right. There are no three-legged horses or cows."

The patient facing chloroform aesthetic moaned in anticipation of what would happen next. Once sedated, Donald watched carefully as the skin was first incised all around the leg, and then a second incision was made closer to the top of the leg through the layer of muscle beneath it. He heard an unpleasant grating sound from the surgical saw that cut the bone two inches up from the initial incision. Blood ran everywhere. Doctor Vorster casually dropped the leg into a box of sawdust waiting beside the operating bench. After cauterizing to stop the bleeding, the muscle and skin were wrapped and sewn with silk suture to produce a smooth stump. The whole procedure took little more than twenty minutes.

Most soldiers survived this ordeal. Donald admired their stamina in withstanding the physical pain, and their ability to quietly accept the loss of a limb. He had never seen such courage, and he felt stronger for being around these men. When he had time, he would take down letters to their families, his poor spelling no longer important. At night he would drop exhausted but satisfied into bed.

The damp spring weather brought on skin rashes. One in particular, army itch, was rampant. The men would appear at the medical tent for treatment, often bashful when describing their afflictions which seemed minor compared to the damage made by a lead Minié ball or a bayonet. But the burning and itching, especially in the groin region, could be fierce. Simpson acted unaware that he had contracted it, but Donald had only to watch him scratching unconsciously to realize the problem. "You've caught the itch," Donald said matter-of-factly one day.

"Nah, it's only a few bug bites," Simpson said batting at determined flies. "Besides, there's no more sulphur ointment."

"I've had success with a salve made with leaves of the pokeweed," Donald offered. He turned to his medicine hamper and pulled out a bag with the leaves he had gathered along the edge of a pasture the day before. "I've made an oil extraction of the leaves and added beeswax to make a salve. The other camps are using pokeweed too. I can give you a jar if you want," he offered.

Simpson looked at him wild-eyed and seemed ready to run. "No way will you get me to use that stuff!

Donald frowned at him. "Fine. Go ahead and itch away. But don't expect my sympathy."

It wasn't long afterwards that Donald caught Simpson going through his bag and removing a few of the young leaves and stems. He was studying them closely, sniffing the leaves and stems and even touching one to his tongue. Simpson turned beet red when he saw Donald watching him.

"I thought I might give it a try." Simpson looked down at the floor sheepishly. "Can't be any worse than the itch, right?" He rushed out of the tent without waiting for Donald to reply.

Donald shouted after him, "Don't use any berries or red stems, just the leaves, and remember to wash your hands after you apply it."

The next day, Simpson came to Donald, his eyes blazing and his palms red. "My whole groin area is bright red now. What was in that salve?"

Donald smiled and nodded. "Didn't you notice that pokeweed sap is red? It's also called inkberry. That's why I told you to wash your hands." Simpson nodded but was his anger was slow to cool. "Is the itch lessening?" Donald asked.

Simpson grudgingly admitted it was, and Donald hoped that Simpson might now encourage the use of the salve rather than discourage its use as he had been doing. Donald had also made a few friends in camp, and they'd reported that Simpson disparaged him to his card playing friends, calling him a worry wart and laughing at his rules for hygiene. Even so, Donald held hopes to win him over. "I could use help making another batch of the salve. If you can find the beeswax, I'll search for more of the pokeweed before it gets too late in the season. The berry seeds can be toxic."

"Where did you learn all this?" Simpson asked.

"We used different remedies on our farm animals," Donald said, thinking of the MacKay farm. "I made a comfrey salve for infected horse feet, and I used white hickory bark or even soot to stop bleeding. Then I learned more during my pharmacy apprenticeships. I saw a drawing of the pokeweed plant in the book at the dispensary. Beneath the drawing, the author had written that it was useful for skin ailments. When I learned that one of the Seneca Indians in our regiment was using pokeweed, and he showed me the plant, it was easy to make my own extract and prepare the salve."

"You talk to the Indians? I never hear them speak English in camp."

"I suspect they understand but pretend not to. I used hand gestures anyway," Donald admitted. "I saw a fellow mashing the leaves, and I pointed to it. He scratched his groin, so I figured out what it was for."

"I suppose I should learn to use herbs," Simpson said, an admittance that was as close to a complement as Donald was likely to hear.

Although Donald was confident of his own abilities, he had never thought of himself as a teacher. The one exception had been Rhoda when she wanted to learn to ride. She took to it so easily, he had been jealous. He never credited his own ability as a teacher but his sister's natural aptitude to ride. "Of course, I'm happy to tell you more. I have books that you may borrow if you agree to be careful with them."

Simpson spent a few nights studying the books, but eventually he told Donald that there was too much information and he could foresee problems finding and making the herbal preparations. Even so, a week later, Donald saw Simpson accepting money for the salve from a new recruit.

"Are you asking payment for that pokeweed treatment?" Donald said.

"What of it?" Simpson responded, clearly feeling no shame. "If I didn't make the medicine, they would suffer more from the itch. And if they don't pay me, why should I make it?"

Donald's face grew crimson in anger, but he knew there was little he could do. He especially regretted showing Simpson where the herb grew as it made it more difficult for him to find his own supply. Searching further afield one day, he entered a hollow below their encampment. The small town of Culpepper had suffered hardships during war, having been relieved of stored grain and animals over the long winter months of Army occupation. Few residents were interested in herbal remedies though, and he found a patch of pokeweed next to a brook. As he gathered the plants, he felt eyes upon him.

"What have you got there, steward?" a gentle voice inquired.

He saw the horse first, a powerful black gelding with wild eyes, snorting and pawing furiously, as if annoyed by the interruption in his exercise. Although dressed unimpressively, the man astride him carried himself with an air of authority. His head was covered by a black slouch hat, his boots were muddy, as was his long frock coat, but he wore the three stars of a General. Donald straightened as he slowly realized he was facing General Grant, a man he had seen only at a distance on the parade field but had come to admire through talk of his exploits. Donald questioned, perhaps for the first time, whether dress was important. It was the deportment of the man that drew his attention, not his clothing. The General sat straight and confident in his saddle, and he talked quietly to the horse whose ears pricked and moved in response to his master's voice. Donald explained he was collecting a medicinal plant to help treat camp itch.

"Ah, that unpleasant malady. And this plant helps?"

"The salve made from the plant benefits the infected soldiers." Donald said. He reached his hand up to the horse that regarded him briefly and permitted him to pat his nose.

"You take a chance with this horse," the General said. "He is thought to be wild and unmanageable."

"I am fond of all animals, sir, and horses in particular." Donald smiled.

"That is something we share," replied the General. "There is another in our Corps, a young farrier, who also has empathy for horses. And a good thing it is too, as many of our mounts have not been previously shod."

"Do you refer to the lad with the bad scars?" Donald asked. He had heard talk of a boy that had successfully stitched up several horses after cuts and bullet wounds threatened their lives.

"Horses aren't bothered by scars." The General smiled wryly. Donald saluted and watched him ride away. He felt an immediate affinity for this man who lacked the usual pretensions of higher ranking officers. Donald had heard that Grant had a knack with unmanageable horses, a talent that was rare in his experience. He resolved to meet the blacksmith that merited such high praise.

CHAPTER 13: 1864, ROCHESTER, NEW YORK

Has anyone supposed it lucky to be born?

After Jack's death, Jessie found herself alternately bored and anxious. She knew she could no longer remain working at the hospital, an invisible woman lacking the dreams she needed to fight the pain of her losses. Her thoughts came back, again and again, to Jack's suggestion that she disguise herself as a man, and she made up her mind to attempt the deception.

She studied men's dress and walk, choosing her clothing to suit her chosen profession of farrier. Women often bought clothing for their husbands, and no one questioned her purchases of used outfits. She knew she would have to leave Galt to find employment. To save money for the move, she rented a room that did not provide board, and secretly ate food left over from the meals served to patients at the hospital. In her small room, she practiced wearing her new clothes and lengthening her stride when walking. She read Shakespeare's *The Merchant of Venice* and saw in Portia, who pretended to be a man, a woman as driven as she felt herself to be. She purchased *The Modern Horse Doctor* and read it twice through, wishing her father were there to answer her questions. Even second-hand, the book cost her dearly. The hardest part in reinventing herself was finding a comfortable pair of boots, her feet being too long for a boy's and too narrow for a man's.

Once satisfied with her disguise, Jessie looked for work. She could rely on what she'd learned from her father, but she would need to partner with another farrier until she earned the money for her own tools and developed a local reputation and references. She realized that staying in the Niagara area would be impossible if she wanted to avoid meeting anyone she knew, so she decided to follow Donald to New York and find work there. She had started, but never finished, letters to him. How could she tell him she dressed like a man because it made her life easier? Her name was chosen with care - Walt for the poet, and Armstrong for her old teacher who would have more than words with her had she caught her outfitted this way.

Once across the border, the demand for farriers increased, many having been hired away by the Northern Army and now working in the great stables in Washington. In Rochester, she began by searching out businesses looking for apprentices and avoiding those that advertised for general iron workers. One business kept several young men busy shoeing and caring for horses. She applied for a position there, hoping her scars would evoke little interest because burns were not uncommon in her profession.

"Sorry, son. But you're a mite slight for a smithy."

"I was hoping you had ready-made horse shoes. I can easily do the rest."

"We have the pre-made shoes." He stared at her hands. "But those burns look recent. Can you still use your hands?"

"They work fine. I'd be glad to demonstrate at the forge." Jessie said, clenching her fists.

"No need to show us. If you don't work out, you won't be staying."

The other farriers were more sympathetic. Her hair now covered part of the scar on her scalp, and she wore a cloth cap except when sleeping. She stayed at a boarding house with the other apprentices. When one of the boys said the food wasn't anything to write home about, she stifled a sob.

After the first few days, her fear of discovery abated, and she began to take more pleasure in her work. She proved she could diagnose and treat foot problems, sew up cuts, and prepare hooves for the shoes far better than any of the other apprentices, although she proved less adept at the heavy forge and wheel work.

But the work load progressively decreased as the cavalry took more horses south. Jessie was told the new apprentices must be let go. Her employer suggested they all enlist. Farriers were in demand, not only in the field but also at the central stables in Washington. In the previous year, the army had recognized the importance of taking care of the horses and mules when it became obvious there wasn't an endless supply. It was said soldiers often went without shoes, but horses never did.

She made up her mind to enlist, but not with any regiment. She wanted to be near Donny, even if his infantry Regiment was unlikely to need another farrier. She wrote to Anne Forbes asking for Donny's address and pretending to be a school pal who had enlisted. Once she knew his regiment, she identified other regiments in the same brigade. The 126th New York Volunteers had an opening for a farrier.

Before she enlisted, she'd heard talk of women who had joined the army and escaped detection by the men of their regiments until bad luck or death revealed the lie. The boys would speculate how this deception was possible, thinking women too gentle, weak, or fearful. Many concluded that the disguised women must be prostitutes kept hidden by the men of their regiment. She tried not to think of Donny, knowing that her chances of meeting him were slim even if she knew the location of his regiment. In spite of longing to see him, she knew he wouldn't understand her decision to disguise herself and join the army. What caused her the greatest concern was her fear that her appearance would repulse him.

Jessie travelled overland to her regiment at the beginning of April. The winter cold had subsided, and there were green shoots of clover and timothy in the abandoned fields. Even so, Virginia was now a desolate country, the trees having been harvested for fuel, plank roads, or cabins, and livestock consumed by the northern army.

She was told there would be no field or arms training for farriers as their work would keep them away from the front lines. The winter camp consisted of rows of evenly spaced tents in various states of disrepair. Seasoned veterans who had spent winter in camp had built more substantial wooden huts that provided cover from the cold weather, but many of the farriers, kept busy day and night, found it more comfortable to bed down on their gum blankets near forges that were fed continuously. The officers did not complain, seeing the advantage of having men close to their work. When it rained, Jessie shared a tent with the forge driver Pringle, a huge Danish blacksmith called Jens Larsson, and a small orphan boy, Henry Lebeau. Larsson pursed his lips as he studied her. "New to this business, are you?"

"I've plenty of experience," replied Jessie, failing to elaborate, "and I'm good at stitching up wounds." She brought out her small kit and displayed the needles, silk thread, scissors and forceps. Larsson nodded, poking his large index finger at the needles and withdrawing his hand quickly.

"Ja, I have seen farriers sew up wounded beasts, but not so much here. Few bother when a horse or mule is shot or cut. They wait to see if the poor creature will recover on its own. Seems a shame." He looked closely at her hands and head. "These are scars from burns?"

Jessie nodded, but turned away before he could question her further.

Within a week, she had stitched up several horses and mules with bullet wounds, scrapes, or more rarely, bayonet wounds. The other farriers were impressed with the quality and speed of her work, but only one, little Henry, asked her if she would teach him. Henry must have lied about his age, she thought, and if he hadn't been so good with handling horses, he would have been sent home. He was shorter than her, and slight in build. His eyes were held open wide, as if surprised, and small red patches coloured his cheeks. Although enthusiastic, he was slow, and he reminded her a little of Joey. He was patient with the horses and would hold their heads, mumbling to them while she prepared a hoof or cleaned and stitched up a wound. She couldn't help smiling when she overheard his conversations with the horses, and her initial embarrassment for him turned to amusement. Larsson once told her empty barrels rattle the most, one of his grandmother's sayings that applied well to Henry.

"What a good brave horse you are. Now stand quiet while Armstrong takes care of that nasty cut. It won't take but a minute. You don't want to go losing more blood." Jessie was amazed to hear Henry carry on for ages in a low sing-song voice that did wonders to relax the horses and mules. With the loud noises from camp and the constant pounding on the anvil, she found his voice soothing too.

The other smithies treated her as a youth who had not yet grown into his muscle and was not much use in the heavy lifting required for their work. But Walt Armstrong's talent in preparing the hoof and hammering the shoes did not go unnoticed, so if she avoided the heavy lifting required for mending wheels and caissons, she made up for it in her work with the wounded horses and mules. The other smithies became used to her scars, and no one complained that she spent little time at the forge thinking she had good reason to fear fire. Larsson partnered with her, performing the ironwork to fit the shoe exactly as she asked and then allowing her to hammer in the nails while Henry held the horse's head. Their efficiency attracted the notice of their sergeant who advised the other teams to watch closely and follow their example.

Larsson asked her early on why she did not send or receive mail. "I've no one left," she'd answered simply. She'd not written to anyone, and now that she'd become Walt, no one would find her unless she wanted them to. Although she'd located Donny's medical tent with its yellow flag and his regiment's colors, she wasn't prepared to face him.

When she told Larsson she was alone in the world, he said, "My grandmother would say, what doesn't kill hardens. You can share Brandy with Henry and me."

"Brandy? Is that your remedy?" she laughed.

"This particular Brandy is." He whistled, and a golden retriever appeared from beneath the wagon. Larsson said to the dog, in a serious voice, "Jessie is our friend." Brandy ran up and placed his paw on her knee, winning her immediate admiration. "He doesn't write or receive letters either." As promised, Brandy became a welcome companion and an improvement, in Jessie's opinion, over the liquor by that name.

Her forth tent mate, Pringle, had tried to hide his disgust when he first saw her scars, and he'd declined to shake hands, thinking, Jessie suspected, she might transmit a disease. His discomfort kept him from talking to her, as if damage to her face and hands had softened her reason, so she avoided conversation with him, and when time allowed, she found solace in Whitman's poems. She knew many did not approve of Walt Whitman's poetry, finding it self-absorbed and even shocking in its honesty, so she kept the small book well-hidden. She'd heard Mr. Whitman worked in an army hospital in Washington, and she dreamed of meeting him one day. His words spoke to her soul and made her loneliness more tolerable.

Pringle was a poor and impatient teamster, and when their regiment was repositioned and they moved east, the horses pulling their wagon could sense his discomfort and balked. She pulled his arm down after he had used his whip once too often.

"They'll work better for you without fear of that black snake," she said quietly, still holding his whip arm.

Pringle shook off her arm, but he stopped using the whip and the horses settled down. They parted company at the Rapidan River, and after the team forded the river, Pringle was holding the reins loosely when the horses spooked at the sound of exploding shells in the distance. The team then pulled the wagon into the line of sight of a rebel sharp shooter whose Minié ball struck Pringle's abdomen. The regiment surgeon removed the ball, but Pringle was unlucky and the wound suppurated. Within a few days, he was dead. Jessie had felt no attachment to the man, but she was sorry he was gone nonetheless. She worried her next tent mate might not be so blind to her subterfuge.

She had good reason to worry. Pringle's replacement, Matt Percy, was a huge, rough man who had a reputation for drinking and brawling. It showed in his mouth and eyes that expressed a look of disdain, and in his stance, chest out and fists clenched. Percy had gawked at her hands when he first met her, and he'd curled his upper lip and said, "Bet you can't even fire a gun with those mitts." But when she stared him down, he was the first to break eye contact.

She judged him to be mean and insensitive, but also likely to yield to anyone who stood up to him. She made up her mind to do that. "I've heard talk around camp," she said. "They say you can start a fight in an empty tent. Don't think I'll take any of it because I won't." She glared and turned her back.

"Kid, you don't want me as your enemy," Percy said slowly, his voice low and threatening. Had she used the right tactic with him? She turned back to hold his stare until he sneered and left the tent. When he was gone, she allowed herself to tremble.

Now she slept fitfully at the end of each day, in spite of her exhaustion. She rejoiced when the regiment sent Percy north to drive a munitions wagon, and Larsson took over driving the forge wagon. But when Percy returned, he was invariably in a foul mood from the effects of drinking and carousing. He'd disappear into the back of a wagon to sleep it off, leaving others to do his work. All she could manage was to keep out of his way. She welcomed dry nights when she could sleep outside with Brandy beside the warm forge and away from Percy.

CHAPTER 14: 1864, THE RAPIDAN RIVER, VIRGINIA

The meeting of enemies, the sudden oath, the
blows and fall

Winter camp broke to jubilation two days later, and the Second Army Corps headed south at the beginning of May. The mood of the regiment was odd considering the men were marching into combat. Donald understood the feeling of relief to be escaping the smells and noise of a camp filthy with spring mud and winter waste. Disease and boredom had taken their toll, and the hours of drilling accomplished little these days except to aggravate raw feet and sore backs. He suspected that apprehension of the upcoming battle was driving the men to impatience, and for some, an overwhelming desire to have the war over. Now that the ground was too muddy to play baseball, even that distraction was gone, and since pay checks had not yet been issued, interest in games of chance had waned.

Donald filled his lungs with big draughts of fresh air as they trooped south, the grass green at the edge of the road and the branches bursting with new leaves. He was thankful for the mist that kept down the dust but didn't cause such a soaking that wagons heavily laden with food, grain, and ammunition became mired in mud.

Doctor Vorster had requested he give up Lancet for the march. A captain missing a foot insisted on leading his men across the Rapidan River, so Donald had reluctantly agreed. Now on foot, he knew enough not to overload his haversack, and his medical kit was stowed on a wagon. But he left his extra blanket and clothing in camp.

Those unwilling to leave their valuables behind eventually abandoned them beside the road as the weight on their shoulders grew too heavy. Others would stop and pick up an item—a half jar of jam, a book, a shirt—but after a mile, it would be discarded. Donald thought of the piles of goods left behind as tribute for the gods in exchange for safe passage south. Divested of the extra weight, his regiment still managed only a few miles the first day before they stopped to camp near a river crossing where hordes of insects were waiting to taste their blood.

Donald had his first opportunity to meet the young blacksmith when Lancet threw a shoe crossing the river with the Captain. Their regiment had a smithy of sorts, but after stopping for the day, he sought out the 126th regiment to meet the boy. A thin lad with bad scars took hold of the bridle, staring at the ground.

"I've heard tell you're good with horses," Donald said. The lad shrugged, as if he didn't care. "General Grant told me himself," he added, and this had the effect of eliciting a blush. The boy took the reins and Donald cautioned him concerning Lancet's behaviour with strangers. Lancet nuzzled an outstretched hand that offered him oats from a pocket in a leather apron. "Of course, if you're going to feed him, that's different." He took a better look at the lad whose clothes hung on his lanky frame. "You look like you could use more food yourself."

"There's only so much camp stew and salt pork my stomach will tolerate," the boy replied, eyes still fixed on the ground as he tied the bridle to a rope strung to a tree from the back of the wagon. Several horses were waiting for shoes. "Return before supper. He should be ready," the boy said in low voice, walking away before Donald could ask his name.

When he went to retrieve the horse a couple of hours later, another smithy delivered Lancet. "Where's the lad?" Donald asked the big man.

"You mean Walt?" the blacksmith asked.

"I guess so. The one with the scars."

"Maybe he's eating. The boy likes to do his own cooking."

"Do you know how he got the scars?" Donald said.

"Forge fire, so I heard. It doesn't affect his work."

Donald nodded and gave his thanks. There was something so familiar about the lad, but the answer eluded him.

Lying awake a couple of nights later, he realized why the smithy seemed so familiar to him. But how was it possible? When he hadn't received letters from Jessie, and his family had heard nothing from the Mackays, he knew something was wrong. Could this Walt really be Jessie in disguise? If so, what had happened to her face and hands, and why hadn't she said anything when he brought Lancet to her for shoeing? Why was she here and pretending to be a boy? Unable to stop thinking about her, he made his way to her camp before dawn. She was lying asleep beside the forge wagon, and he studied her face for several moments.

"Jessie," he whispered, "Wake up."

"What? I didn't hear the bu—". She rubbed her eyes and opened them to focus on his face. "Damn."

"What happened to you?" Donald said, ignoring her expletive. She got up and moved away from the forge. He sat down beside her, removing his cap and wringing it in his hands. He knew he was asking several questions. She remained silent for a moment and then stood up, stuck her feet into her boots, and led Donald away from the wagons.

"You didn't hear about the fire?"

Donald was confused. Was there a forge fire?

Jessie took a big breath and told him what had happened at their farm, stopping several times to answer his questions. "The way I appear now, I am not surprised you didn't recognize me," she said, and he heard the bitterness in her voice.

Why didn't you let me know?" Donald held her hands gently. Her eyes filled with tears and they both stared down at her fingers, once beautiful and agile. Now the skin was puckered with red ridges over the backs of both hands. He ran his fingers over the ridges. "Do they hurt?"

"The sensation is dulled." She was quiet for a moment. "I wanted to write." She glanced up at him briefly and he shook his head but said nothing. He could only imagine what she had endured with the pain and loss of her parents and home, and those terrible scars. His welfare would be at the bottom of her list of concerns.

"Why did you enlist?"

"I get paid to do work I enjoy, and I'm good at it. The Army doesn't look too closely at qualifications, and there was no medical exam. But to be honest, I was hoping to see you," she said, staring at the ground. "I had nowhere else to go."

Nowhere else to go was how he'd felt when Mr. Smith had asked him to leave, but Jessie meant something else. Had she really enlisted because of him? Donald studied her profile in the first rays of dawn, finding it difficult to believe he hadn't recognized her right away in spite of the scars and disguise. "It's only luck you weren't found out before this," he said, his voice sounding sad even to him. "I hear the army is now accepting women nurses. Why not try that?"

"Not with these scars. They'll want pretty nurses to help the men heal faster. I would only scare them."

He nodded absently, realizing from her expression that his response had only added to her misery. "Your father had friends in Chippawa and Galt. Couldn't they help you find a position?" he asked.

"Would your father help? Would anyone help me become a farrier?" Jessie snorted.

"My father would, I think," he said. "It's true your father held different opinions from many in his profession. Not all townsfolk valued his ideas, but I learned a great deal from him, and I will never forget his lessons. I'm truly sorry to lose his friendship and wise council."

"Donny," she sighed, grabbing his hands. "Thank you for saying that. It seems he's still with us when you speak of him that way. You and I carry his knowledge now." Then she turned away. "I joined up because you were here, but now I realize now it's best for both of us if you can ignore me. Remember to call me Walt Armstrong, and I'll pretend you don't know my secret."

"I can't leave you alone in this mess. What kind of friend would I be?" He watched her reaction, but she looked away, as if he'd disappointed her in some way.

"A friend would pretend, if I asked," she said, finally turning to stare into his eyes.

"I don't know, Jessie. I'll think on it." His immediate reaction had been to comfort and protect her. But she was still Jessie and still the strongest person he knew, in spite of what she'd suffered. Her scars had only increased his admiration for her spirit.

Donald left her as silently as he'd appeared. The camp was beginning to stir, and he knew there would be a line in front of the medical tent as soon as the bugle sounded reveille. As he rode Lancet back to his camp, he mulled over Jessie's sad story. Did she think he couldn't help or wouldn't care? Her damned independence was made worse by the fact she'd fooled everyone into thinking she was a man. All she cared about was whether he would reveal her secret. But hadn't she said she'd enlisted because he was in the army? What did she expect from him?

The next time Donald saw Jessie, he caught her swatting flies and swearing as she hammered a shoe onto a nervous hoof. When she saw him, she had Henry take the horse over to the picket line and bring the next one back.

"You'll have to forego cursing when you give up your disguise," Donald said when she came over to him.

"Swearing is one of the few things I enjoy about being a man," Jessie murmured. "Where have you been? I expected you'd show up before now." She was angry at Donald, and he didn't know why.

"I've been considering your request," he said, unhappy about his decision.

"It's like waiting for cannon to fire. What have you decided?"

"Just fix the damn shoe, Walt. I don't like it, but I'll keep your secret." Then she smiled at him. Oddly, the scars didn't alter her smile, and seeing her face light up affected him the way it always had. He felt warm inside, as if he had made the right choice.

Jessie pulled Lancet into line ahead of the other horses. The big blacksmith looked curious but said nothing, and Lancet stood patiently for her while Donny held his head. "This one should stay on for a while, that is, if you're planning on removing another shoe as an excuse for your next visit."

Donald shook his head. "We're breaking camp again and heading south, and I expect we'll become separated for a time. At least, it will be harder for me to find you, and we're both likely to be too busy to visit. Jessie, I'm worried for you. Is there a friend in your camp you can trust?"

"I have friends, but if you're wondering if anyone has questioned my disguise, the answer is no, and I'm planning on keeping it that way."

Donald stopped counting wagons after he reached four hundred, and he had to ask a dozen times before he located the 126th and hunted down the smithies wagons. He didn't think he'd have a chance to see Jessie so soon, but Doctor Vorster sent him to commandeer a couple of empty grain wagons from the cavalry units to use as extra ambulances, and Simpson had brought his mule to pull one of the vehicles back. Commandeering wagons meant to carry grain for the horses was not popular among the cavalry.

"We've passed a cavalry regiment. Why do we need to find the 126th?" Simpson complained.

"I figure the sergeant of the 126th is more likely to be agreeable to having a couple of his wagons commandeered by another New York regiment," Donald said, wondering if it were true.

"I don't see the problem anyway. Once the wagons are empty, who cares whether we send them back to the trains full of the wounded? Then they can get filled up with grain and get sent back here."

"The problem is the wagons don't end up where they started," Donald said. "If the regiment sends back its own wagons with its own men, they come back to their regiment full of grain. When they get used as ambulances, who knows where they'll end up next. It's their horses and mules that suffer and have to go without their feed."

"All we get to eat is hard tack and salt pork. I'm not feeling any pity for horses."

Donald was lucky. The sergeant of the 126th was willing to release a couple of empty wagons but would allow them only one horse. He directed them to the regiment's camp ground. Donald left Simpson to put the mule into the traces of one of the wagons while he went to find Jessie.

Jessie spotted him first and grabbed Lancet's bridle. "Lancet hasn't gone and lost another shoe, has he?"

Donald smiled. "I'm here to pick up a couple of wagons and thought I'd stop by and see how things are going." She looked fine after the day's march, he thought, thin but with a healthy glow. Her stamina had always amazed him, even when they were children.

"Thanks for the concern. We're busy now we've left camp. Those corduroy roads are a bane for horse shoes. The planks pick off a shoe like the lid off a can. I've had to replace four in the last hour, so I don't have time to stop and talk."

Seeing Jessie made him feel homesick all of a sudden. Then Donald realized two men had stopped to watch them. The big smithy walked over, pulling a huge hand out of a heavy leather glove. He introduced himself and said he teamed up with Walt Armstrong. Donald recognized Larsson as the blacksmith he'd seen the first time he visited the regiment. He apologized for interrupting his work, saying he was checking on the lad.

"You've no need to worry. I take care of both boys," Larsson said, placing his hand protectively over Jessie's shoulder.

"That's good to know," Donald said, growing uncomfortable with the pressure of unasked questions. Who was Larsson protecting Jessie from? Living with her, he must have guessed her secret.

"Henry, come say hello to Donald Forbes," Larsson said.

"Are you a friend of Walt's?" Henry asked. Donald nodded, afraid to give up any more information than necessary. "Walt's real good with doctoring horses. Did you bring your horse to get mended?"

"Not this time," Donald said. The young boy seemed a few cards short of a deck, and Jessie would more likely have to watch after him than vice versa. Larsson was a different matter, and his size alone reassured Donald about Jessie's safety. He mounted and rode away, careful not to look back or wave to Jessie. He did not like this situation at all, but he'd given her his word.

Trailing their infantry men, Donald's medical wagon crossed the river and skirted an area covered with scrub oak and tangled undergrowth. Steep gullies were treacherous for men on foot and virtually impassable for everyone else, so the wagons followed the roads while the regiment marched deeper into the brush searching for their enemies. Donald waited until he heard the first volleys of gunfire, and he turned to Doctor Vorster for instructions.

"There's no sense in going out there until it's safe to recover the wounded. The walking wounded will find their way back to us, or they'll have to wait until a truce is called."

They organized the field tent and raised their yellow flag. It wasn't long before they heard distant shouts of commands and rare cries of surprise or anguish. Sounds of cannon reverberated, and the ricochets of hundreds of bullets in the woods made a noise all their own. A fierce pinging racket brought down branches and small saplings. With the unending volleys, Donald imagined even flies were struck down.

Unable to hold himself back, he walked into the brush a few hundred feet before he tripped over a skull. He realized he was treading over human skeletons from a previous battle, partially covered by tangled weeds and roots. He wondered if the soldiers had died outright or had missed discovery among the thick undergrowth, suffering alone for hours before dying. This was not how he had imagined the conflict. His father had described rows of men facing each other over cleared fields. The new rifle had an advantage on a flat plain, but not in this brush. He heard a man call for help nearby, and Donald supported him back to the tent, pressing his hand over a right shoulder pierced by a bullet and leaking a trail of ruby red drops. It brought to mind the childhood story of Hansel and Gretel who marked their path out of the forest with red berries.

Donald's anxiety was pushed aside as he found himself working faster than he could have believed possible. There was no respite from the battle that continued all day and into the evening and seemed to produce a wounded man with each passing minute. The hardest part was deciding who would wait outside the tent and who would be admitted quickly for surgery.

"Don't bother with the gravely wounded, Forbes. Get the orderlies to bring in those with a little life left in them," Clarke said, heading back to the tent to help Doctor Vorster.

"Tell me what to look for," Donald said, sensing his rising panic.

Clarke turned and walked along the line of groaning men occupying the litters. He reached down to a soldier with an abdominal wound to press on his carotid artery. "See this? The artery is not moving and he's not breathing." He waved his hand for the orderlies to remove him. "Now this fellow has regular breathing and the tourniquet is set properly. He goes in. No, that one's too pale, he's lying in a pool of blood, and his breathing is irregular."

"Can't you operate right now?" Donald said.

"Check out his wounds, Forbes," Clark said, his voice lowered. "He has holes through both legs. That likely means two amputations, and with the blood he's lost, there's no hope he'll survive." Donald must have looked doubtful because Clark kept talking. "When we don't have the number of wounded we have today, we have the luxury to treat them all, but after a while, you get to know which ones are likely to make it and which have little hope."

Donald wasn't sure he wanted to develop a talent that let him know who would die by a glance, but as he was standing there, the fellow with the two bullet holes through his legs let out a small gasp and died. That's when he began to smell smoke. The constant shelling had set fire to the dry undergrowth, and he was hearing the screams of wounded men who lay in the fire's path a mile away.

"Why aren't we retreating?" Simpson shouted. "Can't they see we're being hammered?"

Donald detected anger in his voice, but there was fear too. Doctor Vorster shouted at Simpson to quit complaining and get back to work. The surgeons worked long hours without a moment's rest. They stemmed blood flow, amputated arms or legs damaged beyond saving, and administered whisky to those who were unlikely to survive their wounds. The respite between skirmishes allowed time to treat those with more minor wounds and to start making lists of patients to be taken north to the hospitals in Washington. Doctor Vorster had said Washington was receiving two thousand wounded men every day.

Simpson was sent to bury the arms and legs piling up beside the tables, but he came back complaining. "It's near impossible to dig a proper hole out there. The ground is nothing but roots."

"What do you think we dig the trenches for?" said one of the patients followed by a loud guffaw from another.

"Fine, will you carry them up to the front lines for me?" Simpson grunted. Donald was amazed when the wounded men laughed, even those who had contributed an appendage to the pile. He thanked God for opiates.

When a wounded Confederate boy wandered in and asked for help, Donald picked out the small shards of an exploded shell embedded deep in his shoulder and neck and stitched up the larger wounds, but Simpson stood next to him and seemed ready to fire a revolver into the boy.

"We have enough of our own. Send the rebs back to their own damn camps," he ranted.

The battle went on like this for days, and Donald caught a few moments here and there for food and rest. The troops would fight and make headway south, but then veer east and try to manoeuvre around the rebel army to fight again. The regiment was slowly being decimated, and it seemed as if half of the men of his regiment were wounded or dead. No one could say which side had won the skirmishes.

For a few days, they had a reprieve and saw little action while the army moved to outflank the enemy. Donald went to look for Lancet but the horse found him first and greedily nipped at the greens Donald had picked for him. The animal looked fit, with no signs of sores on his back or mouth. Donald was happy the Captain had been careful with him. Lancet tolerated his patting for a few minutes before rejoining the others. The bugle sounded reveille and Donald went to retrieve his pack. The army would head southeast today.

As they moved out, the men covered their faces from the dust of the back roads and the incessant buzz and bite of black flies. Donald's mind wandered to Jessie as they marched through the night and into the next morning. Finally, they rested, waiting for the sounds of battle to announce the next influx of wounded.

When Simpson was not working in the hospital tent, he made salves or foraged for liquor, and according to gossip, was selling both for a good price. Gossip reported Simpson had badly beaten a young private who had complained about the quality of the liquor. Then Simpson and Donald had come close to blows over an incident that started one afternoon when Simpson turned up to work still feeling the effects of his own product. He had failed to clean the surgical instruments. Donald blamed him for the deaths of two soldiers who died of infections several days later. Simpson ignored him, but everyone stepped carefully around the two men, waiting for the harsh words to move to blows. It came the afternoon when Simpson refused to feed his patients.

"I haven't eaten yet," he said, failing to hide his annoyance. "All we've had for days is jerky, and not much of that, either. Why waste food on them when all they do is lie there."

"You'll feed them whether or not you get fed. That's your responsibility," Donald said, his fists clenched by his side.

"Feed them yourself. I'll be up at the front with the ambulance, doing something useful."

Donald suspected he used that excuse to escape camp and forage. "Not this time. They'll be no foraging until you feed our patients." Donald grabbed Simpson's shoulder to pull him back into the tent. Simpson twisted and hit him square in the jaw, knocking him back into the tent pole. Donald grabbed his legs as he slid down the pole, and the two men ended up grappling on the ground. Simpson, heavier by a stone, was not above biting and gouging, and he landed two more solid blows before the Sergeant heard the commotion and separated them. Hearing what had started the fight, he ordered Simpson to feed the patients, and the next day, Simpson was sent to accompany the medical wagon north. As Simpson left, he raised his fist and laughed at Donald, the threat obvious, but Donald was relieved he was rid of the uncaring good-for-nothing for a few days.

When Doctor Vorster found out about their fight, Donald was the only one in camp and so received the brunt of his displeasure. "We have no time for brawls, Private Forbes. Simpson likes to wind you up, we can all see that, but it's up to you to handle him."

"I'm sorry, sir, it won't happen again." For a brief moment, he felt he was back in Chippawa facing Miss Armstrong's tongue.

"I'm appointing you as acting hospital steward, and not because of this recent behaviour. Clarke has completed his exams and will become Assistant Surgeon, so the position of Regiment steward is vacant. Overall, I have been very pleased with your work. It's time you were promoted."

"Thank you, sir. You won't be disappointed." His image of Miss Armstrong scolding him faded. He smiled to realize that Simpson was now his subordinate.

As if reading his smile, Vorster said, "That should help you keep Simpson in line, but don't abuse the privilege."

CHAPTER 15: 1864, BOWLING GREEN, VIRGINIA

We are approaching some great battle-field in
which we are soon to be engaged

The town of Bowling Green was deserted of all white inhabitants, and those remaining appeared jubilant to welcome the northern troops. Jessie's regiment rested near a courthouse hastily cleared out before the northern army arrived. Piles of documents and furniture lay smouldering behind the building, adding to the intense late afternoon heat. Inside the court house, floors were strewn with more papers, abandoned to their fate like the gleaned land they had crossed.

Jessie picked up a sheet of parchment yellowed by age and signed by King George II over a hundred years earlier. "Why did they leave all this behind?" she asked Larsson.

"Why not?" Larsson shrugged, apparently amused that Jessie cared. "They have enough to carry. As grandmother would say, don't put stones on a burden."

"But there are thousands of important documents. It doesn't seem right." She dropped the paper.

Larsson sighed. "At least it will be easy to start a cooking fire."

Jessie was exhausted and had no interest in food. She had lost weight she could ill afford to lose. Everyone seemed shrunken and used up after a few short weeks on the roads. The constant walking had taken its toll on their feet, and the camp salve was no match for the irritation caused by boots that had become alternately wet and then dry and then cracked.

At the mess tent, they were offered coffee to go with their hardtack and jerky, and neither of them wanted to forage for food in the town, knowing there'd be little left worth eating. Larsson suggested finding a place to bed down indoors for a change. Jessie nodded in agreement and they headed back to the courthouse.

The first floor had been commandeered by men of their regiment who had found liquor and were playing cards. Percy saw them and waved them over. "Join the game, why don't you." Jessie saw his eyes glance away from hers and his lips formed a sneer.

"Too tired, boys," Larsson said, and Jessie nodded agreement. As they climbed the stairs, Larsson mumbled more wisdom from his grandmother—better to be alone than in bad company.

The second floor was occupied by those hungry for rest. After bedding down in an empty office, Jessie fell quickly to sleep. She awoke a few hours later when a group of men entered the room, reeking of liquor fumes carried in with the humid air.

"Damn, it's the smithies," Percy said. "They smell like burnt horse shit."

Jessie heard the other men snicker as they slid their packs to the floor on the other side of the room. Heavy snores soon reverberated, and Jessie dropped back into a fitful sleep.

She awoke to the odour of unwashed men and exhaled tobacco and spirits. Larsson snored quietly nearby. She lay motionless, trying to identify the sound that had roused her. Then she heard it again. Someone was pawing through the haversacks they'd placed against the wall. The buckles hit the floor twice more, causing the sound she'd heard, but there wasn't enough light to see who was rifling through their sacks.

Whoever it was had opened Larsson's knapsack and had likely had gone through hers. The only items of value were her copy of Whitman's poems and her stitching kit. But Simpson kept money in his haversack instead of his pockets because he filled his pockets with horseshoe nails that poked holes through them. When the thief crept out of the room, Jessie pulled on her boots and followed him.

She recognized Percy standing in front of a cook fire that had dwindled to red coals. He was weaving slightly, probably from drink, while he examined his loot. It included her book of poetry.

"I didn't know you could read," she said, standing behind him. He jumped and dropped the book. Jessie bent and grabbed it, stuffing it in her pocket.

"That's poetry, ain't it?"

"It's a recipe book for horse doctors."

"Is that all? I found it on the floor where I was sleeping."

"Forget the lies. I saw you going through the haversacks."

"I never did. It's your word against mine," Percy said slyly.

"My word, and whatever you've got in your pockets that doesn't belong to you. Give it up." Jessie held out her hand and wiggled her fingers.

"Damn I will, brat. Keep your distance or you'll meet my fists. They're not all puckered and useless like yours."

"Mine are good with a scalpel."

"Mine are better with a real knife," Percy replied, pulling out a hunting knife that had been sheathed without cleaning. He feinted at her and she jumped back, eliciting a high-pitched laugh of satisfaction from Percy. Someone shouted at them to keep quiet. Before Jessie could cry out, Percy grabbed her arm and swung her body in front of him, waving the knife in her face. She could smell the liquor on his breath, and he was using her to maintain his balance.

"I can get to your throat as easy as your recipe book," he whispered. "Any time I want." She stomped down hard on his ankle with her boot, grabbed his knife hand at the same time, and bit into it. He yelped in pain, and she wrenched the knife from him, wrapping one arm around his neck and pressing the blade tip to his throat.

"Watch out for your own throat," Jessie hissed in his ear. "And give me Larsson's money roll. Hand it over, now, and I won't tell him you took it."

Percy's bleary eyes tried to focus on hers, and he threw down the roll of dollars and spat. "You won't catch me off guard like that again, brat. Better watch your back." He turned and stumbled towards the centre of town.

Jessie picked up the money and climbed the stairs to the second floor, quietly replacing the roll in Larsson's haversack. When she lay down on her blanket, a small sigh escaped.

"Percy took my money, didn't he?"

"How did you—"

"I recognized that bray of his and figured out why you were fiddling with my pack." He was quiet for a moment. "Thanks for getting it back."

"If you want to thank me, forget this. I told him if he gave it back, you'd be none the wiser."

She heard a harrumph from Larsson, but he didn't argue. For the third time, she fell back to sleep.

That night was the last respite for a while from battle. There was talk in camp the war would go on forever at this rate, but they were still slogging south. Jessie had heard Richmond was fortified until it was thought impregnable, and it was now obvious to all that the southern forces would fight them every step of the way.

She exchanged stress and hunger for stress and sleeplessness. Their division had doubled the size of the blacksmith teams when the third division joined them, but they could scarcely keep up with the wounded and lame horses and the damaged wagons brought in for repairs. They thanked God more than once for the forging machine that kept the union army supplied with as many horse and mule shoes as they needed.

Distant sounds of muskets and cannon promised more wounded, and Jessie's mind wandered to Donny whenever things slacked off a bit. She'd seen long ambulance trains heading north with hundreds of wounded, and she wondered if he accompanied his patients or stayed behind to tend to the next unlucky souls.

The morning was oppressively hot, and the black flies near the river were determined to eat human flesh. Jessie's feet felt raw and she coughed frequently, but she would not complain as she was glad to be away from the fields of wounded men and dying animals at Cold Harbor. The images would not leave her mind, and at night, dark dreams interrupted her sleep. Even so, she understood, now, how terror could eventually fade into monotony.

That day alone, she'd shot half a dozen horses too badly wounded to recover, wondering if the rebs would stoop to eating their flesh, but it was the screams of soldiers and animals caught in the burning woods she couldn't push from her mind. No truce had been called to allow the ambulances to enter the brush and recover their wounded, and the cries of distress were impossible to block out. At night, the lucky ones, both horse and man, could make their way to their camps, but many died crying for help. She wished she could talk to Donny, but she had to make do with Henry. The boy was not coping well with the carnage, and she often found him moping or curled up beside Brandy. She had taught him to sew up bayonet wounds on the animals, and they both took solace in this work, even if far more animals died than were saved.

The wagons now followed the passage of thousands of troops over the pike roads made alternately muddy and dusty by unpredictable weather. Few plank roads were in shape to carry the weight of the artillery. When her regiment swung west to leave the main part of the army, Jessie was thankful for clear air. She was told the cavalry would be used to lure the Confederates away from the river crossing where the Army planned to erect a floating bridge. The men complained of being used as bait, but in fact they were lucky to be free of the plodding infantry. Once they separated, she jumped into the back of the farrier wagon and traded sore feet for a sore backside. Henry was there too, trying unsuccessfully to mend leather straps while he bounced with each rut.

"Can you lend me your needle and silk, Walt?" he asked.

"Not for mending, I won't. I need them for stitching up wounds, not repairing old reins."

"Not reins," Henry corrected. "Bridle."

"Bridle," Jessie repeated, massaging her left foot, now freed from its boot. "Next you'll be sewing up your boots with my surgical supplies."

Henry smiled, revealing the gap in his gums where a rotten tooth had been extracted by the company dentist. The loss of the tooth made him look almost old enough to be in the army. "I'll take a new pair from a reb lying in a field."

"I haven't seen the dead wearing much on their feet I'd care to put on mine," Jessie responded. Her own boots were worn through and patched, and she dreaded hunting for another pair after the trouble she'd had finding these ones.

"You've got small feet. Smaller even than mine."

"Runs in the family," Jessie said. "Papa had small feet too. Good thing for a farrier when you think about it. Less likely to get stomped on."

"Yup," Henry looked thoughtful. "I've been stomped on."

Henry was easily distracted and that got him into trouble when he was trying to shoe a horse. He was improving though, and he rarely complained and never took out his frustration on the animals.

By mid-afternoon, she heard shots up ahead. The front of the regiment was miles up the road, but within a couple of minutes, the shooting became louder and fiercer and the wagons slowed and then stopped. Jessie jumped down and saw Larsson heading towards her. "A skirmish, or something bigger?" she called out to him.

"No way to tell from back here. The cavalry should be leading the rebs away from the river crossing. I didn't think we'd see much action for a couple of days. Least ways, I don't hear shells. We'll find out soon enough." Larsson pulled out his pipe as if he planned on staying a while. But the shooting stopped as soon as he had his pipe nicely drawing, and the call came down from the front to move out.

They weren't so lucky at the next encounter. The southern boys had been in position long enough to build trenches near the railroad. From all accounts, it was a vicious battle with hundreds dead or wounded on both sides. No one discussed which side had won the battles unless one side retreated, and that didn't happen with Grant in charge. He'd just go around the reb army.

"I heard we captured over two hundred horses, and a few minutes later, the rebs took them all back again," Larsson said.

"Just as well," Jessie said. "We couldn't feed them anyway."

When they called a truce at dusk, Jessie rode out to the field to tend to the wounded animals. Larsson told her she was foolish to risk a sniper bullet, but she couldn't leave them to suffer. He gave her his hand gun and extra bullets, and she put down twelve horses and two mules that night. One of them had more than a dozen holes she could count, blood congealed in the dirt and covered with flies. Only one mule was left standing by the side of the field, its head hanging low. She led it, uncomplaining, back to camp, but it collapsed and died as soon as they arrived. A small hole behind a front leg had delivered a lethal Minié ball to a lung.

"If you don't want it, I can sell the meat," Percy said, creeping up on her.

In spite of the fact the men were sick to death of hard tack, no one wanted to admit to eating horse. For some reason, mules that ended up in stew pots didn't elicit the same disgust. Jessie shrugged her shoulders, wondering if the starved animal carried enough flesh to make the effort of butchering worthwhile. She couldn't remember when she'd seen a horse or mule with a long tail. At first, she thought the tails were trimmed to prevent tangles in harnesses, but then she realized the starved animals were chewing off each other's hair. She walked away quickly when Percy returned with a huge knife she suspected was borrowed from a surgical tent. He eyed her strangely.

"You could do with more meat on your bones, brat."

"I won't eat any of that." Her stomach roiled at the thought.

"You'd prefer a bite out of me," Percy smirked. Jessie turned away in disgust.

Jens Larsson was watching the proceedings from the entrance to a tent, shaking his head.

"At least make sure he cleans up that ground when he's finished with the carcass. We'll be food for hungry flies."

"Knowing Percy, someone will offer him money for the pleasure of doing his work."

Larsson snorted in agreement, but he looked worried. "Walt, you're not looking fit. You eat next to nothing and your sleep is restless."

"Your sleep isn't so deep either if you're awake to see me tossing."

"I drop off as soon as the bugle sounds taps, but I've been keeping an eye on you."

"Thanks, but I can take care of myself."

"I'm not so sure. I've heard talk of you."

"What kind of talk?" Jessie felt herself go cold as soon as she saw the uncharacteristic look of concern on Jens' face.

"You know what kind. The kind of talk that gets you thrown out of the army for passing as a man. Did you see the article in the Washington paper? They claim more than a hundred female recruits have been discovered and made to, as they put it, resume the garments of their sex. Funny thing is, they didn't say whether they made them leave their regiments." Larsson gave a long guffaw, but Jessie didn't join him in the bad joke.

"You know about me?" she whispered, the blood draining from her face.

"Ja, I've known since the first day. Others would too if they could see past your scars and their own pride. They'd never believe a woman could do the work you do."

"Who else knows?"

"You make the mistake of treating Henry like a child. In many ways he is. He told Percy you remind him of his mother."

"Is that all?"

"That's all it takes. Now Percy is asking questions, and it won't be long before he challenges you."

"What can I do?"

"I see three options. You can leave before he finds out, you can pay him to keep his mouth shut, or you can kill him." Jessie sighed and shrugged. "Without money to pay for his silence and unwilling l to murder a man to hide your identity, you have only the one choice. Have you thought of what you'll do if you have to leave quickly?"

"Sneak off in the midst of a battle, find women's clothes, and then try to get aboard a ship headed to Washington. I haven't thought further than that."

"They need nurses in Washington, and they're hiring women now."

"That's what Donny said."

"Ja, I figured he knew. Can he help you?"

"Do I have to decide now?" Jessie sat down on a stump. She was exhausted and hungry until she smelled the blood of the mule being butchered less than a hundred yards away.

"I wouldn't count on having much time to decide," Larsson said. "We're headed back to the bridge. Maybe you can find your friend there and ask for his help."

But Jessie had convinced herself Percy wouldn't find out her secret if she were more careful. She was surprised when she realized the thought of leaving the army dismayed her.

She was forced to change her mind when she chanced to overhear Percy threatening Jens the next evening.

"If I find out you're lying to me, smithy, I'll let the Captain know you was in on it with her."

"Believe what you want. What do I care if you make a fool of yourself," Jens had replied. But I care, Jessie thought. The thought of Jens and Henry being accused of collaborating in her deception frightened her more than Percy's retribution. He would never let go the fact she'd caught him stealing.

CHAPTER 16: 1864, COLD HARBOR, VIRGINIA

All truths wait in all things

Oppressively hot days were followed by cool evenings that drove damp to the bones. Donald bedded down on the ground next to the surgical tent, padding the earth beneath his gum blanket with dried grass and pine needles. At home, nights were owned by owls, frogs and crickets. Here he drifted off to the sounds of men clanging their cook pots, laughing at bad jokes, or swearing at poor luck in their card games. A few would sing or play their fiddles or harmonicas. These sounds often competed with the noise of conflict— occasional shots of rebel snipers and the screech of feeding vultures and wounded mules.

Camp noises kept his dreams at bay and reminded him he shared the horrors of this war with thousands of men. The sight of bloated, rotting corpses had conditioned him to the dead and the noxious smells that accompanied their decay. He had learned to bring his focus to the living. When he heard a moan, he imagined he could tell whether the man had awoken after anaesthetic, was suffering from the pain of infection, felt delirious from loss of blood, thirsty for water, or desperate for company. Following an amputation, he knew who would survive by the appearance of their wound and the strength of their appetite. Doctoring wounded men wasn't much different than doctoring animals after all.

Those on the mend were sent north to recover in one of dozens of hospitals around Washington. Those whose wounds failed to heal or were thought unlikely to survive the journey, remained in camp. Many realized what was happening and accepted it. Others did not. When asked why they couldn't be transported to northern hospitals, Donald rarely told them the truth. Going north came to have two meanings for him. The wounded went north to the hospitals, or they went north to their just rewards. Either way, they were gone from his care.

Before he fell asleep at night, he tried to push concerns for Jessie from his mind. He would imagine his mother cooking a pudding, a cake, or best of all, a loaf of fresh crusty bread, all his own. He could smell the yeasty dough rising and recall Mama with flour on her nose, saying, "Could you get that bowl down for me, Donny? I've got flour to my neck."

After the first weeks of the spring battles, when so many had died, their regiment had a reprieve from battle. Donald was calmed by the sounds of singing as the troops marched, trance-like, through moon-lit nights. It seemed as if the insects had been lulled to sleep. The regiment bivouacked at five o'clock in the afternoon the next day, and as soon as the medical tent was erected and the yellow flag was flying, Donald faced a line-up of ill men who had missed the morning sick call. Soldiers with the usual symptoms, made worse by the march, looked for relief, if only a bit of salve for their feet. Men with bad cases of dysentery who had managed to keep up with the regiment were given opium. Bandages for superficial wounds were changed. Too many were forced to suffer, not always in silence. The line-up ebbed only when messmates called their friends to a meal that promised something other than greasy dried pork and the hard biscuits they called 'worm castles'. Even then, half of the troops wouldn't bother to eat, choosing sleep instead.

Donald worried constantly about Jessie. At the James River, he learned that cavalry regiments had ridden to the west in hopes of luring the rebels away from the main body of the northern army. He thought the smithies would stay with the wagon train to cross the river, so he was surprised to hear a few had accompanied their regiments. He watched, fascinated, as the huge pontoon bridge was erected and the men started moving across. His regiment was among the few selected to stay behind to guard the bridge, which made them among the last to leave. Long before that happened, Jessie had returned to find him.

"Forbes." a familiar voice said at the opening of the medical tent.

"Ah, Armstrong," he said, realizing immediately there was a problem. "I thought your regiment crossed earlier." The tent held only one patient who was in no state to care what they said.

"We ran into rebels and I'm back with the wounded. Donny, I'm in trouble." Jessie looked around anxiously.

"Someone knows?"

"More likely, suspects, but I can't wait until he's sure. It's our driver, Matt Percy, and he's as miserable as they come. He's got it in for me."

"If the army finds out, they'll send you back north. Is that so bad?"

"I haven't been paid, and I have no money. What will I do when I get to Washington?"

"You can have what's left of my bounty money."

"But what if they think Henry and Larsson have covered for me? My friends will be in trouble. Couldn't I leave here, secretly, maybe with your ambulance?"

"You'll be named a deserter."

"What can they do to me?

"Probably nothing, that's true. We've got only one patient waiting to go north," Donald said, pointing to the man lying silently in his cot. "I'll see if I can get permission to drive the ambulance to the port." It would be easier to transport him before they crossed the

James. "Wait for me at the ambulance at the other side of that rise. I'll feel better when you're out of here." He handed her his roll of bounty money and Jessie squeezed his hand.

Donald thought his plan was simple, but Doctor Vorster had other ideas.

"Send Simpson with the wagon. I'd rather you stay here, Forbes. And do it soon. Everyone else has crossed."

"I could go with the patient and meet up at our next camp," Donald said.

"Give Simpson something to keep him busy. You stay and make sure everything is stowed away properly."

He found Simpson hunched over a camp fire brewing coffee.

"You're to take ambulance to the port before the rest of the regiment crosses," Donald said.

"For one patient?" Simpson grumbled, looking as disappointed as Donald felt. "Why can't you find room for him in another ambulance?"

"We've got another patient from the brigade. Besides, I thought you liked going north."

"I got my reasons to stay put. Let's say I'm not a popular person with the ambulance drivers right now." Donald wondered if he'd stolen something or sold a poor product. Usually he got away with it, but someone wouldn't be appeased. "Where's this other wounded soldier, and what's his problem?"

"I'll arrange to have him brought here. I understand he's pretty much insensible from a head wound." Donald stopped by the supply wagon for cotton bandages and went to meet Jessie at the ambulance with their regimental flag. He told her the bad news that he could not accompany her north. She frowned but said nothing.

"We need to disguise you with a head wound. Perhaps your hands too, he said looking down. "I told Simpson you were unconscious, so say nothing during the trip." All the while, he was wrapping sufficient cotton bandaging around her head to cover all but her eyes, nose and mouth. "I wish we had blood to rub on it."

Before he could react, Jessie had taken out a small knife and cut a scarred area on the back of her left hand. "I can't feel much anyway."

Donald dabbed blood onto the bandages and continued wrapping her hands, leaving the thumbs protruding. When he had finished, he put a little dirt on the bandages on her hands. "You'll do. I don't want Doctor Vorster to see you, so Simpson and I will bring the other fellow on a stretcher out here. We should say goodbye now." He hated to leave her, but it should be a quick trip to port, and she only had to pretend she was unconscious.

"Thank you, Donny. "You do realize all you've done is change my disguise? I'll write and let you know where I am."

"I'll find you when this blasted war is over," Donald said. He drew her into his arms and they held each other tightly. He hoped he was doing the right thing for her. "You know, I believe this is the first time you've needed my help. You are the most capable person I know."

"I don't feel that way now, Donny. Please be careful after I've gone."

Donald helped her up onto a litter suspended over the floor of the wagon. He dropped down from the back of the wagon, and when he turned back, she looked small and vulnerable.

Simpson was waiting impatiently at the surgical tent. Donald motioned for the ambulance driver to help transport their patient to the wagon.

"Make it a quick trip of it. I don't like the look of this fellow," Donald said, lightly touching a pale damp forehead and worrying about sepsis. He didn't want Jessie spending any more time than necessary with Simpson, and this patient's health would suffer from a slow and bumpy ride to port.

"Don't fret. I'm coming right back," he said gruffly.

Donald was packing up the rest of the supplies when a private rushed into the tent.

"Are you Forbes?" he asked, pushing a finger into Donald's chest. The man was wearing the 126th insignia and introduced himself as Matt Percy. "I'm looking for Walt Armstrong."

"What's the problem?" He sympathized with Jessie's need to flee from this man. Percy's state of agitation was disturbing.

"He's gone missing, and we're ready to cross the river, that's what. Not that it's any of your business."

"Have you asked Larsson?"

"He hasn't seen him either, but he sent me here after I pushed him a bit." His leer made Donald's blood run cold.

At that moment, Doctor Vorster stepped into the tent. "Has Simpson left with our patient?"

"Yes sir. He should be back before dark."

"Patient? I saw Simpson with two wounded men in his ambulance," Percy said. Donald paled, bemoaning his bad luck. Of course, Percy knew Simpson. The two men had a lot in common.

"One of the other regiments sent us another patient for transport, sir," Donald explained to Doctor Vorster.

"You should have told me, Forbes. His surgeon will want to know how he manages on the trip north, and I need to keep track of the favours I grant."

"Sorry sir. I'll tell Simpson to report back to you when he returns."

"Be sure you do. What regiment was he from?"

"The 126th," Donald replied before he could stop himself.

"Haven't they crossed already?" Doctor Vorster said, his moustache wriggling in annoyance.

"He's one of their wagon drivers, I believe," Donald said. He heard Percy snort but ignored him. Percy would know all the drivers, of course.

"Fine. See to it the tent is down and packed, Forbes,"

After he left, Percy was still smirking. "Just as I thought," he said, sauntering out.

Donald followed him from the tent and watched Percy as he loitered at the lookout above the bridge. The ambulance had dropped onto solid ground at the far end of the span, kicking up dust as it headed east. He wondered if Percy would get permission to follow it, but the fellow made no move to cross the bridge. Still, Donald didn't take his eyes from him until he meandered back to the wagons. He convinced himself Percy wouldn't care what happened to Jessie as long as she was out of his life.

CHAPTER 17: 1864, CITY POINT, VIRGINIA

Sheath'd hooded sharptooth'd touch!

Jessie lay in the ambulance cot across from a patient who moaned with each bump and dip in the road. There was little she could do to comfort the man without drawing Simpson's attention, and she was meant to be unconscious. Simpson was sitting next to the driver on the bench up front, but she sensed him turn in his seat to glance back at them every few minutes, and she closed her eyes.

Her mind wandered. She'd narrowly avoided being spotted by Percy when he walked by the ambulance after they loaded the other patient, but she'd seen Simpson confiding something to him. Her heart had raced for a moment, but she convinced herself Percy wouldn't recognize her with the bandages even if he looked into the wagon. She focused her mind on what would happen once they reached the port. Should she board the medical steamer as a patient and risk the chance of being discovered as a female before they even left, or should she admit the truth she had been passing as a man? If she was fortunate, maybe she could travel north before they discovered the deception. She wished Donny were sitting up front.

She nodded off in the torpid heat but woke when she realized the wagon had stopped. Simpson was arguing with the driver.

"We'll be staying right here until my pal shows up."

"Don't you want to get your patients to hospital quick?" the driver asked.

"A little delay is all."

The driver muttered about stopping, but then Jessie smelled pipe tobacco burning. Her brain worked overtime trying to make sense of what little she'd heard. One thing became certain. She would be a fool to wait for Simpson's pal to arrive since the pal was likely to be Percy. She swung her feet down from the bench.

"You stay right there, Armstrong," Simpson said.

She froze when he spoke her name. How did he know? She looked down at the harness. If only she could unhook it and jump on one of the horses, she could get to the port first, but Simpson was standing too close. She had to act. Once Percy arrived, there would be no chance of escape. She pulled the bandages off her hands with her thumbs, and looked for a weapon, but all she had was her small knife. She jumped out the back of the wagon and ran up to the driver.

"Help me, please. He's going to hurt me," Jessie cried.

The driver's eyes bugged out as he watched Simpson grab the neck of Jessie's coat.

"Let go the lad," the driver blustered, trying to pull Simpson away from her.

Simpson backhanded him and the driver stumbled, but he kept hold of Simpson's jacket so the two of them pulled away from Jessie and started rolling about in the dust. She ran for the harness and unlatched one side from the wagon, winding the traces around her arms and jumping up onto the horse. She took off down the road, leaving Simpson, yelling, behind her.

Before she was out of sight, she could hear Percy shouting out from a second wagon now in pursuit. She couldn't stop to remove the harness dragging behind them and slowing her horse. She urged the animal faster, but it had no reserves, and Percy gained ground with two horses pulling an empty wagon. He was shouting at her now.

"Stop, or I'll run you and that damn horse down."

Jessie pushed the poor animal harder, crying out in frustration as Percy drew along side. "What do you want?"

"What every man wants from a woman," Percy yelled, throwing his head back to laugh.

She pulled the horse up short and slid off, unhooking a leather strap to take with her. It took Percy longer to rein in his horses, and that gave her time to run up behind his empty wagon and jump into the back as it was stopping. She stumbled up to the front and threw the strap over Percy's head, pulling tight around his neck, but he twisted around and flung her backwards onto the tongue of the wagon. As his weight fell upon her, the wooden shaft hit her head and she immediately lost consciousness.

When she woke, it was dark, her head was throbbing painfully, and the bandages wrapped around her head felt wet and sticky. A fire crackled nearby, and she could hear two voices, Simpson's and Percy's. She kept as still as a wounded raccoon.

"She's unconscious, anyways," Percy said. "But I'm not taking chances. I'll finish her off later."

"Why did you take her clothes?" Simpson asked.

"I had to see, didn't I?"

"I bet you did more than look."

"What? Nah, she's all bones and limp as a rag, and there's blood all over them bandages. That's not for me."

"She looks dead from here. Leave her lie, but I'd burn her clothes so no one takes her for a soldier." Then he laughed. "And wouldn't you know it. Her head was all bound up before she hit it. Convenient, hey?"

"What if she doesn't die, and she makes it to port? It's only five miles off," Percy said.

"With the amount of blood soaking those bandages, she wouldn't make it a mile even if she wakes up, which I doubt she ever will," Simpson said. "If you ask me, she joined up and got what was coming to her. The driver's still back there nursing a headache I gave him, but he saw nothing except a raving patient with a head wound galloping away on a horse. I'm long overdue at camp, thanks to you. And now that horse she took is missing, so I'll have to make it back with one only one animal."

"You're not going on to the port?"

"No point. Both patients are finished."

"You should find that horse she took."

"It'll be miles from here by now, and I can't see in the dark."

"I appreciate your help with my little problem, Simpson. Consider your debt settled."

"Good to hear, but I was hoping you'd share that money you found on her."

"No bloody chance," Percy said patting his pocket. "I've debts to pay, too."

"Don't be gone too long from camp or Forbes will put two and two together," Simpson warned.

Jessie heard Simpson stand up and walk away. The jingle of harness told her his wagon wasn't far off. She said a quick prayer for the driver who'd received a nasty crack on his skull when he tried to help her. Then she made an effort to slow her breathing when she heard Percy approach. He nudged her roughly in the back with the toe of his boot but she stayed still. He bundled up her clothes and boots and threw them in the fire. The heat from the flames felt good and the smoke drove off the insects drawn to her blood. After he moved away and she heard his wagon leave, she slowly rose to her feet, swaying with the pounding pain in her head and dizziness from the loss of blood and the crack on her skull. She used a stick to drag her boots from the fire. They were smouldering but they'd be wearable. The rest of her clothing was finished. She smiled grimly as she remembered her bound head. She removed the layers of bloody cotton and wound it tightly around her torso, shuddering when she remembered how the dead were prepared for burial.

Both wagons had headed to the right, so she started walking left. Her head continued to throb, and she was thankful her bandages had cushioned her against worse damage during the fall. There was only a sliver of a moon to light the way, and she kept stumbling.

The moon had set by the time she saw the lights of the port. Two rows of tent warehouses lined the wharf, and several ships were anchored in the harbour. She prayed one of them was the medical steamer. She was partially covered with thin bands of cotton, and she had no money or identification. She headed slowly down the hill toward the dock, thankful to be alive.

A rotund young sentry stopped her, eyeing her up and down in the light from a smoking oil lamp. He looked terrified. You'd think he was the one standing there practically naked, she thought.

"Could you find me a blanket and direct me to the medical ship?"

She could only imagine what was going through his head as he stood there speechless, shifting from one foot to the other. She wondered if he could see enough to tell she was a woman.

"Wait here," he said and broke into a big man's jog into the darkness. He returned with a moth-eaten blanket and a grumpy sergeant.

"What have we here?" the sergeant said. "Not a ghost after all."

"I need to go to the hospital ship," Jessie said, accepting the blanket from the private and pulling it around her shoulders.

"Hospital ships is for soldiers."

"I'm a soldier, or I was a soldier," Jessie said, rubbing her eyes. She wondered how much longer she could remain standing. Her head was still pounding but she was no longer dizzy.

"Is that 'is' or 'was'?" the sergeant asked.

"Until I had my uniform stolen, I was a soldier," she said.

"Who would steal your uniform?"

"A reb who wanted the shirt off my back," Jessie said, feeling frustrated by the questions. The sergeant harrumphed.

"Hospital ships are for the wounded. Are you wounded?"

"Can't you see I've received a blow to the head?"

"I'll take you down to the ship, but if it turns out you're a reb and you got rid of your uniform to trick us, you'll end up in prison. You best believe our prisons are worse than the war."

"I'm not a rebel. Do I sound like one?"

"Who's to tell? There are rebs all over the west that sound like Yankees, except for that yell and whoop they make. We'll take you down to the ship and they can decide if you're in need of medical attention."

They led her aboard the medical ship where the hospital steward was administering to a dozen patients in cots.

"This one showed up without a uniform and he could be a reb," the sergeant said. The private will stay until you tell him it's alright to leave him here."

The steward motioned Jessie to sit on the bench. He felt her skull and she winced when he touched the large lump above her burn scar, now crusty with blood. He looked into her eyes.

"Pretty bad knock. Any dizziness or nausea?"

"A little."

"Where's your uniform."

"The man who thought I was dead burned my clothes. I saved these." Jessie lifted her feet with the blackened boots. In spite of the heat, she was shivering and glad of the blanket.

He took a good look at her boots and stared at her for a minute before pulling the blanket away. Why are you wrapped in bloody bandages?

"They were on my head. It's all I had to wear." The steward looked at her strangely and then nodded. He didn't ask how her head became bandaged in the first place.

"Someone discovered your disguise, I take it?" Jessie nodded." The steward turned to the private. "That'll be all. This is a woman, and she'll go north with the ship." The private's mouth dropped open. He nodded and left. "Are you alright? Down below that is?" He looked uncomfortable asking the question, Jessie thought. She'd bet he'd never examined a woman and wasn't anxious for the opportunity.

"He didn't interfere with me, if that's what you're asking, but I'd very much like to wash," Jessie said.

"I'll send in a pail of soap and water and the nurse will find you something to wear. By the way, what did you do for the army?"

"I was a farrier," Jessie said. The steward was quiet for a moment.

"That proves you're not a rebel," he said as he left the room. She wondered what he meant.

A coloured woman entered the cabin carrying folded dark clothing, a towel and a bar of brown soap. Jessie hadn't seen a full bar of soap in months. When her arms moved forward to take the bundle, the woman pulled back. She was short and stocky, but full of energy and confidence and a wide smile. Jessie took to her immediately.

"First things first. Do you feel alright?"

"I've seen the steward."

"He's a man, and from what he says, you've been hit pretty bad and had your clothes taken. Maybe something worse happened when you was unconscious?"

"I'd like to punish the men who left me for dead. Isn't that enough?" Jessie pulled the blanket tightly around her, remembering the callous discussion of her chances of survival.

"There are wounds can't be seen, but believe me, they can be felt," the woman said frowning. "I was told you've been passing as a man. Why any sane woman would do that is beyond me. I have a dress you can wear, after you wash. I also brought you a comb and mirror and rice flour to do something with those bruises and that dark complexion of yours."

As if reading her smile, the woman said, "I'll have you know I'm considered light for a coloured lady."

"Thank you. I appreciate your help," Jessie said, unable to stifle a yawn. The woman left and Jessie washed and slipped on a dark brown dress too wide and too short. She used the comb and applied the powder. When she looked at herself in the mirror, she was surprised to see a woman. The thought of wearing powder made her view herself differently. She mused that makeup was a disguise for a woman, just as her clothing had been her disguise as a man. She wiped off the powder. When the Steward reappeared with a Surgeon who was holding a notebook, she stood up shakily.

"What name did you use and what regiment did you serve with," the surgeon asked without preamble.

Jessie answered his questions, including repeating she was a farrier. He picked up her hands and studied her fingers and palms. He seemed satisfied with the calluses and ignored the burn scars.

"We'll have to check on this information. Now, tell me of the attack. Will you name the person or persons involved?"

Jessie had no proof other than her word but wearing a disguise and using a false name meant her word was next to worthless. Besides, naming Percy and Simpson could get Henry and Jens into trouble since they would be considered complicit in protecting her identity.

"I was on my way to port in an ambulance. I don't remember what happened after I banged my head fighting to get away."

"I'll need to confirm your story with your regiment. You can take a bed in the hospital for now and rest. Eat something first, before you faint on me."

Jessie nodded, although the thought of food held no appeal. The pat on the shoulder and a few kind words threatened to release a flood of tears.

When she awoke, the ward was bustling with activity. "It's past time you opened those eyes. We could use your help."

"Help?" Jessie said, rubbing her eyes. She wondered if they had a horse needing attention. The woman looking down on her was not to be ignored. She had a tall body thick with muscle, and if her face told a story, life hadn't been easy. She was unlikely to take any nonsense.

"We're in receipt of two dozen wounded. They need to be settled and seen to."

"I'm not a nurse. I was given these clothes because I had none."

"I know all about that. But you're here, and you were smart enough to pass as a farrier. You can surely do a little nursing. Get something to eat first, and then meet me back here. Don't dawdle."

Jessie stood shakily and realized she'd slept for eight hours. The patients in the cots next to hers were staring unabashedly. The man in the next bed had lost the sight of one eye and cradled a bandaged arm, but he was in good enough spirits to chuckle to himself.

"Did I hear the battle-axe right? You're a farrier?"

Jessie nodded. She could hear the note of respect in his voice and gave him a weak smile. It was all she could manage.

"I hope you won't go nailing any shoes on my feet," he said, getting a laugh from the other soldiers.

His good humour in the face of his wounds lifted her spirits. "How badly do your feet smell? Horseshoes might be an improvement." They were still laughing when she went to find some supper. She enjoyed stewed beef, vegetables and a cup of good coffee. While she would have preferred to sit a while, she headed back to the ward.

"They say your name's Jessie. I'm Abigail. Are you feeling up to helping us with the patients? It will take your mind off other things."

Abigail gave her a meaningful look. Jessie refused to be intimidated by this woman, but she knew enough to take pains to avoid getting on her wrong side. "How do you feel about bedpans?"

"How do the men feel about them?" Jessie asked.

"You can be sure if those men could move their bodies at all, they'd avoid any help in that department, especially from a woman. But it's either the bedpan or changing sheets continuously. I figure if you tell them you were a farrier in the army and have seen it all, they'll be more comfortable with you. You're no snobby rich woman who has never seen those bits or hired a nurse to care for her own children."

"True," Jessie said, remembering the naked men swimming in the Chickahominy River and the times she'd been forced to share the latrine. "How does this work? Do I wait for them to ask for the bedpan or do I tell them it's time to use it?"

"See what works best for you, but don't let anyone tell you to go away. I'm sure you've had horses didn't want to wear shoes."

Jessie smiled at the woman. She felt comfortable with Abigail's no-nonsense approach, but she suspected patients might heal faster if only to distance themselves from this bossy woman. Jessie didn't need to tell anyone she'd been a farrier. The news was all over the ship.

"How do we compare with horses?" one patient asked. Missing both of his feet, he was on her bedpan list.

"Isn't it time you wished *you* had four legs?" She gave him a sympathetic look.

"Now wouldn't that be grand, but I'm happy to have my arms so I can still play my fiddle. Now, that corporal over there could use help writing a letter home."

Jessie nodded at him and went over to the bed. The youth was missing a right arm above the elbow and was struggling to compose a letter with his left hand. "That'll take practice to get right. How would it be if I help you out with this letter?"

A voice boomed over a loudspeaker warning people to leave the ship if not proceeding to Washington.

"I'll return after we leave port," she said.

Abigail found Jessie rinsing bedpans. The woman handed her a slip of paper.

"If you'd take a nursing position when we get to Washington, I can direct you to one at the Arlington Hospital where I work when in town. From what I've seen, I suspect you'll be as efficient with wounded men as wounded horses."

CHAPTER 18: 1864, JAMES RIVER CROSSING, VIRGINIA

Only what nobody denies is so

Donald rushed to pack up the tent and surgical supplies in preparation for crossing the pontoon bridge, but he couldn't relax until Simpson returned and he knew Jessie had been delivered safely to the port.

Simpson didn't arrive back until the next morning, and by then, Donald was frantic. Simpson smirked at him. "What are you getting fussed over? I had a problem with the ambulance after I passed the cut. That patient with the head wound went crazy and ran off on one of my horses. The other patient up and died, and the driver and I buried him right there. We had to bring the wagon back with only one horse, and it took forever."

Donald glared at him. There was no way to tell if Simpson was lying. He was too practiced at it. "Where's the driver?"

"Here I am," an old man said. A blood-soaked bandage covered his head and he was swaying slightly. "Simpson conked me on the noggin, for no good reason if you ask me."

"Don't you remember? The head patient was as mad as a swarm of wasps?" Simpson said, slapping him on the back in a less than friendly fashion.

"Yeah, that I do, but you grabbed me and tried to pull me away from him. Then you conked me over the head with the butt end of your revolver." The driver was glaring at Simpson.

"You're imagining that. You slipped and hit your head when that patient grabbed a horse and took off," Simpson said.

Did you see the patient take the horse?" Donald asked the driver.

"I don't remember. Both horses was gone when I came to."

"Was Simpson gone?

"For a while, but he showed up later, saying he was off looking for the other horse."

"What happened to the other patient, the one that didn't run off."

"Dead when I come 'round. Looked real peaceful lying there. We buried him when Simpson got back." The driver sat down next to the wagon. "Look here, I need to lie down. My noggin's ready to explode."

Donald told him the tent was packed but to pull himself under the wagon with a couple of blankets until they were ready to harness the horses. Before he went to find Larsson, he asked Doctor Vorster if he would take a look at the driver.

Larson was sitting on the back of the forge wagon. When Donald asked him if he'd seen Percy, he told him he was sent to drive munitions the day before. Donald closed his eyes and squeezed them together, willing the awful truth to go away.

"I thought you were here to ask about Armstrong," Larsson said, looking perplexed.

"Percy's the one who knows where to find Armstrong."

"What do you mean?" Larsson sat up, his face turning red. "Tell me. I know the truth about the boy."

Donald glanced around to see who might be listening in on their conversation, then explained about bandaging Armstrong to go by ambulance to port, and that Percy had figured it out. "Percy must have followed Simpson."

"That's bad news. Percy and Armstrong have been at each other's throats. If he found Armstrong, no telling what he'd do."

"Simpson's says Armstrong stole one of the wagon horses and rode off. I don't believe him for a minute."

"Simpson?"

"You know him?"

"He and Percy are close, and usually up to no good. Simpson owed him money but Percy's was waving folding money a while ago. He said Simpson had paid his debt."

"Where would Simpson find money on the road? He didn't even make it to port. And where's Percy?"

"Knowing him, he'll be sleeping in the back of a wagon. As grandmother would say, he who sleeps does not sin. I'll bet he's never nursed a single blister on this march. When we set up camp tonight, we'll find him and get to the bottom of this story. If he's done something to Walt, he'll have a lot more to deal with than a blister."

Donald agreed to meet Larsson later, and he rode back to the hospital wagons. He considered telling the whole story to Doctor Vorster but could see no advantage until he knew more. That's when Doctor Vorster called him over.

"Forbes, what's bothering you? You've been running around all day."

"I'm concerned about the loss of the two patients yesterday."

"Do you doubt Simpson's story?"

"Sir, it doesn't ring true." Donald looked around and saw Simpson sitting astride his mule and smirking at him.

"We're past the cut-off to the port," Doctor Vorster said, sighing deeply. Have Simpson show you were he buried the patient. Then go on to the port and see if the other patient arrived on that lost horse." He turned on the bench and shouted back to Simpson. "Did you hear me Simpson?

Simpson wasn't smirking now. He nodded sullenly and turned his mule around to head to the cut-off. He kept looking back at Donald but said nothing. They started off down the road.

That's the grave over there," Simpson said, pointing to a bump with fresh soil a few feet off the verge. Wagon tracks ran close to the site.

"Show me."

Simpson and the driver had done a poor job covering the body with a thin layer of soil and leaves. He bent over and used a battered metal canteen to scrape the soil from the top of the mound. Donald was able to recognize the patient's face, now home to a variety of insects. Thank God it wasn't Jessie, he thought.

A mile down the road, Donald spotted more wagon tracks going off the verge into the bush. There was a lone horse hobbled by its own traces.

"Is that your missing horse?" Donald asked. The poor animal looked too tired to graze.

"Yeah. It's him," Simpson agreed. He dismounted and went to the animal, untangling the traces and tying them to the rest of the harness. He looped one of the traces around the pommel of his saddle.

"Whose wagon tracks are these?"

"Couldn't say," Simpson said, shuffling his feet.

Donald walked around the wagon in a tight circle and then again in a larger circle. He found a camp fire with ashes and pieces of fabric. The charred wood was still warm. "There's been a recent fire. Someone was here last night."

"Now that you mention it, that's right. I stopped to make coffee when I couldn't find the horse."

"But you didn't see who made the wagon tracks?" Simpson shrugged. "It looks like cloth was burned in here."

"I might have started the fire with a few bandages."

Then Donald saw something gleaming and his anger erupted.

"Bandages with brass buttons?" Simpson couldn't meet his eyes. "What did you do to her?"

"Her?"

"Don't play me for a fool. The horse you said she took is standing here, and there was another wagon. Percy was here too, wasn't he?"

"Maybe he was and maybe he wasn't," Simpson said, his eyes ranging around the fire. "Does the Doc know you lied to him about the extra patient?"

Donald could feel his face flush. "Get on your mule. We're going to the port." His mind couldn't stop churning. Why would they burn her clothes? Was she buried somewhere near here, or had she abandoned her uniform to head north? Talking to Simpson was pointless.

It was late afternoon by the time they got to the port. The hospital ship wasn't at anchor, so Donald and Simpson rode directly to the hospital tent. The sentry waved them past when he saw their green armbands. There were only two occupied beds in the tent and a large coloured nurse was leaning over one of the patients. She stood up when she heard them talking.

"Don't tell me you got more patients. The ship left and it won't be back till Thursday," she said, pointing into the tent wall as if they could see through to the vacant berth.

"We're looking for a lost patient." Donald realized too late he should have thought this through.

"Now there's something you don't hear every day. How did you lose him?"

Donald ignored her question. "Did anyone show up here last night or this morning?"

"Lots of people been through here. We had five ambulances and a half dozen supply wagons I knows of. But I can't say I've seen any lost patient. What kind of wound did you say?"

"Head wound," Donald said, glaring at Simpson who smirked at his discomfort. "This man said the patient stole a horse from his ambulance."

The nurse stood, hands on hips, and stared at them for a long time. "Rode off, you say? Sure this was a Union soldier?"

"Yes, ma'am, I'm sure." It was hard not to miss the anger on her face. Her lips were pursed and a deep furrow formed between her eyes.

"Someone walked in here last night. No uniform though and no horse."

"Was it a woman?" Donald said quietly, hearing Simpson choke.

"Didn't you say it was a soldier you lost?"

"She was disguised as a man, but she worked as a farrier with us."

"Not much of a disguise when you ain't got clothes."

"Was she alright? Did she go north with the ship?"

"I don't know if I want to say anything mo' to you boys. You wait here and I'll go get the Sergeant."

After she left the tent, Simpson looked livid.

"Now you've gone and done it. They'll put the blame on us."

"Blame? For what? What did you do to her?"

"Nothing. It was her falling off the wagon caused the head wound. I thought it was funny you had her head all wrapped up in those bandages, and then she goes and smashes her own noggin. Lucky she had those bandages is all I can say cause there was a load of blood."

"When did she hit her head? You said she ran off with the horse." Donald suddenly felt calm, as if the flurry in his brain settled down so he could think through the problem at hand. The wound couldn't have been too bad if she had managed to walk five miles, he told himself.

"I told you, she ran off on the horse."

"The horse is back there, and the driver said she asked for his help. Why did she need his help?"

"The driver got it wrong."

"When did she hit her head? Did she fall off your wagon? If she did, how did she get away on the horse?"

That's when Simpson hung his head and looked sullen. "You won't get another word from me."

The tent flap opened suddenly and a grim-looking Sergeant entered with the nurse on his heels. "I heard all that, by the way, so don't try to sell me a different story, either of you."

"Was your missing 'patient' called Walt Armstrong by any chance?" the Sergeant asked, looking down at his notebook.

"Her real name is Jessie MacKay," Donald replied. "She's a friend of mine."

"Is she your "friend" too?" the Sergeant asked, eyeing Simpson.

"I was supposed to get her here, I mean get him here, but he ran off."

"It sounds like you might have made her "run off"," the Sergeant said. "Did you hit her over the head and take her clothes, too?"

"Who did she say did it?"

"She wouldn't say."

Simpson smirked and Donald's face went beet red. He wanted to do was choke the life out of him. Before the Sergeant could stop him, Donald rushed at Simpson, pushed his back to the post and slammed his arm up against Simpson's neck. "Tell me what you did!"

Simpson squirmed out of his hold and pushed him away. The Sergeant had a handgun out, ranging between the two of them. "It wasn't me. It was Percy," Simpson shouted. Under the stares of Donald and the Sergeant, he admitted, "When she ran off on the horse, he took after her in a wagon and caught her. Then she fell off his wagon and hit her head. Accidental-like. She went unconscious, and Percy thought she was dead."

"What would Percy know? He's only a teamster. Did you examine her?"

"Nah, Percy came back later and said he'd dealt with her. That's all I know."

"You're a liar. You told me you had coffee at that campsite where we found her horse. That's where Percy caught up with Jessie, isn't it? You must have been there."

"I never touched her. She looked dead."

"You took her clothes and burned them in that fire."

"Percy must have done it after I left."

"But you were the one that told Percy where to find Walt."

"I didn't have too. Percy figured it out by himself."

"There's no way you're innocent in all of this." Donald rushed at Simpson and punched him hard in the jaw. The Sergeant pulled him back as Simpson slumped to the floor.

"Who is this Percy?" the Sergeant asked.

"He drives the forge wagon for the brigade," Donald said, his fists and jaw clenched. He wondered why Jessie hadn't told them who attacked her. "You're sure she didn't say who was responsible?"

"She refused to name anyone, but Martha spoke to her. Maybe she knows more." He pointed to the coloured nurse.

"She said nothing to me neither," Martha said, shaking her head and clucking her tongue. "She lost blood, but she weren't concussed, or at least not bad, and she didn't complain one bit. She had a good sleep last night and half the morn, and I heard the head nurse, Miss Abigail, had her up helping the wounded before the ship left port."

Donald shook his head and gave a little smile. "That's Jessie. Nothing keeps her down long."

"Give me your names and regiments, and the full name of that Percy fellow too," the Sergeant said coldly. "I'll be letting your commander know you were here today, and why."

Donald and Simpson, heads down, walked back to their horses and started back to the Regiment. Simpson was smart enough to keep his mouth shut, but as they neared the camp, he lagged further behind.

"Keep up, Simpson. I'm reporting this to Doctor Vorster, and I want you there when I do."

"Shouldn't you find Percy first? News travels fast around camp, and he'll get clean away if he hears you're looking for him."

"You mean if you run off and tell him?" Donald said, halting Lancet to wait for him. Lancet would have no trouble keeping up with the mule if Simpson decided to make a run for it, but Donald suspected Simpson wanted time to work up a story for Doctor Vorster. He did have a point about Percy running off, but if Simpson was with him when he found Percy, he'd be facing the two of them. Maybe Larsson could back him up.

"Fine. We'll find the 126th wagons first." As soon as he said that, Simpson rode up beside him.

They turned right at the cut-off and picked up the pace. Within a couple of miles of passing what seemed an endless line of supply wagons, Donald saw the large figure of Larsson and the slight figure of Henry atop a forge wagon.

"Isn't it Percy's job to drive the forge wagon?" Donald said when he drew up beside the wagon. Simpson shrugged. They rode up alongside. "Walt made it to the port and is heading north on the hospital ship," Donald said to Larsson.

"Good to hear," the blacksmith said gruffly, taking a glance at Simpson and Henry. Donald realized he wasn't going to jeopardize Walt's disguise if the others didn't know.

"Walt was hurt though. Where's that low-life Percy?" Donald said. Larsson shot him a look, and Donald nodded when he realized that Henry was absorbing every word.

"He said he was driving ordnance across the bridge. I can't say if he spoke the truth."

"He's up in front of the 126th wagons then?"

"As far as I know, and we won't see him until we stop for the night. Maybe not till the morning."

Donald had hoped Percy would be driving the forge wagon and he could enlist Larsson and Henry's help if Percy tried to run, but the line-up of wagons extended miles ahead, and he didn't want to face Percy alone. "Percy attacked Walt, and Simpson helped him," Donald said.

"I didn't do anything," Simpson roared out. "It was all Percy's doing."

"You didn't help either," Donald shouted back. "Percy will likely run if he hears I'm looking for him."

Larsson eyebrows floated up and his face darkened. "Did Walt lay charges?"

"No," said Simpson and Donald in unison.

"Then you have a problem. Percy has no reason to fear you, and Simpson will back anything Percy says."

"I think Percy stole the money I gave Walt." Donald said.

"You can't prove that either, I'll bet," Larsson said, looking glum.

"You'll be in more trouble than Percy and me." Simpson smirked. "You're the one that lied and did all the bandaging, and the Doc knows that. He doesn't know what happened later because it's only hearsay with no charges laid. That right's, isn't it Larsson?"

"Afraid so, Forbes." Larsson looked like he wanted to say more, but not in the hearing of Simpson and Henry. "Come back later, after we've stopped for the night."

"I have to tell Doctor Vorster, and he'll tell the Colonel, and then it will be all around camp. Percy will get word of it."

"Why?" Simpson asked. "Larsson and I won't talk. Just tell Vorster the other patient is on the boat north."

"Haven't you forgotten the Sergeant at the hospital? He's got our names, and Walt's. Besides, there's no way you won't tell Percy."

"I won't if you promise to keep my name out of it," Simpson said, running his finger in the shape of a cross over his chest.

"Your word is worse than worthless," Donald said, shaking his head. "Come on. We're going back to report to the doctor."

Simpson shrugged. "You'll wish you hadn't."

The sun was starting to set before Donald tracked down Doctor Vorster who was changing a bandage on the arm of a captain at the back end of one of the medical supply wagons.

"There you are, Forbes. What took you so long?" He eyed Simpson's bruised cheek and frowned.

"I have to tell you about the patient we sent from the 126th," Donald started.

"This is all his doing," Simpson said. "It was his idea."

"What idea?"

"The patient was a woman, working in disguise as a farrier with the 126th," Donald said, glaring at Simpson. "She came to me because she was worried someone had discovered her disguise, someone she feared would hurt her. She asked me if I could get her to the port on an ambulance."

"Why didn't you tell me? She would have been sent back to Washington."

"She's a friend I've known since childhood. She was worried about implicating me in the deception, as well as others she works with, and she thought it best to leave quietly."

"You've known for a while about her deception?"

"A few weeks, sir." Donald stared directly in Doctor Vorster's eyes, willing him to understand the truth of the situation.

"Where is she? Is she the one who rode off on one of our horses, Simpson?"

"That's right, he did," Simpson said, "but we got the horse back. Could I speak to you in private, sir?" Forbes has had one go at me today, and you should hear my side first, since I was the one who was there."

"Please wait a moment, sir," Donald, said, interrupting Simpson. "He was involved in hurting the woman."

"I have to hear him out, Forbes. Go get something to eat or water that horse. I'll listen to your side of things later."

Donald walked Lancet over to the corral, removed the saddle, and led the horse down to the river for a drink. The sky was dark but it was still uncomfortably hot. He could hear a few of the men laughing downriver as they cooled off in the refreshing water. The drone of insects and slap of hands on wet flesh sounded like an odd form of music. He wished he could sit at the edge, hang out a rod, and pull in a catfish. Without pausing to think, he stripped off his clothes and plunged into the river. A large sigh escaped him as his skin hit the cold water, and he relaxed until heard a guffaw from the shore.

"I thought I'd find you here with that horse of yours. The doc wants to talk to you now, and he's not happy with you." Simpson laughed at Donald's predicament. "I wouldn't keep him waiting."

Donald took his time getting out of the water. He was exhausted and couldn't stop wondering what had happened to Jessie. Then he realized Simpson had gone off to tell Percy all about it. He scrambled up the bank, swearing that he had to search for his clothes in the dark. When he was dressed and had tied Lancet to the picket line, he went to face Doctor Vorster.

"What did Simpson tell you sir?"

"Never mind that. I want to hear your version of what happened."

Larsson had been right, Donald thought, as he watched the surgeon press his fingers into his temples. Donald told him what had happened.

"You say this Percy is responsible for the attack? But as this woman, Jessie, didn't formally accuse anyone, then I don't know what you can do, Forbes. You should have told me right away. In many ways, I see this as your fault."

"But Simpson set her up for Percy, sir. Simpson owed him money."

"She's gone north without laying charges, so there's no proof of any of that. You should be glad she was not hurt too badly. I understand they had her acting as a nurse on the hospital ship."

Donald glared at him. "This isn't fair, sir."

"Perhaps not, but I consider this situation finished, and I don't want to hear another word from you, or hear you've hit Simpson, again. Do you understand me, Private?"

Donald mounted Lancet and headed back up the road. He needed to talk to Larsson, if only to commiserate with him. The fact Doctor Vorster would do nothing about Percy or Simpson made him want to pummel both of them. How could Doctor Vorster blame him? If he hadn't gotten her away from camp, Percy would have found a way to get at her.

He found Larsson and Henry working at the forge. Larsson had a swollen red eye starting to turn blue, and he nodded sourly at Donald as he continued to use the bellows to push air into the coals.

"Percy showed up," he said.

"I figured that," Donald answered.

"He'd talked to Simpson, and he was feeling mighty smug." He paused to look up at Donald. "Is it true nothing will be done?"

"I don't know why you're surprised. You're the one who told me it would go this way."

"Even so, not even a reprimand?" Larsson shook his head and winced. Donald hoped Larsson had done as much damage to Percy's face as Percy had done to his.

"I'm the one that got the reprimand."

"Grandmother would say it's not one person's fault if two people argue."

"The doc told me not to hit Simpson again, but he said nothing about hitting Percy."

"That's because Percy isn't part of his regiment. Feel free to knock him about. I felt better when I did, I can tell you, but he's expecting you to show up," he said, looking up to see if Donald understood his meaning.

"Hitting him is not enough for me. He took the money I gave Jessie, and I want it back."

"You'd better hurry then. He was planning on starting up a poker game."

Percy spotted him first. He was with a group of men lounging near a smoky fire, and he was occupied shuffling a pack of well-worn cards. The fire was there to keep the insects at bay because the men surely didn't need the warmth. "Joining the game, Forbes? Maybe you'd like to win your money back." He laughed and the others joined in. Donald suspected they had all lost money to Percy, although not in the same manner as he had.

"I've come to reclaim it, and not by playing a game." He could feel the blood pumping in his neck.

"Bounty money, wasn't it? How do we feel about bounty money, boys?"

"Stolen bounty money's alright," one of the men offered, causing them all to laugh again.

"I'll tell you what," Percy sneered. "You leave now and I won't give you what I gave Simpson."

Donald felt his face engorge and he ran forward, fists raised. "You're nothing but a low life. You won't get away with it." Donald threw a punch but Percy dipped low, picking up a flaming brand from the fire. He rammed it towards Donald, laughing when Donald jumped back.

"She was skinny and covered with scars. That your type, is it?"

Donald's anger flamed like the brand, and he was blinded by rage. He leapt at Percy, landing a solid punch in his jaw before the heavier man could react. Percy fell back, tripping over a log that hadn't been there a moment before, hitting his head in the process. A small Derringer pistol, carrying a single deadly .44 calibre shot, dropped from Percy's pocket and quickly disappeared into the crowd. Not all these men were his loyal supporters. Before Percy could stand up, Donald straddled him and began pummelling his face and chest. Percy shouted for a knife, but thankfully no one obliged. When Donald's fury had abated, Percy could only moan and spit out bubbles of blood. Donald inverted his pockets and had reclaimed his roll of bills before Percy could push himself to his knees.

"This belongs to her, not you."

"A woman that ugly needs it." Percy spat out, but the look in his eye said he was anything but resigned to the loss.

Donald grabbed Lancet's reins, leapt up on his back, and headed back to camp. He knew the story would be all over camp in minutes. Now he'd inherited Jessie's foe, and he didn't need Larsson to tell him to watch his back.

CHAPTER 19: 1864, OUTSIDE PETERSBURG, VIRGINIA

The pleasures of heaven are with me, and the
pains of hell are with me

Larsson was bending over Donald's make-shift bed, breathing hard, sweat dripping from his chin. His bruised face looked swollen and painful. "Forbes, I'm worried Henry's gone and done something stupid."

They'd marched towards Petersburg that day, the heat, dust and blue bottles their constant companions. It was nearing ten o'clock at night before they were allowed to stop, and it took another two hours before the medical tent was erected and supplies readied. Battle would likely start by dawn they were told, and the troops were grabbing what little sleep they could. Donald had drifted off, listening to the sounds of the wounded men who were too ill to travel north when he felt a hand on his shoulder and his name whispered in his ear. Larsson was staring down at him, his lungs still gulping for air.

"Henry never stopped asking — where's Walt. He'd heard talk that Walt was a girl and Percy hurt her. I told him Walt's alright and gone north, and then he keeps asking if I've had a letter yet. I've told him it's too soon for that, but the boy wouldn't leave it alone. I got angry at him and sent him off. I haven't seen him since before supper."

Donald was sitting up and rubbing his face as he considered the problem. "Have you spoken with Percy?"

"He claims not to have seen the boy." Donald now rubbed his eyes briskly, trying to get his mind working faster.

"Is Henry likely to go north and try to find Walt?" Donald asked.

"He's slow, but he knows what happens to deserters. It's my guess he went after Percy, and Percy found him."

"But we've been on the road all day." How could the boy have found the energy to hunt down Percy after a twelve-hour march? "Isn't Percy driving a wagon?"

"He said he was sleeping all day in the back of a wagon, and that would be just like him, but he could have dropped off the wagon anytime and hopped back on when it suited."

"Ours wasn't the last regiment to cross the James. The Fifth Corps is behind us. Henry could be back there, I suppose, but we'll never find him in the dark."

"I figure he might call out to us or be limping up the road. I came to ask if I could to borrow your horse." Larsson looked hopefully at Donald, the light from the oil lamp shining on his blackened eye.

"It's best if I go after the boy. If he's hurt, I can offer medical treatment. There's a moon tonight too, and that'll help. Where were you when you last saw him?"

"I'd say a mile east of the old Court House."

"I'll go back that far and start working my way forward. Where's Percy now?"

"A poker game, so he won't bother you. Take Brandy. The dog will find Henry if he's out there."

The retriever was lying patiently outside the tent, and Donald helped himself to a large knife from the surgery, picked up his medical basket, and took his leave of Larsson. He didn't own a rifle, but it would be of little use if you couldn't see to fire. He was lucky to have two good companions, the horse and the dog. "Come on

Brandy. Let's go find Henry." The dog rose willingly and followed him to the corral.

As he neared the Court House, the road was empty and silent, the dust having settled from the last of the troops on their way south. He knew his silhouette in the moonlight would make him a target for a sniper, and calling out to the boy would identify him to whoever might be watching. Still, there was no other way, and at least Percy was occupied making up his lost money back at camp. When he first shouted out Henry's name, Brandy barked and began to range out along one side and then the other side of the road. Donald shook his head in amazement at the dog who understand what was needed. They continued up the road, and a mile past the Court House, Brandy barked furiously.

Donald jumped down off Lancet and followed the sound of the barking into the woods beside the road. When he reached the dog, he saw the outline of a body lying still in the brush. He didn't need to see the body to know it was Henry. Brandy was whimpering, his muzzle snuffling at Henry's legs, and then he lay down next to the boy. When Donald touched Henry's head, it felt hot and sticky. The boy was alive but barely conscious, and when Donald lifted his head to give him water from his canteen, Henry's eyes fluttered open.

"Is that you, Forbes?" It was a good sign the lad recognized him, Donald thought. "I was hit on my head."

"Do you know who did it?" Henry asked for more water and when Donald touched the back of his head to lift it, the boy winced. The bones of the skull felt intact, suggesting a cut in the skin was responsible for the pool of blood congealed beneath his head. Henry struggled to get his words out.

"I was following Percy to ask if he hurt Walt. I saw him go off the road and I went after him. He's a bad man."

"Did you see anyone else?"

"Only Percy. My head hurts something awful, Forbes."

"I don't doubt it." You're lucky to be alive, Henry. We need to get you back to camp. Do you think you can sit my horse?" The boy nodded, winced again, and tried to stand before sitting back down.

"I'll bring Lancet here."

He managed to push Henry up into the saddle, but the boy was too dizzy and weak to hang on alone, so Donald mounted behind him and took the reins. They started to walk back down the road.

A mile from camp, they approached a turn in the road and Brandy growled. Donald slowed and that's when he heard the report of a rifle from the hillside in front of them. At the same moment, Henry's body pushed back into him and the boy slumped down in the saddle, emitting a small moan. Brandy barked and took off up the hill. Donald urged Lancet to pick up his pace. Another shot rang out and Donald felt a sting as the bullet grazed his upper arm. He thought he could hear the dog ripping at clothing, and then he heard cussing in a voice that could have belonged to anyone. Fearing for the dog's life, Donald shouted out for Brandy. The obedient animal loped back to the road, apparently none the worse for the encounter. Donald urged Lancet to a trot, praying the boy was not badly wounded and the horse could manage the double load. By the time he made it to the hospital tent and jumped off the back of the horse, Henry's lifeless body slid with him. Doctor Vorster came out immediately, took one look at the lathered horse and the dead body, and shook his head.

"What now, Forbes?"

Donald explained why he had left camp, and how he had used the dog to find Henry. "The boy was following Percy and got hit on the back of his head. Then, when I was bringing him back, we were shot at by a sniper."

"The boy went after this man Percy, the one who you say attacked your friend?" He watched Doctor Vorster rub his temples and sigh. "Were there any witnesses to any of this?"

"Henry said no one else was there."

Doctor Vorster bent over the body, opening the shirt to look at the blood-covered chest. "Other than what looks like a rifle bullet to the chest, there's the one blow to the back of the head."

"The butt of a rifle or gun, do you think?"

"Something like that."

"What if Percy's rifle is bloody?"

"Not good enough. We're in a war. There's blood on a lot of guns. Give your report to the Sergeant of his Company, but unless you've got a witness, there's not much they'll be able to do."

"I'm sure the shot that got Henry was meant for me."

"That wouldn't surprise me. I heard you fought with Percy. You've made an enemy, Forbes. Our regiment has the whole Southern Army gunning for them. All you have is one man after you, and you've brought it on yourself. I can't say I'm sympathetic."

Donald nodded. "Percy's figured out all the angles. Wait a moment. There's the dog." Donald said. Doctor Vorster raised his eyebrows. "The dog tussled with the man who shot Henry." Brandy lay exhausted behind Donald's feet, but raised his head when his name was spoken.

"You want to use the dog as a witness?" Doctor Vorster looked incredulous and shook his head. "You need sleep, Forbes. You look like you haven't slept for days. When the fighting starts in a few hours, I'll need you to forget all this and concentrate on the wounded."

Donald knew he couldn't sleep until he told Larsson what had happened. He led Lancet to the picket line. An old teamster, seeing to his own horses, took pity on him, or maybe it was the state of Lancet, and offered to wipe him down, feed and water him.

"Maybe you'll do the same for me someday," the teamster said, "when I take a bullet."

Donald nodded absently and walked towards the 126th wagons. He knew their flag by now, and even recognized a few of the men. But

Larsson found him first. "I can tell by your face. Either you didn't find Henry, or you found him dead."

"Not exactly. I found him alive, but Henry was shot dead on the way back here." He watched Larsson's face drop.

"Where's Brandy?" Brandy hearing his name ran up to Larsson and the two made a fuss over each other as Donald explained how Brandy had found Henry. Larsson, his back to Donald, seemed frozen in a crouch beside the dog. "Was it Percy who shot him?"

"I couldn't tell in the dark, and I rode out of there fast. Besides, I thought you said Percy was playing poker."

"Turns out he quit the game early. I asked around, and no one knew where he went." Larsson sat down heavily on a log, burying his face in his hands.

"Henry saved my life. That bullet was meant for me," Donald said.

"Poor kid couldn't keep out of it. I told him we'd take care of Percy, but he wouldn't listen." Donald could see Larsson blamed himself for not doing a better job of protecting Henry. Or Jessie, for that matter.

"I have to tell your Sergeant what happened last night, but Doctor Vorster says we have no case against Percy, and he's right. Unless he was seen whacking Henry or firing on me, there's no proof he did it."

"I don't need proof, and you'll be busy when the fighting starts. Let me see to this."

"How will you take care of it?" Donald asked. He was worried for Larsson. Jessie would never forgive herself if Percy killed her friends when she had the chance to name him as her attacker.

"Lots of things can happen during a battle. Leave it to me."

Donald was having trouble fighting his mounting exhaustion, and he couldn't think straight when he told the Sergeant his story. There was more than a little disbelief written on the Sergeant's face, but he said nothing and wrote down the particulars of Henry's death, asking for clarification when needed.

"You haven't given me much to go on, Private. I'll talk to Percy, but I doubt I'll get anywhere with him."

"What about the dog?"

"What dog?"

"He fought with the man who shot Henry. We could see what the dog does when he meets Percy."

"Not much use, unless you've got a talking dog."

Donald headed back to his camp. There was the occasional rifle shot from the southwest but no sounds of heavy artillery. He desperately needed a couple of hours of sleep to function, and he tried to put all thoughts of Percy and Larsson out of his mind as he spread his blanket under a tree. The heat was just bearable but the sun hadn't begun to do its worst. He passed out as soon as he lay down.

The sound of steady artillery woke him after noon. He prayed the battle would be decided quickly and would not extend for days like so many others. When he entered the stifling hospital tent, Simpson surprizing him by expressing concern.

"Doc said you had a run-in on the road, and that little kid was shot while you were bringing him back."

"Don't say you're surprised," Donald replied morosely. "I'd bet it's your friend who's responsible."

Simpson frowned, but did not protest. Donald wondered if Percy's behaviour had now crossed the line, even for Simpson. The ambulance attendants began to bring in the first of the wounded, the pace increasing as the afternoon progressed. The box with the limbs had to be dumped twice into a hole someone had the foresight to dig.

"I need help with the chloroform, Forbes."

Donald looked down at the wounded patient, and was shocked to recognize Percy, eyes pinched shut with the pain of two bullets, one in the shoulder and one in the torso. His breathing was ragged and his skin pale from the loss of blood. Simpson stood next to him, bug-eyed with surprise.

"What's wrong with the two of you? Take care of the chloroform, Forbes. We need to stop the bleeding and get at those bullets."

"It's Percy, sir."

Doctor Vorster looked down at the man. "Two shots at close range. They missed the heart and lungs but could have nicked the liver. And you, Simpson, isn't this your teamster friend?" Simpson shrugged and shook his head. "I can't believe he was at the front lines. It's his bad luck he was brought to this tent, that's all I can say." Doctor Vorster worked the bullet probe into the shoulder wound, eliciting a moan from his patient. "More chloroform, Forbes," he said impatiently, twisting the bullet forceps into place to remove the first bullet. Donald put his questions aside and continued his work.

After Percy was moved out of the surgical tent, Donald tried to get his mind around the events of the day. It must have been Larsson who shot Percy, he thought, but Larsson didn't seem the type to shoot a man, even one he hated. He might beat him to death though.

"I saved you some grub," Simpson said, holding a tin plate with bread, boiled meat and a cup of black coffee.

"Thanks," Donald replied, surprised by the offer and realizing he hadn't eaten since the previous day. "Where did you get fresh bread?"

"They finished repairing the track to the port, and the first train came in with supplies an hour ago. Look, Forbes, I'm sorry about Percy."

"I'm not."

"I don't mean his getting shot. I mean what he's been doing. He doesn't care a damn except for himself. Seems nothing's beneath him."

"It took you a while to realize that," Donald said. "Henry might still be alive if you had told the truth."

"I didn't think he'd sink as low as he did. Looks like he got what he deserved, anyway."

"He's still alive?"

"Still breathing."

"I'm putting him on the list to go north tomorrow."

"Shouldn't he recover here for a few days? The wounds could open," Simpson said. Donald was surprized Simpson considered this possibility. But maybe there was another reason to keep him close. Maybe Percy knew who shot him.

"You told me the train is here. That's an easier ride than the ambulance."

"I don't care what you do with him," Simpson said.

"Send him north," Doctor Vorster said, having overheard them. "The sooner he's out of this tent, the better." He gave Donald a shrewd look and left. Donald ate a couple of bites of the greasy salt pork and put the plate down. He felt ill from the heat and insufficient sleep.

Simpson grudgingly agreed to watch the wounded during the night, and Donald finished scouring the surgical benches and removing the detritus. Exhausted, he fell asleep next to the tent, knowing he should have told Larsson about Percy, but concerned what Larsson might do if he heard Percy was still alive.

The next morning, Donald woke to the sounds of battle and noises from the recovery tent. He quickly washed his hands and face, noticing, but ignoring, the swelling surrounding his bullet graze. He made the rounds of the wounded, lifting them up to drink water or beef broth brought in by the orderlies, changing their bandages, and feeding those who would take food. The train would be ready leave with the wounded men at noon.

"You feeling alright, Forbes," Doctor Vorster asked.

Donald felt a sheen of sweat cooling his brow and realized his upper arm was throbbing. "I have swelling in the bullet graze."

"What bullet graze?"

"After Henry was shot, someone fired again, but he missed."

"I wouldn't say he missed. Let me take a look at that arm." Donald removed his jacket and shirt. The wound looked angry. "Why didn't you clean this properly yesterday?"

"We were pretty busy, sir. I guess I forgot."

"Something tells me you won't forget again." Doctor Vorster took a clean cotton rag and poured alcohol over the wound. It stung fiercely, making Donald's eyes water. The doctor wrapped his arm and touched Donald's forehead. "It's only a graze, but an infection has set in and you're running a fever. Make sure you clean and change that bandage twice a day."

"I can hear cannon."

"It's not our boys this time. Our Regiment took a solid hit yesterday, and they'll be out of action for a while."

The ambulances made four trips to the train to transfer all the wounded. Donald made sure Percy was taken aboard with the first group, and he waited to ride with the last patients. By the time the train was loaded, Donald was feeling unsteady although his arm no longer throbbed. He sat down with the wounded men from his Regiment. It was terribly hot and humid, even in the moving train, and he couldn't manage to swallow enough water to slake his thirst. He offered cups of water to the few men who were awake and happy to be leaving the war behind them. In spite of the bumpy ride, he fell asleep and had to be prodded by a patient when the train stopped. He stood up, feeling no better. When he looked over the men hanging in rows of stretchers facing him, Percy was staring at him and smiling. Two bullet holes and the bastard was still smiling, he thought.

Donald recognized the coloured nurse in the receiving tent next to the dock, and she remembered him too. "Don't tell me you've gone and lost another patient?

"Not this time. Not yet anyway," he said, thinking a couple of his patients might not complete their journey. "I've got fifteen from the 111th Regiment to go north." He handed her the sheet with their names and details. Two who had been unconscious had the foresight to pin their names and addresses to their jackets before the last battle. He'd seen that done more often since the fighting at Cold Harbor when days passed before a truce could be called to remove the wounded and dead. Men were buried where they fell, often in unmarked graves. "I have another question for you. Is this the same hospital ship that took Jessie MacKay to Washington last week?"

"If you mean the Jessie MacKay who was passing as a farrier, ask Nurse Abigail Morgan on the ship. She spoke to me this morning about Miss MacKay."

Donald smiled at his good fortune and thanked her. Finally, something had gone right today.

He saw to the transfer of his patients and when the men were settled in beds lining the walls of the paddle wheeler, Donald went to find Percy. When Donald touched his arm, Percy opened his eyes and eventually focused on him. The smile reappeared, but it was more of a grimace, Donald realized.

"Who shot you?"

"Not saying," Percy whispered, closing his eyes.

Donald reached out to shake him again when an arm took his firmly. "Let him sleep," the nurse said. She stared as his armband. "You should know better."

"Excuse me, but I must know who shot him." He hoped it wasn't Larsson. Maybe he only needed to know it wasn't a random attack by a rebel sharpshooter, and being a scoundrel had consequences.

"He'll tell you when he's ready." The woman looked formidable, and she stood with her ample arms crossed, waiting for him to leave.

"I don't suppose you'd be Miss Abigail Morgan?" he asked, hoping he hadn't ruined any hope of finding Jessie.

"What if I am?"

"I'd like to talk to you about another matter, if you have time."

"I can give you a couple of minutes, but that's all."

"Could we talk outside the ward, please?"

Miss Morgan was stopped twice for advice before they made it to the stern. Donald was impressed to see the ship was equipped as well as a hospital and had its own surgery and drug dispensary.

"How can I help you?"

"I understand you met Jessie MacKay last week. She's my friend, and I know she went north but I haven't heard from her yet. Can you tell me whether she's alright, and where I might find her?"

"Assuming you know about the attack, how do I know you weren't the one who attacked her?"

"I certainly wasn't, but you might direct that same question to the man you were protecting back there," Donald replied, affronted she would accuse him.

It was the nurse's turn to look surprised. "You were asking who shot him. It wasn't Jessie if that's what's worrying you. I know for a fact she's working at a hospital in Washington."

"How is Percy doing?"

"I doubt he'll make it. I suspect internal bleeding."

Donald nodded. "I would have guessed that by looking at the pallor and sheen on his face."

"Have you looked at your own face recently?" She wasn't smiling, and when he didn't answer, she laid her palm on his forehead. "You're running a fever. Do you have any other symptoms?"

"Dizzy, maybe a cough."

"Have you received any wounds recently?"

"A bullet grazed my arm a couple of days ago, but it was sore only briefly."

"Let me look at that." She led him aft to a small dispensary off the ward and removed the dirty bandage. "I can tell from the scab this was infected, but it seems to be healing." What she didn't say is infected wounds could cause brain fever. "Is your neck stiff?"

"Not really, but my stomach's complaining, no doubt from bad food."

"We all suffer from that now and then. Will you be going back to your regiment today?"

"No, I'm staying until tomorrow. I have to place an order and pick up surgical supplies. If I had an answer to the question I asked Percy, I could take it back to his commander. And if I could impose upon you once more, perhaps you could deliver a letter to Jessie for me?"

"That I am willing to do. Give me the letter before you leave tomorrow." Donald noted she did not offer to provide Jessie's address. As he turned to leave, he asked, "Will you talk to Percy and ask who shot him?"

"I'll apply no pressure, but I've seen many who want to unburden themselves when they believe the end is near."

Donald left the ship and wandered along the shore of the James River. Even in the few days since he'd last been here, many changes had taken place. Two new wharfs were nearing completion, and the wooden frame of a large hospital was taking shape. Outbuildings were going up all along the walkways. He could smell fresh bread from a bakery even this late in the day, and dozens of linen sheets were drying on lines near a makeshift laundry. All the smells made him nauseous. He found a shady spot to sit and within minutes, he was asleep.

He woke up coughing and rolled over onto his side, hugging his knees. The sun was close to setting and he hadn't picked up his supplies order. He rose unsteadily, brushed off his clothes and swayed slightly as he lifted his knapsack and medical kit.

"A little too much to drink, eh?"

Donald searched for the high-pitched voice and found a very short man staring up at him. He wore a blue velvet suit and a bowler hat, and he carried a cane with an intricately carved ivory pommel shaped like a lion's head. Donald wondered briefly what this man did for a living. Saying he felt ill seemed an admittance of weakness. It was better to let him think he was drunk. "Do you know which storage house stocks the surgical supplies?"

"I can tell you which tents or buildings stock food, drink, or women. That's the limit of my knowledge, but I've found it to be adequate." The small man smiled happily. "I'm George Pratt, by the way. I run the bawdy house. Pratt's Pretties."

"Of course, you do," Donald smiled back. "Where is that located?" The man pointed to the left. "I'll go this way then," Donald said, turning his back on the man and walking towards a large complex of buildings.

"Wait," Pratt said, jogging to catch up. "I saw your armband. One of my ladies is in need of your skills."

"There's a hospital ship in port. Take her there. Or try the receiving tent. I'm not a surgeon, only a steward."

"I've tried. They won't help her. Besides, you carry a medical kit," George said, pointing at the leather knapsack.

"I can remove a bullet or sew up a wound. I know nothing of women's troubles."

"She's been stabbed, silly girl. I knew her mouth would get her into trouble someday. Still, you'd think a good smack on the backside would be enough. Couldn't you have a look at her and see if you can help?"

Donald stared down the wharf. He realized it was too late to pick up supplies. He felt a little better, now that he was up and moving around. Maybe he could help the girl. "Take me to her."

"Thank you. I'll make it worth your while, even if you aren't able to help her". Pratt looked as if he might be attempting to leer at him, but it missed the mark and came off looking strangely angelic. Donald shrugged in response. The way he was feeling, a soft bed appealed more than a willing woman.

When they arrived at the house, the sun was setting and a few customers were ogling the women lolling outside on the porch swings, less for the breeze than the attention they would attract. Pratt led him up to the second floor where a woman lay moaning on the floor.

"Can't you find a bed for her?" Donald asked.

"She's bleeding, and besides, we need all the beds for business," Pratt said, not the least embarrassed by his insensitivity. Donald's dreams of a soft mattress evaporated.

He knelt down and felt her pulse. It was strong, and there was little blood beneath her. He lifted her shift and found a single stab wound to her left breast. Blood was still dripping from the wound, but slowly. "How long ago was she attacked?" he asked.

"An hour, I'd say,"

"The knife hasn't punctured her lung, although it could have scraped a rib."

"Damn good thing she's well endowed, then."

Donald nodded, thinking a breast that size could absorb a four-inch blade. "I can give her morphine and sew up the wound."

"She'll be alright then?"

"It's hard to say. If the wound stays clean and there's no corruption, she should recover."

"How soon will she be ready to work?"

"Maybe a month?" He watched Pratt's face drop.

"I can't keep her a whole month without money coming in."

"Can't she serve beer downstairs?"

"I thought you said she couldn't work for a month."

"I meant she shouldn't be doing her usual business. Nothing too strenuous, if you catch my meaning."

"That's different, then. Can I leave her with you?"

"I'll take whiskey first," Donald said.

"Now? I thought you'd want it afterwards?"

"It's not for me," Donald frowned. Pratt sent him another unsuccessful smirk.

"She's already insisted on laudanum, but suit yourself," Pratt said, heading downstairs for the whiskey. Donald took out his surgical kit and threaded a needle. He sprinkled morphine powder into the wound and lifted the woman's head to allow her to drink the whiskey. She smiled back at him and spoke for the first time. She was missing her two front teeth, probably a result of insulting another customer, Donald imagined.

"This is the good stuff." With the whiskey and laudanum doing their work, she cursed only twice while Donald worked. Her wound had stopped bleeding, a good sign, but he would need to bind her breast so it didn't move and break open the stitches. One of the other girls offered to help lift her while he wrapped strips from a linen sheet tightly around her chest.

"Tell her to remain on her back for several days."

"But Mr. Pratt said she wasn't supposed to work." Donald saw the girl smirking at him. Her version of a leer was much more successful than George Pratt's.

Downstairs, Pratt grabbed Donald's arm and drew him over to the bar. "What'll you have? I gave Nelly the good stuff thinking you might take a sip yourself."

"Do you have water?"

"Water? Is that it?" He went behind the bar and stood on a crate while he filled a large glass from a jug under the counter. Donald drank greedily, placing the glass down on the bar only when it was empty. Before he could leave, Pratt grabbed his arm again and whispered, "Which one will you have. She's on the house."

"Not this time."

Pratt looked offended. "Maybe you should see a doctor yourself. By the way, the place they keep the surgical supplies is a quarter mile to the south. It's the same building they store the boots and uniforms."

Donald had started walking down the wharf when the girl who had helped him with the patient ran up behind him.

"Mr. Pratt sent me with this." She pushed a bottle of Old Crow whiskey at him, curtsied, and ran back the way she'd come.

Donald was attempting to shove the bottle into his knapsack when Miss Abigail stopped beside him. "Drinking is the last thing you should be doing in your state, Private Forbes."

"It was a present."

"Why would a woman like that give *you* a present?"

At least she didn't leer as she said it, Donald thought. He wiped the sheen off his brow and coughed. "I stitched up a friend of hers."

"You should be taking care of yourself, not some slattern. How are your bowels?"

Donald smiled and shrugged, thinking no woman had asked him that question.

"Tell me. Do you have the flux?" she asked impatiently. Donald shook his head. Neither of them said anything. They were both considering the possibilities. "If you don't feel right tomorrow, I think you should accompany us north. I'll ask our surgeon to write a letter to yours explaining the situation. Meanwhile, return to the ship with me." She wasn't about to take no for an answer.

Donald followed her back to the ship. She found him a bed and offered him a clean night shirt. He declined. He couldn't remember when he'd last bathed, and he shuddered at the thought of peeling off his dirty clothes and then having to put them back on again in the morning. As he drifted off to sleep, he remembered he hadn't written to Jessie. It was just as well, he thought, since he didn't want to tell her Henry was dead and Percy was on his way to Washington.

He woke up the next morning coughing uncontrollably, his ribs straining outward from the effort, the tendons tight with pain. Gradually the urge subsided and he looked down the row of men. He felt no movement from the ship, so they must be in dock. Men in the adjacent bunks were enjoying porridge, but the smell made him nauseous. He couldn't remember when he'd last eaten, and as he swung his legs to the floor and tried to rise, a wave of dizziness overcame him and he sat down abruptly. He'd seen similar symptoms in camp, although fever and cough could mean many things. At least he didn't have dysentery, he thought. He was sitting hunched over, feeling sorry for himself, when Nurse Abigail stopped by his bed.

"I fear I have camp fever," he said.

"I thought so last night when I heard you coughing. Typhoid pneumonia, I'd say." She laid her palm on his forehead. "Your fever is down a little, but it will come up again this evening. You need rest more than anything, I expect. I have quinine for you." She offered him a glass with the bitter liquid. "I should tell you Percy died during the night," she said, watching his face.

"Did he say who shot him?"

"He admitted to shooting a young boy, by accident, so he claimed. He was upset by that, and it was weighing on his mind at the end."

Donald nodded, thinking of the night when a bullet meant for him had hit Henry's chest. He should be relieved Percy was dead, but the only emotion he could elicit was anger.

"I did ask who shot him, but all he said was it was a person he considered a friend. I heard no more from him after that."

"He had only one friend that I know of." Donald wondered if Simpson could have shot Percy. The series of events played out in his mind. But why would Simpson do that? Surely, not for a little money. Perhaps he was worried that he'd be next? He stood up shakily. "I've got to get back to camp."

"You're in no condition to go anywhere." As if on cue, he felt a shudder as the paddle wheel started to turn and the ship began to pull away from the dock. "Besides, it's too late."

CHAPTER 20: 1864, ARMORY HOSPITAL, VIRGINIA

Cushion me soft, rock me in billowy drowse

Donald had lost track of time and had only a vague sense that he'd been carried by stretcher from the ship directly into a hospital ward. He remembered fighting to get out of bed, but when he'd tried to stand, he stumbled and fell.

It was dark now, with only a small lamp glowing at the end of the ward. He heard a familiar voice say his name, and he turned his head to look up at Jessie who was holding a candle and a cloth-covered bowl. She looked beautiful, her blonde hair peeking out from under a white cap. Her green eyes, full of concern, were glowing in the candlelight.

"I've been dreaming of your smile. Where did you hide it?" He struggled to keep from coughing. Jessie's lips were shaky and he could see her eyes filling with tears. "It's really not so bad. Seeing you, I feel stronger." But the look in her eyes told him he was not on the mend.

"Don't talk. You need to rest." She laid her hand on his head and her touch felt wonderfully cool. "Are you warm enough?"

"Tell me how you've been." He wanted to watch her, and he needed her to take his mind off the pain tormenting his chest.

Jessie tucked the blanket around him and found a stool to place beside his bed. "I've talked with Abigail, and she said you came looking for me after I'd left port. She also told me Percy died." She paused, and Donald saw her considering her next words. "Do I have you to thank for that?"

"Someone else got to him first." He watched her nod and look away. When she turned back, she was smiling.

"I can thank Abigail for finding me a job at this hospital, and for telling me you were here, but I was so surprised to learn you were ill."

Donald wondered why she was surprised. She'd been the one to tell him how everyone eventually caught something, a bullet or an illness. He tried to absorb what she was saying.

"She didn't know me, but she found me employment. I don't know what I would have done without her help. I'm living with a few nurses in a house right on this hill, so it's very convenient. They have everything we need here. It's more like a small village really. You would be amazed at the size of this hospital." She stopped talking suddenly and looked down at her hands.

"I got our money back from Percy." He motioned to his haversack, thinking that he didn't get it back as much as fight to get it back. "Please take it now. It may not be safe here."

"I'll keep it safe until your better," Jessie said, searching and finding not only the money but the bottle of whiskey. She drew it out and studied the label. "Should I keep this for you as well, or would you like a wee dram now?"

Donald started to laugh, but it turned into a paroxysm. When he stopped coughing, he said. "I was thinking of giving it to Miss Abigail. Could you do that for me? If it weren't for her, I wouldn't have found you, and now you've told me how much she has helped you."

"I'm happy to, although I doubt she would take a drink. I'll tell her it's for medicinal purposes, shall I?"

Donald laugh sounded more like a sigh. "I'll be better in no time. Please be patient with me."

"You won't get any better if you keep refusing to eat," Jessie said. She picked up a bowl covered with a cloth napkin and wafted the aroma towards him. "This is proper chicken soup, and I've made it myself so you can't say no."

The smell made him queasy, but he thanked her and let her spoon the warm broth into his mouth. His stomach roiled, and after four spoonfuls, he said, "That's enough for now, please. Perhaps I'll take more later. It's very good." He could see lines of concern on her face.

"Those lies may work with others, but I can tell you've swallowed it for me, and that's fine because now you've got a little food in your stomach to fight the fever. Others want to take something out of you. I had to shoo away the surgeon with his lancet, ready to cut a vein."

"Good for you. Your father would have been proud." Donald felt guilty when he wished his father were there to take care of him. The fever obviously enjoyed living in his lungs, and it behaved as if it had no intention of leaving. They had moved his bed away from the other patients as his coughing had caused complaints by those wishing to rest. "If Papa were here, he would say he'd seen far worse at sea, and then he'd tell a story to make me laugh."

"Don't talk. Let me see if I can come up with a story for you." Jessie looked off into the distance, the corners of her mouth turning up as she recalled a humorous incident. He was amazed she could devise an amusing story when her life, of late, had been anything but happy.

"I have one. It's concerning little Henry." Donald closed his eyes briefly. He realized she didn't know of Henry's death. She wouldn't hear it from his lips.

"A couple of months ago, although it seems more like a lifetime, we'd stopped after a long march on a very hot day, and we got the coke fired up hot enough to melt iron. We fitted a few shoes before the sun sank too low to see. The regiment was camped close to a creek that ran into the Chickahominy River, and I thought I might run down and cool off before trying to sleep. As you might imagine, a score of naked bodies filled the creek, so I kept walking upstream until the creek turned a couple of bends and I could no longer hear the men laughing.

"There were plenty of frogs croaking, and mosquitoes were buzzing as they searched for a meal, but even so, it was pure pleasure to be away from the camp. It was a little past sunset, but still as hot as a forge oven, and I shed my apron, pants and shirt, and walked into the cool water wearing only my vest and drawers." She looked at Donald and raised her brows. "I would have shed them too, but I was worried I'd give the mosquitoes too much flesh." Donald smiled at the image but said nothing. "There I was, floating blissfully on my back in the middle of this lazy creek, looking up at the stars and wondering what you were doing at that very moment.

"That's when I heard someone on shore, stripping off clothes and wading into the water. I panicked for a moment because there was only sliver of a moon that night, and all I could see was a pale blur. But then I heard singing and I recognized the voice. It was little Henry, sitting alone in the shallows on his naked backside, singing with such a pure little boy's voice. But his choice of song was odd. Have you ever heard a song called Jingle Bells?" Donald shook his head, and the room swam as he did so. "Neither had I, only it features a sleigh and snow, so it was well out of season. Henry thought he was alone, and I didn't say a word until after he'd finished singing. When I said 'Hello Henry, it's me Walt,' he came close to jumping out of his skin. I asked him why he wasn't bathing with the others. Can you imagine what he said?"

"That they'd object to his song?" Donald suggested.

"I'm sure they would, but that wasn't his reason. He said he didn't want the others to see his *tattoos*. By then, I'd made my way over to him, and he obligingly stood up and bent over so the moonlight lit up his back and backside. They were covered with tattoos."

"What kind?"

"Everything imaginable: mermaids, three or more types of flowers, an anchor, and at least two sailing ships, fully rigged. He told me his father made a living in New York City creating tattoos on the arms of sailors. He practiced his designs and experimented with inks on the backsides of Henry, his brother and cousins, none of whom had stepped off land. Can you believe it? His father told them the designs would be well-hidden from all but the loves of their lives!"

"Now that would make an amazing family photograph," Donald said, choking back his cough. "Did he ask why you were there alone?"

"No, but he did ask why I was swimming in my vest and drawers, and perhaps he imagined I was covered with tattoos as well." They both laughed at the image. "I said my underclothes needed a good wash and wearing them was the easiest way to do it. He accepted that explanation, and I guess it was too dark to catch me in the lie." She paused for a bit, her face becoming more pensive.

"I know Henry isn't the brightest penny in the bottle, but when I asked him why he chose that song, he said singing about snow made him feel cool, inside and out. It occurred to me he might be smarter than he looks. We both started to sing his song, Jingle Bells." Her face lit up with her smile at the memory.

It wasn't easy, smiling back at Jessie and knowing Henry had died by a bullet meant for him. He'd clutched that slight body in front of him, never realizing Henry's backside was a colourful canvas. Even Doctor Vorster, who had looked closely at the bullet wound in his chest, missed finding those tattoos. Funny how you never see what you aren't looking for, he thought. His eyes strayed back to Jessie.

"Did Henry tell you how he came to be in the army?" he asked.

"He joined up with his brother who died at Fredericksburg. Larsson took him under his wing after that."

Donald felt suddenly exhausted and unhappy. The story, meant to be amusing, had only served to remind him of the loss of a boy Jessie had cared about. She hadn't asked what had happened to Henry, but he knew if she did, he would lie to her. He turned his face to the pillow trying to stifle another coughing fit.

"I should go now and let you rest." Jessie took his hand and squeezed hard.

When he awoke, she was sitting beside the bed staring into the distance. She turned to him, and he watched her face light up with a smile. "Are you with me, now?" she asked. He began to cough, and lifted himself on one elbow, feeling a desperate urge to clear his lungs of the fluid that had accumulated during his sleep. His ribs ached from the effort and he lay back, exhausted. His body seemed to grow smaller and more vulnerable.

"What will you do when the war's over?" Donald asked, his voice a whisper.

"I've been dreaming you and I would go back to Chippawa and start a small veterinary business, and maybe find a few acres close to your relatives. We have what's left of your bounty money, and our pay. It isn't much, but if we find a partner willing to share a forge and equipment for the shoeing, we'll get by. Oh, I realize there aren't many opportunities to remove bullets or sew up bayonet wounds, but we have lots of skills to draw on now. It won't be only horses."

"I'd like nothing better," Donald said, and he meant it. He remembered telling his father he didn't want to leave the farm. He expected Papa saw it as his fear of the unknown, and maybe it was, at least initially. There wasn't much point in going elsewhere when all he needed to be happy was right there in Chippawa. "We could marry, if you'd have me."

"Would I have you?" Jessie said. "Donald Forbes, I've chased you all over this country, across the damn border, and cornered you in this hospital bed, just waiting for you to ask." Tears were flowing freely down her face.

Her hands were in his, the ridges of the scars comforting him, even when he closed his eyes. He always knew when he was holding his Jessie. He made a silent prayer that he would be allowed to keep the promise. They kissed quietly, the room suddenly still around them. He listened as Jessie talked about going back to the Welland Hotel to earn money to buy a forge oven and anvil for her work. He fell asleep to her voice spinning dreams he wanted to share. In his dreams, his parents and Rhoda were there with him. Jessie was right, he had been a fool, but if he recovered, everything would be different.

His fever rose steadily towards evening and well into the next day. He lost track of time and Jessie's visits. At times she would sit and describe the events of her day or tell him what was happening in the large room surrounding them; who was sitting up and looking brighter, which nurse comforted and which scolded her patients to get well. Her visits melted together, her voice growing more anxious. She laid wet cloths on his brow and lifted his head for water. They both knew his body was fighting a determined enemy. His lungs kept filling with fluid, making it difficult for him to speak, to breathe, and eventually, to make sense of her words. He liked it best when she took his hand and pressed it to her heart. He wanted to stay that way forever. Eventually, though, his own heart stopped pumping.

Jessie kissed his forehead, as cool now as the James River He didn't look like the Donny she knew, but more like the older man he might have become.

I'm so sorry, but he was too worn down to fight off the disease." Abigail had placed a comforting arm around her shoulder.

Dozens of wounded men lay in cots pressed against hastily-constructed walls. Most were older than Donny and some would suffer his fate. Jessica was certain Donny would recover. After all, hadn't he sipped some of her soup last night? Did he know he was dying? That was the most painful thought of all. Selfishly, she'd given him no time to reflect on his death, or his life for that matter. Instead, she'd saturated the air between them with a weave of endless plans for a bright future together.

Abigail lifted the sheet to cover Donny's face, signaling the attendants to remove his body. Jessie struggled with an urge to grab the sheet, hating to lose sight of him under a what amounted to a white flag signaling surrender. Her friend sighed deeply, drawing a grumble of annoyance from a patient in a neighbouring bed. "This bloody war must end soon," Abigail murmured.

"Not soon enough," Jessie said, her voice louder and angrier than she'd expected.

"What will you do now?"

"Forgive me. I must be alone." She felt dizzy and sick with anger, wanting only to ignore the question she'd refused to let herself consider. She fled the ward with its smells and clamour, running from the hospital towards the river. Tears flowed freely, and in her blind rush, she tripped over a root and sprawled under an oak tree, her fists pummeling the soil in frustration as she sobbed. She knew when she returned to the ward, his body would be gone to make room for another. There was always another. She would be expected to care for that man, too, because the world didn't care. She had an answer to Abigail's question. "I'll be alone."

Slowly her sobs subsided. She lifted herself up and brushed off her dress and apron. Then she noticed the trunk of the oak tree had two sets of carved initials surrounded by a roughly carved heart. She imaged the initials were hers and Donny's and her fist smashed into the bark. "Damn it all. Why did it have to be you, Donny?" With her back to the tree, she slid down and slumped on the ground, her face buried in her arms. She was so sure he would recover because she couldn't imagine her life without him. It hurt too much to think of him. She must keep occupied.

Jessie spent many long hours that summer visiting Donald's grave on a Virginia hillside. Dozens of bodies were laid to rest there daily, and she would walk among the stones looking for Percy's grave and thinking she might like to defile it. But her heart broke again when her eyes chanced on a stone carved with Henry's name. She searched out the details, surprised to learn they he had died of gunshot wounds a few days before Donny had arrived in Washington. Did Donny know about Henry, and fail to tell her? Did he think she wouldn't find out? Abigail suggested she write to the Colonel of her regiment and inquire how Henry died. A long month went by, and the letter she received was terse and provided little insight, telling her Henry was seen by the 111th regiment surgeon, Doctor Vorster.

"Why would Doctor Vorster have seen Henry?" she asked Abigail. "That was Donald's regiment, not Henry's."

"You'll have to write to Doctor Vorster to find out why. He may be the only one who knows what happened."

"Another person might know. Donald worked with a man called Simpson, and Simpson was friends with Percy. Why do you look so surprised?"

"Before Percy died, he said someone he considered to be a friend had shot him."

"I don't see why Simpson would have shot Percy."

"Why not write to Simpson, too. He might ignore your letter, but then again, he might tell you how your friend Henry died."

They took another sip of whisky. They had toasted Donald twice. Abigail told her how Donald had come by the bottle of Old Crow, and Jessie had laughed for the first time since Donald died. It tasted all the better for it's history.

She wrote to Doctor Vorster first, receiving a letter back within the week.

> *Dear Miss MacKay,*
>
> *You say you were a friend to Donald Forbes, and I do know he was a friend to you. I miss him daily and I wish he had found the strength to recover from sepsis.*
>
> *He told me the story of the deception he devised in an effort to secure your safety, and also of your unfortunate fate whilst travelling to the port. He believed Private Percy was responsible for your attack, but he lacked the proof. Percy's punishment is irrelevant now as I understand he died of wounds en route to the general hospital. He appeared on our operating table after a battle on the 15th of the month. I do not know who shot him, although it was not Forbes because he was with me all day.*
>
> *The boy Henry had died two days earlier of a shot received while Donald was bringing him, wounded, back to camp. The lad had been hit over the head and was riding with Donald when a sharpshooter killed the boy. Donald believed the person who hit Henry and later shot him was Percy, but again he lacked proof.*
>
> *You ask about Private Simpson, as you say he was a friend of Percy's. This may have been true at one time, but Simpson was angry when the boy was killed, and I can tell you he showed little concern when Percy went under my knife. The blacksmith you mention, Larsson, still works with your regiment. I prefer not to speculate on the meaning behind Percy's last words.*
>
> *I sincerely hope your life is less exciting these days. I did hear you were an excellent horse doctor and your efforts were appreciated by your regiment, many of whom still refuse to believe you are a woman.*
>
> *Yours,*
> *Doctor P. Vorster*

Surgeon, 111th NY Volunteers

Jessie read the letter several times, convincing herself Doctor Vorster believed Percy had killed Henry and Simpson might have shot Percy. Abigail persuaded her to write to Larsson. She chose her words carefully as she was concerned that Larsson may have been involved in shooting Percy. She preferred to think it was Simpson. Larsson's reply set a few things straight.

Dear Walt Armstrong, as that name is how I remember you,

I was taken aback to hear your friend Forbes had died of disease. He was in good shape when last I saw him, but I've witnessed many fall ill and die within days so I should know better than to be surprised. Fate is fickle. I know he meant a lot to you, so I hope you will stand fast and fend off the doldrums sure to follow. That is what I've tried to do after Henry was killed, although I admit I'm not making much headway.

I did not shoot Percy. Reading between the lines of your letter, I suspect that's what you might have been hinting at. I did look for him to give him a good taste of my fist. He was shot by someone else before I could find him, and for that, I can only thank the man.

You ask after Simpson, a friend to Percy and a man Forbes said was involved in your attack. I've seen him only once since this all happened. We looked each other straight in the eye and said not a word. I have my own idea about who killed Percy, but I'm not going to accuse that lazy son of a gun. Maybe he got pushed too far by Percy who took satisfaction in everyone's pain, especially when he made himself the cause of it.

I hope you will write to me here and let me know how you are doing. It looks as if we'll be dug in for a while outside this accursed city while we try to close down supplies to the rebs. I'm so tired of this sport. I miss you and Henry something fierce, but I try to take comfort in the fact you've both got out of this situation. As grandmother would say, shared joy is twice the joy and shared grief is half the grief. Brandy says to be remembered to you.

Your friend,

Jens Larsson

126th NY Volunteers

Jessie showed the letter to Abigail as they sat on the hospital veranda on a hot summer evening. "I believe Larsson didn't shoot Percy. It's strange, but I don't care if I ever know the truth of it. I'm glad Larsson has a clean conscience." Jessie looked down at her hands. The calluses were reduced and the scars had faded a little. "He's luckier than me. I blame myself for Henry's death."

"This man, Larsson, doesn't blame you."

"If I'd named my attacker that night when I arrived in port, Henry wouldn't have gone after Percy. I believe that's why Donald said nothing to me of Henry's death, and I'll have to live with that." Abigail took her hand and gave a short squeeze.

CHAPTER 21: 1864, ARLINGTON, VIRGINIA

The smallest sprout shows there is really no death

Mary, one of the nurse's aides, handed Jessie a small manila card with Doctor John Forbes' name printed on the front. "You'll find him under the big oak beside the veranda."

"Thanks, Mary. I've arranged to take the afternoon off. Nurse Morgan knows."

Jessie looked down at her uniform. It was reasonably clean considering she'd bathed four patients that morning. There was no time to change, but when she removed her apron, the brown dress was passable. She took time for a quick glance in the wall mirror. Her hair had grown to her shoulders, and it covered the scar at her hairline and partway down her neck. She could no longer see Walt in the face that stared back at her. Jack would say she was a woman with an interesting scar and a look of determination. But there wasn't a lot of joy in her life these days, and spending the afternoon with Doctor Forbes was unlikely to bring much pleasure either.

Doctor Forbes was sitting on the bench beneath the tree, staring into the distance. He ignored a large yellowed oak leaf that spiralled down beside him, a portent of the fall season. As she approached him, he raised his body slowly. A fall body too, she thought.

"Jessie," he said, grabbing both of her hands in his. He must have felt the ridges because he looked down and studied them, more as a doctor might than a concerned friend. He seemed lost for a moment, perhaps remembering what he could of the Galt fire, or perhaps considering what to say to her. She tried to make it easier for him.

"I am so pleased you have come. Let's sit here a while and talk."

He smiled and sank back down, his hands still holding hers. "It took no time at all to travel here by train, yet I feel, sitting here, that I am so far away from all I know." His gaze turned to the field behind the hospital, covered with brown grass. "Donald walked from Culpepper down to Petersburg in less than two months."

"Walking turned out to be the easy part," Jessie said, regretting her words as soon she said them.

"I've seen my fair share of blood and killing, but what is happening here…"

"I thought I understood the reasons for the war before I joined, but I was wrong," Jessie said. In her mind, she could hear the men complain of the carnage and repeatedly ask each other why the war wasn't over. There seemed to be an endless supply of young men marching stalwartly into battle. "Some say the wrong generals were in charge at the beginning, but I wonder if the North simply lacked the heart for the fight and kept delaying the deciding battles. The South was protecting a way of life, and that is always a stronger motivation than trying to take it away."

"Very perceptive," Doctor Forbes replied. "I'd like to think Donald mulled over those questions."

Jessie looked at him closely. What father wouldn't be pained to think his son had died for a few hundred dollars of bounty money. "I know he felt strongly that slavery was wicked, but the killing made no sense to him. We both wondered whether this country would be able to heal its wounds after the carnage."

"A good question and one that should be of concern north of the border. We worry the Americans have endured five years of terrible war and may have become accustomed to it. A huge industry has developed to supply their armies with weapons, clothing and food, and that industry will press for new battles. Perhaps they'll consider heading north to complete what they attempted fifty years ago."

"I suspect people wish fervently for a little peace."

"You're right. Any sensible person would never want to endure another day of war after seeing one close up, and especially one such as this." Doctor Forbes paused to tap out his pipe, fill and then light it.

"Tell me. How is your wife coping, and Rhoda?"

"Anne is bereft as you can imagine, but Rhoda has spirit, like you Jessie, and she has taken charge of the household. I think it helps her cope with the loss to keep busy. Is that true for you too, Jessie?"

"I suppose so. With my nursing duties, there is little time to dwell on what might have been." She didn't add that the long nights provided plenty of opportunity to count her losses. She wrote and received frequent letters from Jens Larsson that helped to fill a void. She knew his heart better as a woman than she ever had as a man.

"You said in your letter that Donald is buried near here. Could we visit that place?"

"I'd planned to take you there, but it's too far to walk," Jessie said. She'd walked to the site several times, but Doctor Forbes would not be able to manage with his poor knee. "There are horse cabs at the hospital entrance." She took hold of one of his arms and walked slowly towards the front of the hospital.

When they arrived at the cemetery, Jessie waited to be helped down by Doctor Forbes. She missed wearing pants and simple clothes made for action and independence. After they alighted, they stared up at a stately mansion in sore need of repairs.

"This property was taken from General Lee for unpaid taxes, they say. Those are Mrs. Lee's roses you see next to the house," Jessie said.

"The roses are fertilized now with the young men of this nation. I must remember to tell Anne."

Jessie set a slow pace towards Donald's headstone. She often brought a flower or two to place beside his marker, and she removed the withered one still lying there.

"I see they've spelled his name wrong," Doctor Forbes said. The marble marker read 'Forbs'.

"He's missing his 'E'," Jessie replied. She wondered if Doctor Forbes would find this upsetting.

"He was never awarded an E on his report card either," Doctor Forbes mumbled. "But I had a fine letter from Doctor Vorster. He said Donald was an excellent steward." His eyes wandered over hundreds of stone markers. "They say all one should hope for is to die without debt or sin. That is easier to do if you die young." He walked around the area looking at the other markers. "All these stones show young men from different states, both north and south. He won't have known any of these boys, I suppose. Not that it matters."

For a while after Donny died, she had placed part of the blame on Doctor Forbes, although she knew that was unfair. Many things had conspired to end Donny's life prematurely, and his father's expectations of his son were only one of them. "I believe Donny was happy in his work, and he was good at it. Maybe that's why he managed so well when many others barely got by."

"He had a capacity for the healing arts, as you know, Jessie. I couldn't dissuade him from fixing little creatures and wanting to work with your father. He would have been a good surgeon too, had fate been kinder, but what do you mean, he managed well?"

"He did his job well, never complained, and he made sacrifices for his patients and his friends. Eventually those sacrifices included his health. He was able to adjust to the hardships of war far better than others. I give you credit for that. Donny loved to tell your navy stories at school and I heard a few repeated in camp. I remember how he described in great detail how you amputated a limb. At the time, I thought he did this to terrify us, but now I think your stories helped him to prepare and cope for this war. Had he been more selfish, I expect he would have survived." She had considered telling him her story and the roles Percy and Simpson had played in his demise, but she thought better of it. Perhaps it was because she couldn't face more blame right now. Her own loss was too fresh. She paused and then asked, "You know why he joined the army, don't you?"

"Anne and I knew he wasn't happy as a clerk, and he was caught up with claiming that bounty money."

"He planned to use the money to pay his tuition to veterinary school."

"He still held to that notion, did he?" Doctor Forbes said, eyebrows raised. "I thought his work here would have changed his mind."

"Perhaps it did. I believe he was very satisfied helping wounded soldiers. It's as if the war helped him find himself or live up to his expectations of himself." Still, she wondered whether Donny's experience of war time medicine would have prepared him for city practice.

"But you, Jessie, you are treating people now, as a nurse. Do you feel this is how you wish to spend your life?"

"My plans are the same. I still want to care for horses, and to work in the country." Let him think of that what he may, she thought.

Doctor Forbes only nodded. "When Donald was younger, he used to say he preferred animals to people. Perhaps he changed his mind, but I am not surprised if you have not. Your mother, God rest her soul, once described you as being as tenacious as a badger." They both smiled.

"When Donny and I met during the war, and considered our future after it ended, I thought we might work together with animals." Jessie wiped a tear from her cheek and bit her lip to check the flow. "I'm less sure I want to work on my own." She wiped away more tears, and then turned to face him. "But I will do this. It may take me time to save enough money for my barn and my equipment, but I will do this. I won't allow myself time for self-pity." She remembered how her nurse friend Abigail had employed the tactic of hard work with her, and many others, to such good effect.

"I have no doubt you will, my dear." Doctor Forbes said, taking her hands. "I came down here for other reasons as well. I wanted to see you and visit Donald's grave of course, but I also needed to reclaim his stolen bounty money. You may know how determined he was to win back his full bounty when the war was over, so I felt obliged to do this for him. I found the boy whose place he took, and talked to his father, and I was able to extract the money owing to Donald. I have the two hundred pounds promised to him."

Doctor Forbes looked so proud of himself, Jessie thought. It couldn't have been easy, asking for what amounted to blood money. Perhaps Donald's death made it more likely the other boy's father, whose son was spared that fate, would willingly pay the bounty. "Donny would have been happy to have that made right. When he first enlisted, he planned to buy you a new suit of clothes with some of his bounty money. Remember how he so enjoyed wearing stylish clothes?"

"I never understood his longing for finery," Mr. Forbes said, smiling. Jessie watched his fingers as they clutched his worn jacket, patched on both elbows.

"He told me once that stylish clothes made him feel more confident, and people would think more highly of him if he dressed the part," Jessie said. "But during the war, he met men he respected who cared not a fig for their appearance, and that changed his mind."

"Then I suspect he would have changed his mind concerning how to spend his money." A smile played over his lips, "And that's good, because I have my own idea of how the cursed bounty money should be spent." Dr. Forbes used his good foot to brush away some dried leaves from Donald's grave.

"I wish you could have met Donny in the Army," Jessie said. "He was not the same boy we knew. He was a man you would have been proud to call your son."

Doctor Forbes bent his head down and ran a hand over his eyes. "I was always proud of Donald, although I regret I never told him so. My father was hard on me too, and often he'd quote to me those lines, 'Spare the rod and spoil the child'. I never hit Donny as my father hit me, but I was overly demanding, and now it's too late to make amends." Jessie watched as he shook his head vigorously, as if to dispel those painful thoughts. When he turned to her, she sensed his resolve. "Donald wrote to us about the difficulties you've weathered, my dear. It bothered Anne and me, thinking of you managing alone after the fire, with no recourse but to reinvent yourself as a man and enlist in a foreign war. Donald was amazed at how well you coped, your spirit never seemed to lag. Jessie, there is only one thing left for me to accomplish on my journey south. I want you to have Donald's bounty money to spend as you wish."

Jessie was astonished as she allowed the idea to sink in. "I could set up to be a horse doctor?"

"If that's what you want. We have a blacksmith in Chippawa, but he knows precious little of horse ailments and seems more interested in making iron doo-dahs than shoeing or doctoring horses."

"Papa believed no one would bring their horses to a woman."

"I don't hold with that. If you do a good job for them, they'll make use of your talents. In my profession, skills, not appearances, are what matter. I can't see why it would be any different for horse doctors."

Jessie couldn't keep the smile from her face. She should have realized Doctor Forbes wouldn't care a fig for appearances and would value competence.

"You look like a different person when you smile, Jessie."

She remembered Donny saying the same thing, and how her smile made him feel warm inside. It had been a long time since she'd envisaged a future for herself that could elicit a smile. She took Doctor Forbes arm and they wandered back to a waiting cab.

ACKNOWLEDGEMENTS

I am far from an expert in American civil war history and have undoubtedly fallen short in several areas. I hope my readers will be forgiving.

Much of the history that informed this book was available on the internet from excellent government sources and websites of individuals. Other sources included: Martin W. Husk, *The 111th New York Volunteer Infantry: A Civil War History*; A.J. Bollet, *An Analysis of the Medical Problems of the Civil War*; Paul Fatout, *Letters of a Civil War Surgeon*; G.W. Adams, *Doctors in Blue*; Annie Wittenmyer, *Under the Guns*; John C. Knowlson, *The Complete Farrier or Horse Doctor*, and Joseph Janvier Woodward, *The Hospital Steward's Manual*.

Special thanks go to my husband, Eddie Durand, who supported me throughout this process and was a willing companion on our road trips to retrace the movements of the 111th New York Volunteer Infantry during the Overland Campaign in 1864. Thanks go also to my mother, Avro Flett, who instilled in me an admiration for our Canadian ancestors, and to my lifelong friends and readers of my drafts, Carolyn Olive and Sandra Marshall.

ABOUT MARGARET DURAND

I was born in Montreal in the middle of the twentieth century, met my husband at graduate school, and worked in academic research in the United States and Canada for almost forty years. Since retiring, I volunteer with local environmental groups and develop my life-long passion for fiction writing through courses and practice.

I currently reside in Victoria, British Columbia where I recently completed a book of short stories of the near-future entitled *Best Not to Look*. Please visit my website at www.margaretdurand.ca where I have included a short prequel to *Blood Memories.* It introduces Donald, age nine, and his family.

Blood Memories was short-listed for the 2015 Cedric Literary Awards.

www.ingramcontent.com/pod-product-compliance
Lightning Source LLC
Chambersburg PA
CBHW020552180626
46810CB00007B/2477